The Magic in this Other World is Too Far Behind! 1

Gamei Hitsuji
illustration=himesuz

"Good grief.
I guess I don't
have a choice..."
Yakagi Suimei

"My goodness... Surely it's in poor taste to stalk someone like this. That's behavior befitting the pitiful and foolish stray sheep..."

"It couldn't be... You noticed me?"

"*Azure Engraved Beheading!*"

"The heavenly sky which dyes all
in its perfectly clear blue light.

The invisible horizon where sea and sky are one.
For only this moment in time, that boundary lies within my hand.

Sever the blue sky.
Its name is the dazzling blue azure!"

contents

The Magic in this Other World is Too Far Behind!

1

The Magic in this Other World is Too Far Behind!

Volume 1

Gamei Hitsuji
illustration=**himesuz**

THE MAGIC IN THIS OTHER WORLD IS TOO FAR BEHIND! VOLUME 1
by Gamei Hitsuji

Translated by Hikoki
Edited by Morgen Dreher

This book is a work of fiction. Names, characters, places, and incidents are the product of the author's imagination or are used fictitiously. Any resemblance to actual events, locales, or persons, living or dead, is coincidental.

Copyright © 2014 Gamei Hitsuji
Illustrations by himesuz

First published in Japan in 2014 by OVERLAP Inc., Tokyo.
Publication rights for this English edition arranged through OVERLAP Inc., Tokyo.

All rights reserved. In accordance with the U.S. Copyright Act of 1976, the scanning, uploading, and electronic sharing of any part of this book without the permission of the publisher is unlawful piracy and theft of the author's intellectual property.

Find more books like this one at www.j-novel.club!

President and Publisher: Samuel Pinansky
Managing Editor: Aimee Zink

ISBN: 978-1-7183-5400-5
Printed in Korea
First Printing: April 2019
10 9 8 7 6 5 4 3 2 1

Prologue   The Magician Yakagi Suimei

Felmenia Stingray was one of the proud court mages of the Kingdom of Astel. Born as the second daughter of Earl Stingray, she was a girl of noble lineage who was brought up without ever knowing want or hardship. After discovering her high mana capacity as a child, she took to studying magic under an old man known as the sage. Even as a young girl, she was considered a genius who peered into the abyss of the ways of magic.

Ten years passed as she studied magic with the sage. Under his tutelage, Felmenia plumbed the depths of magic that were ordinarily said to take thirty years minimum to comprehend.

"From this point on, there is nothing more I can teach you. Using your wits, discover your own way of magic," he'd told her at that point.

And after that, Felmenia's life became quite busy compared to her time studying under the sage. For the caliber of her magic research, she was appointed as the youngest initiate of the court mages. The amount of regular work entrusted to her could not even be compared to the invitations to evening parties, unfamiliar jobs, and tea parties with noble ladies she received. Ever since she left the sage's cave where her time was exclusively devoted to the study of magic, her life had been nothing but a series of new learning experiences.

Her busy life left her with little time for sleep and brought her hardship like she had never known, but it was so fulfilling that she hardly minded. She already felt a great sense of accomplishment. She felt alive. She was no longer a little noble girl trapped inside a cage like a bird; she felt like she was making a difference as a vital cog of her country. And so she continued her busy but rewarding way of life. Several years after parting ways with the sage, Felmenia made a major discovery. In the middle of one of her jobs as a court mage where she'd been tasked with subjugating a major threat of monsters and demons, she came upon the truth of the flame that was unbeknownst to man.

Yes, at the tender age of fifteen, Felmenia arrived at the truth. The true flame that all fire desired to be. She discovered that which could burn all things to ashes—the white flame. After trembling with joy for a moment, Felmenia reported this to her teacher and His Majesty the King. She even received words of high praise from both of them for her grand achievement.

But it wasn't just the white flame she'd discovered. That was the moment she also discovered value in herself. This was what she truly desired. It was the validation and self-worth she'd been chasing all along. It spurred her forward, and she resolved herself to continue to forge down the path of magic.

From that point on, Felmenia continued in her magic work, amassing a great number of achievements for her service to the kingdom. From defeating demons in the north, to exterminating an enormous monster enshrined in the desert, to reforming magical scholarship within the country, to her appointment within the Mage's Guild, which served as a platform for even more academic change… For nearly everything she did, she was showered in admiration from anyone and everyone. The gratitude of the people, the envy of her colleagues, and the words of expectation hanging over her from her father and mother were all the greatest honors she could imagine.

That was how Felmenia had lived until now. Her prodigious life of achievement eventually earned her the recognition of being the foremost mage in the kingdom, made all the more remarkable by her young age.

But even Felmenia, who prided herself on being the kingdom's strongest mage, was unable to lift a single finger against the young man standing before her now.

The full moon shone down from a darkened sky decorated by the glitter of the stars in the king's favorite courtyard of Royal Castle Camellia. It illuminated the young man dressed in black, who proceeded to mock her scoldingly.

"My goodness... Surely it's in poor taste to stalk someone like this. That's behavior befitting the pitiful and foolish stray sheep who know nothing of the truth and providence of the world, you know?"

This young man who spoke in unfamiliar terms to her was one of the good friends of Reiji, the summoned hero. But unlike the young woman who'd also arrived with them and consented to participating in the Demon Lord's subjugation together with the hero, this completely plain young man had rudely refused the king's request and demanded to be returned to his own world.

With a perfectly straight face, he'd claimed to be a normal person. He said he had no special powers worth mentioning, and for that reason, refused to fight against monsters, demons, or evil. And he especially scorned the idea of being sent after the Demon Lord. Insisting he wouldn't fight, he demanded to be returned home with all sorts of colorful language. That was a few days ago, after which he'd proceeded to lock himself in the room he'd been granted.

Overcoming the confusion and fear threatening to crush her after being suddenly summoned to this world, his female friend had loudly announced that she would accompany the hero on his quest. But not this young man. He continued to insist on being left alone and sent home. It was a joke. He was a coward. And a selfish one. How could he even call himself a man? Not just the high-ranking castle officials like ministers and generals, but all of the castle staff down to the lowliest maid and soldier ridiculed him mercilessly behind his back.

But... what was the truth of the matter?

Felmenia bet her pride on her white flame, the perfection of fire magic. But it was woefully insufficient to win against this young man, who had dispelled it with a mere snap of his fingers. And now he stood over her, overflowing with tranquil mana that was so overwhelming it felt like it might just turn her to ice.

"Now then, little miss mage. Is it my turn yet?"

It was in that moment that Felmenia Stingray learned what her self-worth really amounted to.

This young man was strong and clever. His plain appearance was a lie. A disguise. He was so sly that the people who looked down on him with pity and scorn were the true fools. He was not to be underestimated.

No, this young man was a monster who resided far deeper in the abyss of the ways of magic than the sage who taught her. He possessed many secret arts within him that she was no match for as she was now. He had such absurd skill and knowledge that it seemed he could take out even the hero who'd received divine protection in the summoning ritual, all with ease and a scornful laugh.

There was no mistaking it. He was a mage at the summit of his craft.

"…Who are you?"

Felmenia asked him that in a trembling voice. The young man fiddled with something atop his hand with a bored expression and replied to her flatly.

"The magician Yakagi Suimei."

That would be the first time he properly introduced himself.

Chapter 1 I'm Not Something You Just Summon!

"Owowow…"

It had happened so suddenly that there was no chance to prepare, and the price for not being ready was the pain he was feeling in his rear end. Suimei could only leak out his anguish with a pained complaint.

He had been caught completely off guard. Even though he'd had a premonition that something would happen beforehand, there was just no predicting how suddenly. And without any warning, he hadn't even been able to make a proper landing. Worse yet, the floor was hard. It felt like stone pavement or tiling. Suimei had fallen square on his bottom, and his tailbone was screaming in pain.

Suimei wondered briefly what had just happened. But there was no need to think back on it too seriously; it had only happened moments ago. While walking home from school with two of his friends, a magickal teleportation circle had suddenly appeared on the roadside and forcefully sucked them in. Then, after being teleported, he was rudely deposited on the floor. That was one of the perks of sudden teleportation he could do without.

…This is definitely a huge blunder…

Living in the concrete jungle of the modern world, Suimei had been walking down the secret path of magicka. Though he'd only been at it for a modest twelve years, he'd achieved a certain level of skill and was proud of that. Yet even he, a savvy modern magician, had been caught in someone else's magicka so easily.

He had sensed it—seen it right in front of his own eyes, even—but was unable to respond appropriately in time. He'd simply stood there blankly in the single second it had taken for the spell to ensnare him. What could he call such a failure other than a blunder? He was ashamed and disappointed.

And that only made things worse. Humiliation and pain compounded within him, manifesting as tears in the corners of his eyes. Suimei then looked to either side of him for the friends he'd been with just a moment ago.

"Owowow…"

Beside Suimei, who was brushing off his butt, was his friend Shana Reiji, who appeared to be dealing with the same pain Suimei was going through. Reiji had dyed brown hair with every strand neatly styled into place, as well as a sweet countenance and slender figure that could render women weak in the knees. Spotting him, Suimei called out to him.

"Hey, Reiji, you okay?"

"Yeah… Somehow. How about you, Suimei?"

"My butt hurts. A lot. I think it's broken clean in two…"

"Hahaha, you too—Wait, Suimei, are you the only other one here?!"

Reiji laughed brightly at Suimei's foolish joke, but only for a short moment. He then immediately realized the absence of the third person who had been walking with them, their friend Anou Mizuki, and raised a panicked voice.

Briefly looking around, it certainly seemed she was missing. She had been with them just moments ago, but was now nowhere to be found. The cylindrical room was enclosed by stone walls and was atmospherically lit by old-fashioned candlesticks. All they could see was a sturdy-looking door across from them, and a pattern drawn on the stone floor beneath their feet—a teleportation circle.

"Y-Yeah... Mizuki isn't here, huh?"

A bit confused himself, Suimei could only mutter in response to his increasingly anxious friend. Reiji's expression grew dark as the questions continued to mount in his mind.

"What happened...? And where is this...?"

"Yeah, I don't know where this is either. But it seems that someone wanted us here, however weird and rude it might have been. That much... I do kinda understand."

"...Could it be because of this?"

Following Reiji's dubious gaze, Suimei looked down at the floor where the large magicka circle was and inspected it once more. Inside the large circle, another circle about a quarter of its size was drawn at its edge. The geometric shapes drawn within didn't conform with the traditional four elements, nor did they conform with the five elements of the Chinese philosophy of wu xing. Words were scribed around the rim of the circle in a language that Suimei had never seen before. He could tell that the circle was similar to what was used with spirit communication and summoning magicka, but it would have to be his secret.

After all, Reiji was a completely normal boy. Suimei and Reiji had known each other since middle school, but Suimei had never introduced him to the mysteries of magicka that existed in their world, much less revealed the fact that he himself was actually a magician. He was oblivious to such things, meaning everything he could guess about the circle beneath them came from manga and anime subculture—the world of fiction.

"Probably, right?"

"Really…?"

Reiji looked dumbfounded in response to Suimei's barefaced acknowledgment of such a possibility. Granted, the situation certainly seemed to warrant that level of disbelief. Even Suimei's expression was tinged with a certain sense of incredulity.

"Hey, Suimei, doesn't this situation… How do I put it…? Doesn't it seem awfully familiar?"

"Yup. The light novel Mizuki lent me the other day definitely went something like this."

"Thought so. This feels like the kind of setup where you're suddenly summoned to another world and asked to defeat a Demon Lord. Or something like that."

"Nope, not doing it. I'm not even considering that a joke right now."

Suimei grimaced like his stomach was in pain. Reiji's expression was riddled with complex emotions, but he managed a somewhat dry laugh.

"Hahaha… But you know, even though I know it's impossible, I dunno… I kinda feel like that's what's going on."

"Reiji, are you being serious right now?"

"Mm."

"Hey, don't just nod and 'mm' me…"

Exasperated by Reiji's simple nod and deduction, Suimei averted his gaze for a moment and began to use magicka to analyze their surroundings without letting Reiji catch on. As things stood, he wasn't fully willing to buy in to such a fantastical straight-out-of-a-book scenario, but if they truly were in another world, something about the place should be different enough for him to tell.

Though it was impromptu, Suimei prepared his spell and started processing the information it gathered for him. Gravity here was normal, and there was no major difference in the composition of the air. It was insignificant enough to think that they'd just been transported to a different locale. However...

The mana is thick here... Is it because of this room?

Mana, otherwise known as aetheric, was the source of mystical power that existed naturally in the atmosphere, and it was particularly dense here. Such density was comparable to that found right on top of ley lines in the earth or within holy temples and circles.

However, that alone wasn't enough to convince Suimei that this was a different world, not to mention that it was an absurd idea. It was more likely someone selected a place with dense mana so that they could activate this magicka circle.

But more importantly, Reiji should have no techniques to observe and no way to perceive the irregularity in mana. If he felt that something was strange, it was likely something else.

"What makes you say that, Reiji?"

"Just one way or another, I feel like I've become really strong."

"Wha...? Aaah, is it that? Did your brain blow a fuse, my dear Reiji-san?"

"Listen, it's not like I'm telling you I'm receiving radio waves or something. Just watch."

With those words, Reiji reached out of the circle and lightly struck the floor. There was a smashing sound disproportionate to the strength of the gentle blow, and the stone floor shattered to pieces so violently that it sent debris flying.

"Th-That's kind of idiotic..."

Seeing it happen right before his very eyes, Suimei could only stare in wonder. Reiji may have been the all-around, good-looking, good-at-sports perfect guy, but this just wasn't right. It wasn't possible. The requisite amount of power required to render stone to pieces like that... Doing that should have required a good impact with serious weight and force behind it. It literally shouldn't have been possible with just a poke. This was unreasonable even for a strong, perfect guy like Reiji. Yet in spite of all this, he was acting as if it was all quite natural.

"See? I did it."

"'See?' My ass! Don't move the plot forward in such an ominous direction..."

It certainly did seem ominous. If this was truly a forced summoning to another world...

Indeed, Suimei was now sure they'd entered an unknown dimension. Someone with skills that overleaped his had brought them here. The art of physically reinforcing a body in addition to summoning it was no simple ritual, but... Turning that over in his mind, Suimei suddenly realized something else. As a magician, it was only natural that he took to analyzing the mana and any sort of magicka that had been involved. But even so, all things considered, he was the one being extraordinarily casual about the whole thing.

"So how about you, Suimei?"

"...No, nothing seems different for me."

He knew Reiji was really asking if he'd undergone some sort of strengthening as well, but Suimei had answered honestly. When he tried clenching his fist and gathering his mana, there was no hint of any change.

That had to mean Reiji had been the one summoned as a hero to defeat the Demon Lord. There was no point in summoning Suimei here. But just as he slumped his shoulders, the magicka circle beneath their feet suddenly began to glow. Reiji's expression abruptly shifted to one of unease.

"This is…"

"Tch, it's activating! Are we being transferred again, or maybe…?"

"Something is being summoned?!"

Reiji understood the implication quickly. In fact, he hit the nail on the head and put himself on guard accordingly. A magicka circle smaller than the one on the ground then suddenly appeared in the air.

"It's coming!"

"Wah!"

A voice came from the circle, and Reiji swiftly took action the moment a shadow emerged. He seemed to have realized what was coming out, but demonstrated a level of agility far beyond what he was previously capable of in responding to it. Was it the result of the physical reinforcement? Either way, Reiji managed to catch Anou Mizuki, the girl who had fallen from above without warning.

"Mizuki!"

"Wah… Reiji-kun, what…?"

"Good for you, Mizuki. Thanks to Reiji, your butt was saved."

Thus, the three friends were reunited again in this unknown place.

★

"You're kidding. Seriously…?"

"Yup, that seems to be the case."

After catching Mizuki, Reiji explained their current predicament to her and what he'd deduced about it so far. Mizuki seemed to be thrown for a loop at first, but was predominantly glad that she wasn't alone. Encouraged by the presence of her two best friends, she gradually came to terms with the current situation. Her willingness to accept it rather than deny it showed both boys that she had some guts.

"Hmm… Okay."

"You accepted that all pretty fast, huh?"

"Well, the two of you are pretty calm about it. If I'm the only one who breaks down, can you imagine how embarrassing that would be? And besides, since we're already here, what else is there to be done? We have to accept it one way or another."

Mizuki seemed to have a refreshing take on it all, and explained herself to the boys while fiddling with the unseasonable red muffler around her neck. She had long, black hair and gentle, coal black eyes. She had a certain look about her that gave the impression she was a dainty and fragile young woman. Yet though she looked rather meek, she apparently had quite a stout heart inside her. The boys had only known her under normal day-to-day circumstances, so it seemed there was plenty they still had to learn about Mizuki. Reiji then smiled at her.

"Mizuki, you're pretty tough, aren't you?"

"Huh? A-Am I?"

Having that smile directed at her, Mizuki finally caved. Her face turned bright red. This kind of exchange was typical for them, including Reiji being unaware of the effect he had on girls.

And just like that, the strange and potentially frightening situation they found themselves in was diffused by a completely inappropriate atmosphere. Determining it was counterproductive, however, Suimei decided to change course and get things back on track.

"So, Mizuki, I want to ask you something."

"What's up?"

"Well, about this situation that we're in now… If it's nonsensically similar to those novels you read, then after this…"

"Mm, yeah. Someone important from this world should appear. Or possibly…"

What could it be? The first part of her reply was definitely what he would have expected from reading one of her books, but what was this about another possibility? She made it sound like there was another direction this could go, so Suimei prodded her for more details without pause.

"Is there something else?"

"In one of the books I read, the hero was summoned somewhere else… And if we were following a plotline like that, that would mean we're in the Demon Lord's palace right now."

"You mean starting right at the climax?"

"Yeah, the last dungeon."

"Ugh… Isn't that a bit much, honestly?"

Suimei let out a disheartened groan. In the majority of novels like this, after being summoned, the hero must face several trials, twists, and turns before defeating the Demon Lord at the end of the story. But what Mizuki was suggesting meant that they'd be starting from there, right at the climax—the final boss.

That thought didn't thrill Suimei. It meant they'd be in serious danger, and this wasn't exactly where he wanted to spend his last breath. Reiji, on the other hand, began questioning Mizuki in a calm tone.

"If memory serves, that's the kind of story where they defeat the Demon Lord right away, then return to live in the new world as heroes, right?"

"Yup. Then they either challenge the next powerful enemy, or end up getting involved in a war between countries though…"

"Okay, but the situation that we're in right now..."

"I wouldn't be surprised if it's something similar to what Reiji-kun was thinking."

"Oh my god..."

Mizuki's assessment left Suimei quite dejected. His discontentment left his lips as a pained sigh. This sounded more and more like it was going to be a huge pain. If what Mizuki was suggesting was true, it would only be inevitable that he'd get dragged into it. And since Suimei had other plans, this would end up being a major speed bump for him.

"Anything's possible. I guess we'll see, huh?"

And the moment Mizuki said that, Suimei could hear something—using his ears that were enhanced with magicka—coming from outside the room. Erasing his presence, keeping alert, and killing any excess noise, Suimei called out to the others.

"You guys."

"Huh?"

"Yeah, I know."

"Oh? Is that also a result of your strengthening?"

"I think so, but if so, how are you able to hear it, Suimei?"

"My, uh, ears have always been good... Actually, this isn't the time for that."

Suimei brushed off the question with a light joke. He and Reiji were on the same page now, but Mizuki had yet to grasp the situation.

"H-Huh?"

"Mizuki, someone's approaching right now. Quite a few people, actually."

Reiji recognized the distinct sound of many footsteps approaching. It seemed that the strengthening effect didn't just make him physically stronger. And once he gave Mizuki the short of it, Reiji positioned himself in front of her with the intention of protecting her while he focused on the passage that lay beyond the door. Mizuki shrank back in anxiety, and Suimei also put himself on guard next to Reiji.

"Now then, just what is going to pop out…?"

"Hopefully it's someone important from this world rather than the bad guys."

"Are you kidding, Reiji? Hopefully it's our classmates with a sign that says 'Surprise!'"

"…"

Reiji didn't respond to Suimei's all too optimistic humor. Was it because the footsteps were drawing ever nearer? Or was it because he was hoping for something other than that? Maybe Reiji honestly believed the best-case scenario would be if someone important walked through that door. Suimei had no way of knowing what he was really thinking, but now that the footsteps were just on the other side of the door, it would only be a matter of seconds before they saw who it really was.

Suimei cast a fleeting glance to his side. He could see Reiji lower his stance, ready to spring into action at any time, and Mizuki stepping back so that she wouldn't get in his way. As for Suimei, rather than stiffening up at the prospect of danger, his heart was pounding at the thrill of the unknown. He was in his element right now, and that was his natural curiosity as a magician at work.

Suppressing his excitement, he quietly inspected the belongings he had with him. He'd been brought here completely unprepared, so he had nothing other than what he usually carried on his person.

I have my bag, inside of which is a chain accessory, a vial of mercury, cards, my suit, the gloves of discord, and a little of the Yakagi secret medicine... Frankly, I'm a little unsure about whipping any of that out, but...

If something happened, he wouldn't have a choice. Because Reiji and Mizuki were used to peaceful everyday life in Japan, Suimei was the only one with combat experience among the three of them. He'd had his fair share of run-ins in the underworld. He certainly wanted to keep that and his powers a secret from his friends, but if that came at the cost of their lives, he wouldn't hesitate to reveal himself. Even in the worst case, though he would feel guilty about it, there was the option of manipulating their memories.

The three of them each tensed up as the footsteps came to a complete stop. The brief moment after that seemed to last forever. But eventually, the door finally opened with the sound of something heavy being dragged across the ground. Reiji immediately readied himself.

"Tch!"

"Mea firma aegis."

[My solid shield.]

With that, Suimei put his defensive magicka on standby. It wasn't out of the question that whoever it was would suddenly attack upon seeing them. Better safe than sorry, after all.

What appeared in the doorway was a group of armored men who didn't look particularly friendly. From what Suimei could see, however, they looked to be human. They didn't appear to be monsters, demons, or other evil beings, so that much was a relief, at least.

The armored group then stood along the wall, forming orderly ranks while facing the three friends vigilantly. Just what was going to happen? Suimei kept his magicka at the ready, but the wall of armored men parted. A young woman with blue hair wearing a pink dress, and a second girl with silver hair wearing a white robe the color of a polished pearl then appeared.

"Huh…?"

"Hmm?"

Both girls tilted their heads to the side in unison, looking as though something completely unexpected were unfolding right in front of them. Then the girl with the blue hair leaned in and began quietly whispering to the other one.

"White Flame-dono, was there not supposed to be a single summoned hero?"

"No, it is just as you say."

"Yet there are three people present here…"

"I-Indeed there are… About that, this is merely conjecture on my part, but let's just assume one of these three is, in fact, the hero. I would imagine then that the other two simply got caught up in the hero summoning."

"But how could that be? I've never seen records of such a thing happening. I've never even heard of it."

"Neither have I, Your Highness. Yet even so, here three people stand before us, so…"

"The probability is rather high, you mean."

They were talking privately to one another, but Suimei could overhear them thanks to his enhanced hearing. He expected Reiji could hear them as well, but wasn't sure he could understand what they were saying. What they were speaking, after all, wasn't Japanese, or any other language from Earth, for that matter. It was a strangely rhythmic language. And even though he didn't know what it was, Suimei could still decipher it.

Figuratively speaking, it was like the words were being rearranged in his head into a language he knew well, or something to that effect. Since it was considerably intuitive to him, it was difficult to explain in words. The reason for it was likely because of the kind of spell that was cast on them when they were summoned. It was only a theory of Suimei's, but he didn't have much else to go on. The reason why didn't matter all that much right now. More importantly, it was convenient.

And then, judging that there was no longer any need to remain on guard after hearing the words "hero" and "summoning" from their conversation, Suimei discreetly canceled his magicka. Reiji also seemed to relax as he came out of his stance. Suimei then turned to Mizuki.

"Hey, Mizuki, it seems this was a bit of a surprise for them too. Is this kind of development normal?"

"Well, yes. There are stories where the friends of the summoned hero are caught up in things too, but…"

Mizuki suddenly looked troubled, like it was hard to explain further. Suimei was left hanging. Just what was it she was afraid to say?

"Mizuki, are you worried about something?"

"Um, in this kind of scenario, one of the hero's friends—in our case, that would be one of us—usually forms a pact with an evil god and becomes the antagonist."

"What the hell, seriously? Now an evil god's going to show up for no reason? Why?"

"I'm not really sure myself…"

Mizuki trembled with anxiety. Frankly speaking, Suimei wanted to do the same thing. No, he just wanted to run away. He just couldn't get his head around why something as extreme as an evil god would suddenly show up.

He might have been able to understand if it was just an avatar or some other manifestation of its power, but actually summoning an evil god would cause deaths in the thousands. Even if the summoned hero somehow managed to scrape by on bare luck, they would have a dangerous incarnation of evil eyeing them forever after that. And people rarely ever got that lucky twice. Without some sort of intervention, it seemed the hero would still meet an unfortunate end eventually. And that wasn't what Suimei wanted. Thinking about it sent a chill down his spine. While Suimei was lost in his own thoughts, Reiji continued questioning Mizuki.

"The antagonist? Why would one of you end up fighting with me?"

"In this scenario, either me or Suimei-kun would come to oppose your way of thinking, Reiji-kun, and end up making a pact with the evil god as a way to fight against you."

"What…?"

Reiji went visibly pale upon hearing Mizuki's explanation. He was dumbfounded. Seeing his response, Mizuki desperately tried to backpedal.

"But, but I would never do that, Reiji-kun! I don't hate you! I l-l-l-l-lo…"

She must have been too embarrassed to say it directly to his face. Her voice steadily trailed off until it was completely inaudible. Reiji then awkwardly turned his head towards Suimei.

"Th-Then… it's you, Suimei?"

"Heh, to be honest, I've always secretly thought you were a real bottom-feeding braggart who should just drop dead."

"—!"

A dark passion could be seen filling Suimei's eyes as he spoke, and Reiji was left at a loss for words.

"I'm kidding…"

"S-Suimei…"

"I really am kidding. If I hated you, why would I have gone out of my way to keep your company for the last six years? Just think about it."

"Th-That's right. Th-Thank god…"

Hearing that Suimei and Mizuki were on his side, Reiji now let out a sigh of relief. And while the three of them were having that exchange, the blue-haired girl called out to them with the dignity of a graceful princess.

"Um, excuse me. I apologize for the interruption, but would you mind speaking with us?"

"Oh, of course."

Reiji politely agreed, and the young woman with blue hair and a prominent forehead gave a graceful bow before introducing herself.

"I must truly apologize for calling you forth so abruptly. I am the second child of His Majesty King Almadious Root Astel, king of the Kingdom of Astel. My name is Titania Root Astel, and here with me is the one who strove to bring you here on this occasion…"

As if to show she had someone else to introduce, the girl with the large forehead, Princess Titania, lightly turned to the side. The robed girl she was speaking of took a single step forward.

"I am Court Mage Felmenia Stingray. It is a pleasure to meet you."

This was the young lady the princess had called "White Flame" in their earlier conversation. She had beautiful silver hair that reached her waist with neat braids hanging down next to both her ears. Her slightly angled eyes seemed to convey a sense of pride. She made a lasting, intense impression, but she also had some rather charming, likeable features. As befitting someone who called themselves a court mage, mana was fluidly flowing through her body. The same was true for the princess, but this woman seemed far more adept at its control.

Wait, this woman is the one who summoned us here? That son of a…

Before him now was the person responsible for their current predicament. Feeling nothing pleasant at making her acquaintance, Suimei grumbled to himself. Once the girls finished their introductions, Reiji stepped forward and politely returned the gesture.

"Thank you for such a courteous greeting. My name is Shana Reiji. If it is more common here to put the surname last, then please feel free to call me Reiji Shana. These two with me are my good friends. To my right is Mizuki Anou, and to my left is Suimei Yakagi."

Exactly when did he learn to be so formal? Princess Titania and Court Mage Felmenia responded quite admiringly to Reiji. They were rather dignified themselves, but they seemed to be pleased with Reiji's manners. When she had the chance, Mizuki stepped forward next.

"Allow me to introduce myself. My name is Mizuki Anou…"

When she was finished, Suimei took a step forward too.

"I'm… Suimei Yakagi."

He kept things short and sweet. He didn't really have anything else to say, and he could tell this was the kind of situation where he should avoid saying anything imprudent. Titania then passed her gaze over the three of them, and closed her eyes as if deep in thought. And then…

"Reiji-sama, Mizuki-sama, and Suimei-sama, correct? The reason that we have summoned you under such circumstances… You see, there's something that we must ask one of the three of you."

"What is it?"

"We need you to destroy the Demon Lord Nakshatra, the leader of the demons who currently threaten the peace of this world."

The moment Princess Titania said those words, the three friends all gave each other knowing looks. Suimei was then the only one that put his hand on his forehead and looked up at the ceiling like he wanted out.

★

Summoned to another world, greeted by a princess and a court mage, then asked to save the world. It was practically textbook. The three friends were able to keep up appearances on the surface, but each of them truly felt like they'd had their legs knocked out from under them.

"Man..."

"Wow..."

"Oh my god..."

In the end, they weren't able to keep it together after all. Each one of them broke into a different kind of sigh. They now looked like they were at their wits' end from the shock of it all, and Titania began questioning them in a somewhat bewildered tone.

"And so, I must apologize for the abruptness of it all, but which among you is the esteemed hero?"

"Um..."

"That's..."

In response to her question, Reiji and Mizuki looked at each other with troubled expressions. There was no way they would know if they were heroes or not. How could they? As far as they knew, they were just ordinary civilians. If anyone had asked them if they were heroes otherwise, they certainly would have said no. As such, there seemed to be no answer to the question posed to them now. But they couldn't just stay in the dark; things would never progress that way. And so Suimei decided to step in.

"Can I ask something?"

"Yes, please feel free to ask anything you see fit."

"Is there something that would indicate who the summoning target was? Like a sign that should prove that one of us is a hero?"

"Proof of being a hero? A sign, you say?"

Suimei nodded, and Titania looked over to Felmenia. Felmenia met her gaze and nodded, then turned towards Suimei to give him an answer.

"Yes, there is such a thing. The hero who is summoned by the ritual is given divine protection by the Elements upon crossing worlds, and should house tremendous power within their body. In other words, one among you should feel power flowing within you unlike anything you've ever experienced... Does one of you not match that description?"

"If that's how it is, I think that would be me. Since coming here, I've felt like I became much stronger—stronger than I could have ever imagined."

The soldiers in the room began whispering amongst themselves and let out a collective "oooh" at Reiji's response. It was true that Reiji seemed to be the only one who'd gotten any power when they were transported, but be that as it may...

She said "by the Elements," didn't she?

Suimei scrutinized the girl's words internally. Elements, elemental, elementary... Such words in the world Suimei was from were used to describe chemical elements, or more esoterically, the four or five arcane elements. Earth, water, fire, and wind made

35

up the traditional four, and including the void made it a more conceptual five. These words and the things they represented played an extremely important role in magicka.

Yet the way Felmenia had phrased it made it sound like she was referring to a living being. Even though magicka could work hand in hand with spiritual religious faith, and even though the core of its practice was calling on spirits for power, the nuance was a little strange.

But they were in another world now. There was no guarantee that things worked exactly how Suimei would expect them to. If they were identical, there would be no need for the division between worlds in the first place. There had to be some reason these two worlds were separated—something that made this one different. Perhaps the difference was Elemental...

"So then you are the esteemed hero?"

"Well... Yes, I think so."

While Suimei was ruminating over the Elements, Titania's intoxicated eyes fell on Reiji. It appeared she had some special feelings for this "hero." Of course, it didn't hurt that he happened to be quite handsome. Seeing her looking at him like that, Reiji was somewhat taken aback. Even more so when Titania suddenly grabbed his hand.

"Hero-sama, though it is truly presumptuous of me, please... I'm in your hands!"

"H-Huh?!"

"Y-Your Highness?!"

It seemed that the girl in the white robe, Felmenia, was just as surprised by this sudden outburst as Reiji was. She called to Titania in a fluster, and it was only then that she seemed to realize what she'd said. The princess then let go of his hand as she blushed a little.

"Goodness… You have my deepest apologies, Hero-sama. I of all people shouldn't be acting so impertinently in a situation like this… Well, now then, I believe His Majesty the King will explain things in the audience chamber, so please give us your reply then."

"U-Understood."

Still caught in the vortex of confusion, Reiji somehow managed to collect himself and offer an acceptable answer. Felmenia then took a step forward towards him.

"H-Hero-sama, allow me to introduce myself once more. My name is Felmenia Stingray."

"Ah, yes. It's a pleasure to make your acquaintance."

"I believe we'll be seeing a lot of each other from here on. It's an honor to work with you. I'll be in your hands as well."

"What? Oh, yes, of course…"

Felmenia nonchalantly echoed the princess's sentiment as she bowed, and Reiji replied politely despite not really grasping what was going on. Titania, however, cleared her throat in a rather forced fashion.

"Ahem, White Flame-dono…"

"M-My apologies. I'm getting ahead of myself."

"Now then, please come this way, you all. I will personally show you to His Majesty."

At Titania's command, the soldiers once again fell into line and opened a path for Suimei and the others.

★

After following the soldiers down an unfamiliar and gloomy passage for a ways, the group emerged from the dimly lit stone hallway into a bright and dazzling marble passage with ornamental candlesticks dotted along the walls. Unlike where they'd been previously, this area was elaborately decorated and neatly kept. Here and there were works of art, paintings, and ornamental suits of armor that gave the place a truly splendid atmosphere. It was unlike anything they'd ever seen before.

But that was perhaps to be expected—this was another world. It truly seemed to be one of fantasy, swords, and sorcery. But from what he'd seen of it and its people so far, Suimei had already formed some rather strong opinions.

Apart from the unnamed soldiers who were escorting them, they'd met two young women—a princess and a court mage. Titania, perhaps because of the charming impression he'd made on her, was walking with Reiji and talking to him nonstop. She'd started by asking about the world he'd come from, and then moved on to asking about his age and his specialties. Her high spirits and incessant chatter made her look like a girl walking together with a boy she had fallen in love with. Suimei was a little jealous.

Mizuki was too, albeit for different reasons. It wasn't like she was Reiji's girlfriend, but out of all the girls he knew, she was definitely the closest thing. It was certainly what she wanted to be. And now a beautiful girl—a princess, no less—had suddenly jumped in the way and was vying for his attention. It didn't really show on her face, but Mizuki was pretty down about it.

But then there was the second girl, Court Mage Felmenia.

"Do you need something?"

"No, nothing in particular."

39

For a while now, Felmenia had been glancing back at Suimei, staring in particular at his abdomen. Suimei finally shot back with a question in a slightly sharp tone, but Felmenia simply turned back around like it was nothing and stayed that way. In his mind, Suimei let out a groan.

Was it a failure to keep my magicka on standby? From the looks of it, I'm guessing she saw through me and knows I can use magicka now...

It was one blunder after another for Suimei, it seemed. Right now, he just wanted to dig a hole to hide in, but he knew he'd never get away with that.

The existence of magicka and magicians was a secret in the world Suimei came from. It had to be. In the modern era where science was king, magicka was considered heresy. The zeitgeist made sure to stamp out anything that might stand to dethrone science, and that included magicka. But in this world, how were its users regarded? This girl who called herself a court mage was walking alongside a princess who was clearly her social superior, but it was hard to tell what her standing was otherwise.

Outright using magicka would be a quick and easy way to get the answers Suimei wanted, but it was a bad idea. He didn't want to out himself to Reiji and Mizuki like that. And it was exactly because he wanted to keep them in the dark about his talents that his first priority now was finding a way to keep Felmenia from talking. He would have to think of some countermeasures.

"Here we are. This is the audience chamber. His Majesty awaits, so let us go forth."

Titania indicated the door they'd arrived at. It looked large enough that even giants could pass through it, not to mention how extravagant and grandiose it was. One of the soldiers who had been attending them called out to another guard stationed at the door. The porter then muttered something, and before long, the door slowly began opening.

"Whoa!"

"Huh?!"

Reiji and Mizuki both gasped when they saw it. It was undoubtedly a surprise to them to see a door opening unassisted. The porter wasn't touching it, and it certainly didn't look like an automated door. Not having any idea what was afoot, Reiji asked Titania about it.

"H-How did it open?"

"...With magic? Was it to your liking?"

"Ah, I see, there's magic here, huh?"

"'Here?'"

"Magic doesn't exist in our world, you see."

"Is that true?!"

"Yes."

"That must mean this is your first time seeing it, is it not?"

Seemingly pleased by how impressed Reiji sounded, Titania was grinning ear to ear. Felmenia, however, seemed to be panicking a little. She quickly began to assert herself to Reiji.

"I-I can accomplish such a mean feat with ease."

"Really?"

"Despite how I may look, I am one of Astel's proud court mages, after all."

"Wow, Felmenia-san is also amazing, huh?"

"W-Well... Heehee..."

It was difficult to tell if Reiji was genuinely impressed or if he was just being polite, but Felmenia suddenly became bashful. Was she weak to flattery? Perhaps anyone would be if the summoned

41

hero praised their skills. The disparity between her normally intense aura and the carefree smile on her face now was amusing, if not charming. On the other hand, Mizuki's eyes were still sparkling at the sight of the enormous door opening.

"Amazing... So magic really does exist..."

It seemed she was quite interested in the bigger picture. But as a girl who loved fantasy novels, that much was expected. This was right up her alley.

Suimei was paying attention to the magic as well, but as a magician, he was naturally more invested in the details than Mizuki was. He hadn't quite heard the chant that the porter had used, but he easily had a handle on the spell's composition, the deployment of the formula, the manifestation of its power, and the activation effect.

Wind, right?

What opened the door was simple magic—a wind spell that consisted of three verses, which had physically pushed the door to open it. The porter's control over the spell was splendidly fluent. He must have been an exemplary magician, but...

Hmm, but I wonder... Why wind? Why go out of the way to utilize an element as an intermediary and increase the workload just to open a door? No matter how you look at it, using a three-verse chant so impractically is just completely over the top, isn't it?

Rather than being stunned at the fact that magic existed, he was puzzled at how inefficiently it was being used. The porter was talented, certainly, but Suimei could only describe what he'd done as wasteful. Optimizing the available mana, he could have invoked a movement spell, and that would have been that.

Suimei just couldn't figure why anyone would use a wind spell to achieve the same effect in a roundabout way. It would increase the length of the chant that much more, and increase the mana required for the invocation.

And since a spell like that took more time and mana than necessary, Suimei couldn't see any merit to it. Speaking frankly, a task that simple shouldn't have even required a chant. If Suimei had done it—or if any other magician he knew had done it—opening a door with magicka shouldn't have taken any more effort than snapping his fingers. He decided not to dwell on it, but just how much excess mana had been wasted merely to open a door? Honestly, Suimei just couldn't get his head around it.

Maybe the porter just likes going the extra mile for flair?

He left it at that. Perhaps the royal porter simply enjoyed being showy. If that were the case, it would be a little easier to understand. He had no real reason to nitpick the man's style anyway, but whenever Suimei saw magicka in action, he had a habit of analyzing its practicality and efficiency. But while he was turning that over, Titania suddenly started talking to him.

"Suimei-sama, you are not surprised by magic, are you?"

Crap.

"Oh, me? I'm just too shocked to say anything... Hahaha."

"Oh my, is that so? Just wait until you see the court mages training right before your eyes—you may just lose the strength in your legs."

"Is it that amazing? Wow, I can't wait to see it..."

"Heehee..."

Titania giggled in a cheerful, yet ladylike manner. This was indeed all surprising to Suimei, but not in the way she assumed. As she and Suimei continued to talk, Felmenia called out to her.

"Your Highness, it is about time."

"Yes. Now then, Hero-sama, Mizuki-sama, Suimei-sama. Please follow me."

With that, the group followed after Titania as she passed through the open door. On the other side was an enormous hall. The large, rectangular room had thick stone pillars piercing through it. It had clearly taken much more work to make than the passage they'd used to get there. This, apparently, was the audience chamber.

"Wow…"

"Amazing…"

"Oooh…"

The three friends couldn't help but ooh and aah in admiration. The audience chamber was just that impressive. Even Suimei, who had been underwhelmed by the magicka earlier, was completely fascinated by this.

Sitting atop a throne at the raised center of the innermost part of the audience chamber was a rather intense-looking man who radiated an air of authority. This was likely the king, Almadious Root Astel. He had neatly-groomed, short, golden hair and a splendid beard. To his side was an elderly man who appeared to be his advisor. On either side of the throne was a line of other important-looking people as well.

Titania proceeded directly forward without even offering a glance at anyone but the man seated on the throne. Then, after ascending a single step of the raised platform, she knelt before the king. Following her example, Felmenia also knelt down. Deciding to take a hint from their actions, Suimei and the others followed suit in a hurry. Once everyone knelt down before the king, Titania finally addressed him.

"I, Titania Root Astel, have brought forth the hero summoned from another world by the hero summoning ritual."

"Excellent. You have been of great assistance, Titania. However, why are there three heroes present?"

The king clearly seemed puzzled, but it was Felmenia that answered his question.

"You see, Your Majesty, the other two in the hero's company are friends of his. It seems that they were also caught in the ritual and dragged with him at the time of the summoning."

"What?! They were dragged with him?!"

"Yes, Your Majesty. Most likely."

With that, the king's intense expression became one of utter shock. The murmurings of "How could that be?" and "I've never heard of this" grew louder from the other people present. The king then turned to address Felmenia properly.

"Is such a thing truly possible? The hero summoning ritual has been performed by various countries for centuries, but I have never once heard of such a thing."

"That is... I am but a fledgling with limited knowledge, Your Majesty, but I cannot deny the presence of the people who stand before you now. And as such..."

"You're suggesting we have no choice but to believe it."

"Yes, Your Majesty."

After his exchange with Felmenia, the king's expression turned grim. With that, Mizuki whispered to the others.

"He's talking about this summoning thing like it happens all the time, even in other countries. Does that mean there are people like us all over the place?"

"Based on what he said, maybe. But more importantly, just how many Demon Lords are springing up in this world...?"

Suimei replied with a disconcerted expression to Mizuki's question. He felt sorry for anyone else who'd been snatched out of their own world, but if they'd really had to summon that many heroes that many times... something was seriously, outrageously wrong here.

"Moreover, our situation seems to be a first for them."

"Ahaha... We're the ones people should be feeling sorry for..."

As they finished their whispered exchange, the conversation between Felmenia and the king came to an end. His grim expression was now resolute as he turned his gaze on the three friends.

"Hero-dono, I must apologize for calling you to such a place so abruptly. I am the thirteenth king of the Kingdom of Astel, Almadious Root Astel. And this is my castle, Royal Castle Camellia. Though I can only imagine how you must feel attending a royal audience with no prior notification, I implore you to be at ease."

The king sounded rather gracious as he spoke, and when he was finished, Titania whispered something into Reiji's ear. Suimei assumed she was cluing him in on how to properly address the king, but in complete contrast to that expectation, Reiji stood bolt upright in apparent shock.

"What?!"

Suimei was bewildered, and it seemed everyone else was as well. The room was abuzz again. In short, the unthinkable had happened. It might have been hard for a modern person to understand, but in a medieval country like this, kings held absolute authority. They were regarded nearly as gods, and to stand in front of one so casually without permission was a flagrant act of disrespect. Surely nothing good would come of it.

"It is alright. The hero is an esteemed gentleman who has been summoned from another world to save ours. We should be the ones respectfully yielding to him. You needn't worry about him addressing my father on equal standing."

"I-Is that so…?"

Picking up on Suimei's tense apprehension, Titania whispered to him to reassure him. Based on what she said, it seemed everything was fine. He'd been terrified for a moment there, but this was a relief. Reiji then bowed before the king and began speaking.

"My name is Reiji Shana, Your Majesty. I am honored to have been granted an audience here on such an occasion."

"So you are the hero from another world?"

"Yes, Your Majesty."

As Reiji confirmed his identity to the king, the others in the room began excitedly talking again, saying things like "So that gentleman is the hero?" and "What a sublime countenance!" When their enchanted praise finally died down, the king then directed his attention to Suimei and Mizuki.

"Then the two back there must be the hero's good friends?"

"Yes, I am his friend, Mizuki Anou."

"I'm Suimei Yakagi."

While still on their knees, Mizuki and Suimei looked up to answer the king. Since they weren't heroes, they decided against standing like Reiji had.

"I see. I do apologize for summoning you with him. For our mistake, though it is truly to our benefit, I do hope you find a way to forgive us."

"But of course."

"Yeah…"

Still regally seated atop his throne, the king asked for their forgiveness. As king, it was likely the best he could do in the way of an apology, but it honestly didn't sound like much of one at all. Suimei was a little peeved.

Yet once again, the crowd gathered in the room was astir with whispering. This time, they said things like "Such words from the king are more than they deserve," and "Such exceptional compassion!" It was almost the complete opposite of the way they'd talked about Reiji.

"Ehem… I have many matters that I would like to discuss with the hero, but I believe that this is enough for today's audience. This has all been quite sudden, and I do believe that Hero-dono is still perplexed by it all."

"I…"

"Hero-dono and friends, there will be a banquet in Camellia's reception hall after this. Please attend once you have yourselves settled in, and we will move on to the more serious matters at hand tomorrow."

It seemed some entertainment was in order, and the real business would wait until after an evening's rest. That consideration seemed to be the king's real apology, and in the end, he perhaps may have been overdoing it. Upon hearing the word "banquet," the atmosphere in the room seemed to lighten up. But there was one person unwilling to let the conversation go.

"No, Your Majesty. If possible, I would like us to move on to the serious matters at once."

"Is that truly alright, Hero-dono? You have only just arrived. Surely you haven't steeled yourself yet, have you?"

"That much is true… But, in the end, I know that this is something I must do. I would like to know the details of the danger I must face sooner rather than later."

"…I understand. If you wish, Hero-dono, we shall speak of it now."

After sinking deep into thought for a moment, the king agreed to Reiji's request. It wasn't the answer Suimei was hoping for.

Aargh... Damn this goody two-shoes!

With a sour face, Suimei angrily muttered to himself. This was a terrible turn of events. Things were developing too quickly. The pacing of it all was absurd. The three friends hadn't even yet had a chance to properly discuss things together. Spurred by panic, Suimei tugged on the cuff of Reiji's trousers from his kneeling position.

"H-Hey, Reiji! What are you thinking?! If you talk about this now, he's going to want your answer now. Did you think about that? Actually, isn't it obvious that—"

"It's fine, Suimei. Leave this to me."

"Forget that. We should—REIJIIIIIIII!"

Before they could finish discussing it, Reiji took a step forward and shook off Suimei's hand. Suimei quietly but mournfully called after him. To Suimei, what the king was going to ask Reiji to do was unconditionally unacceptable. Going off and defeating a Demon Lord in another world... Just what kind of fantasy was this? It was crazy to go and pick a fight with an opponent whose combat force and battle capabilities were completely unknown. Moreover, there was nothing that said they actually had to do it even though they'd been summoned here.

And on top of everything else, Suimei had a reason for returning home right away. He still had the thesis that he stubbornly promised to complete for his departed mentor, his father. Certainly, it was true that the magicians who secretly maneuvered in the underworld were destined to put their lives at stake, but that didn't mean they felt like throwing down their lives for just anything. And Suimei was dead set against this.

Suimei stared at Reiji's back as he stepped forward, full of anxiety. There was no way any rational person would accept such a ludicrous request, but this was his friend, the abnormally softhearted Reiji. Suimei couldn't deny the possibility that Reiji just might actually agree to it. That was the worry that pulsed through Suimei's mind as Reiji approached the king.

"How much have you heard already?"

"When we arrived, Her Highness requested that we defeat the Demon Lord. Other than that, we have yet to hear anything."

"I see. Then... Gless."

The king turned to the elderly man at his side and gave a nod in Reiji's direction. It must have been a signal. The elderly man—Gless—then stepped forward.

"I am the Kingdom of Astel's prime minister, Gless Dillez. To begin with, I will provide you with a rundown of the current situation."

"Please do."

"Far north of Astel, by a distance that could fit two countries, lies a land of intense cold called the Kingdom of Noshias. Noshias served as the bottleneck between demon and human territory, and for a long time it was known as the northernmost stronghold of humanity. It held off the demons' advance in our world. That is, up until half a year ago. The royal capital fell in a sudden and unexpected demon assault. After that, Noshias was no longer able to maintain itself as a country, and perished accordingly."

Prime Minister Gless's expression turned grim as he continued.

"Despite its harsh climate, the people of Noshias boasted strength that was in no way inferior to the people who live on the plains. I have heard that their army was also very powerful, but they could hardly make a stand against an army of demons over a million strong. A great country was cast into utter ruin in less than a month."

Mizuki then hesitantly spoke up.

"Um, by ruin, you mean… What about the people of Noshias?"

"The demons have no need for human prisoners. At the time of the attack, the majority of Noshias's people were slaughtered by the demons. The ones who survived were then picked off by the demons' human hunts. There are a lucky few who have survived to this day, but the population of Noshias has been decimated."

"Human hunts? No way…"

"That, I'm afraid, is simply how these demons are. They despise humans and treat them like prey. They are completely evil beings with no merit to speak of other than their raw power. Rather than come to a compromise at the negotiating table, they would sooner use one to strike at us."

Hearing Gless's explanation, Mizuki's face paled. The very idea of a "human hunt" struck fear into her heart. It wasn't all that hard to swallow what Gless was saying, but it was thoroughly unpleasant. Knowing genocide was on the table, it was quite clear the demons of this world were different from the sort that commonly appeared in novels. There was no working together with creatures of that ilk for peace or the greater good.

"After that, thanks to the oracle of the Church of Salvation, we were able to confirm that a Demon Lord has taken over the demon territory. The Demon Lord's name is Nakshatra, and if left at large, the demons will eventually annihilate humanity."

Gless paused briefly before continuing again.

"Faced with the prophecy of the annihilation of humanity we received from the oracle, the countries all gathered and held a conference to discuss countermeasures against the demon invasion.

However, with the fall of Noshias and the reported size of the demon army, many of the proposals presented to break the deadlock were withdrawn. It was just a demonstration of how we as people lack the means to oppose the demons that tower over us in strength and number."

Gless then suddenly turned his gaze towards Reiji.

"Accordingly, the nations all agreed to resort to the summoning ritual that has been passed down since time immemorial to summon a hero from another world. Normally, the hero summoning ritual is something only the Mage's Guild and the Church of Salvation are privy to. Its use is strictly forbidden without their consent, and only when humanity is so threatened is the ritual held. After all, if each nation performed the hero summoning ritual indiscriminately with their own national interests in mind, the entire world would be thrown into chaos."

"There are that many crises in this world...?"

Reiji wrinkled his brow. He may also have been secretly screaming internally, "This world has too many damn crises threatening humanity!"

"Yes. From what the knowledge passed down to us tells us, there have been two occasions where giants that threatened to eat all living beings appeared; three occasions where a tyrant attempted world domination; and like now, there has been one other instance of a Demon Lord appearing. This marks the seventh occasion that such measures have been necessary. And so to avoid the impending crisis, including the Kingdom of Astel, four countries are to carry out the hero summoning ritual."

"Four countries..."

Suimei leaked out a mutter at that unexpected statement. He wasn't a fan of the idea that there were other pitiful people out there who were having the absurd favor of subjugating demons pushed on them. Surely there were multiple summonings as a failsafe in case someone refused, but that also meant that there was no reason the burden of saving this world had to fall on Reiji's shoulders.

"And so the ones that were summoned here would be us, right?"

When Reiji asked for confirmation, Gless closed his eyes and nodded.

"It is just as you say."

Then Gless's expression turned from grim to grimmer.

"Currently the invasion of the demon army has slowed, but in the near future, not just this country, but the entire human world will be trampled underfoot by that massive demon army. We will all fall like Noshias if nothing is done."

The color ran from Gless's face, and his voice became somber. It came off as a piteous act to invite their sympathy. It was sly and repulsive, but thinking of the summoning on an international stage, failing to provide a hero would likely be seen as a dishonor that would hamper the people's faith in Astel. As the prime minister who had to think of the future of his country, he was acting with good intentions, but Suimei was unable to suppress the fountain of irritation bubbling up within him. Allowing a pause after Gless's explanation, the king spoke up once more.

"Hero-dono, would you somehow be willing to accept the task of saving us all?"

"..."

"What say you?"

Reiji cast his eyes downward like he was deep in thought as the king asked again for his answer.

What's the deal, Reiji? It's obvious that you should...

Naturally, Suimei, who had no intention of ever getting involved, secretly prayed to Reiji. As a magician, Suimei had learned a few combat techniques to protect himself and his research, but had no interest in taking part in an actual war. He thought it should go without saying, but he didn't want to die, either.

As if trying to put those anxieties to rest, Suimei devoted his prayers earnestly to the great living god Shana Reiji that stood before him. Everyone was waiting with bated breath for the hero's answer. And after a long, silent moment, Reiji firmly raised his head.

"I will undertake your request."

Thought so. He would never agree to that. There's no way he would—What?

To be clear, Reiji had indeed just said the words: "I will undertake your request."

Wait... Hey, hey, hey, hey, heeeeey!

Reiji agreed. He went and did it. Suimei had to wonder for a moment if his ears were playing tricks on him, but no. Reiji had honestly agreed to do it.

"Excellent! Then—"

"WAIT RIGHT THEEEEEEEEEEERE!"

This couldn't happen. Drowning out the king's delighted voice, Suimei's shriek reverberated through the audience chamber. It was so loud that even Suimei was surprised at himself. Everyone else gathered in the audience chamber froze up, completely aghast. Though he had just disrespected the king by screaming over him, it was so sudden and unexpected that not a single person threatened him for his actions. Even our softhearted hero looked like he had no idea what to do.

"Wh-What's the matter all of a sudden, Suimei? Raising your voice like that..."

"It ain't sudden, and of course I'd raise my voice, you dumbass! Mr. 'Oh, yes, I'd gladly march to my death for you,' did your fucking brain rot?! You just said you were going to beat the shit out of a demon army that's—let me remind you—about to destroy the world! Millions! We're literally talking millions of demons! I'm not the one who's in the wrong here for raising my voice! You are for accepting this crap without even consulting with me or Mizuki first, damn it!"

Suimei's breathing became rough as he railed at Reiji without hesitation or pause. He was in an agitated state, but Reiji looked at him and replied with his usual straightforward expression.

"It's exactly because of that army of millions of demons that the people here are suffering, and things will only get worse if nothing is done. That's why the people of this world have called on their last hope, a hero. And that hero is me. That's why I'm here, so I need to do everything I can for these people."

"Listen, I'm trying to tell you it doesn't have to be like that! We have no obligation to these people!"

"Sure we only came to this world today. Just like you said, we have no obligations here. But we're all human, and that connects us. Where is your sense of solidarity? We're bound together by something more important than obligation, aren't we?"

Reiji spoke in a philosophical and somewhat cool manner. How was he, a mere high schooler, so articulate on such an important platform? Suimei wanted to grill him about that for the next hour or so, but…

"You've certainly got a point, but… Actually, no, that doesn't have anything to do with this! What I'm saying is that there's no reason *you* have to be the one to do it!"

In the heat of the moment, Reiji's lofty speech was so compelling that Suimei was about to concede, but he countered with what should have been most obvious. Reiji was a student. Unlike Suimei, his only real experience with violence added up to brawling with the neighborhood delinquents. He wasn't incapable of fighting, certainly, but no matter how he tried to cut it, he stood no realistic chance against a trained army. But in spite of it all, Reiji shook his head and settled the matter with a bad joke.

"You don't know that. Right now, I'm overflowing with an amazing power. With this, I very well may be able to defeat a Demon Lord."

"What the hell are you talking about, you moron?! This 'amazing power' of yours 'very well may' do absolutely nothing! A great scholar once said, 'Fights are all about the numbers, bro!' Ever heard that one before?! I don't care how strong you are, this is basic math, man! It's you against a million!"

"I'll never know if I don't try. We already know that people summoned here have saved this world before."

It was true they'd learned that much so far, but it was entirely possible those stories were just legends passed down from generation to generation.

"Maybe they just got lucky."

"But it's precisely that luck that represents an undeniable truth. And honestly speaking, I can't just abandon those in need. It may not be sensible, but I want to help the people of this world."

"Reiji. Again, you're..."

Suimei was slightly discouraged at Reiji's earnestness. Pitied it, even. This was Reiji's disease. The moment he saw someone in trouble, he would throw himself into the fray for their sake. That's just who he was, and he hadn't changed since the day Suimei met him.

He would go about trying to save someone and get people like Suimei involved, but in the end, he would save everyone. He was strong, and his only real weakness was being unable to look the other way. That was Shana Reiji. Suimei, who had been by his side for years, knew his true nature quite well.

"Suimei... If you don't want to help, then I won't force you. Honestly, I'd feel better if you were with me, but I'm the only one who obtained power as a hero. This falls on my shoulders, and I'll understand if you don't come with me."

"You damn... It's a matter of principle. Of course I don't want to go, but it's not just...!"

"Mm, I know. You're worried about me, right? Whenever I don't think things through, you're always the one who's there to straighten them out for me, after all."

It was sly of him to say that so kindly. It was moves like that that were the reason Suimei could never actually put his foot down, and would always end up going along with him before he realized it. But this time...

"I'm absolutely not going. I don't want to get involved in any of this, and I don't want to die."

In the end, he just couldn't do it, not even if he was only tagging along. No matter how he thought of it, it was far too reckless.

"Mm. Sorry, Suimei."

"If you're actually sorry, you shouldn't have accepted in the first place, damn it."

Suimei could only reply with a mix of exasperation and resignation to Reiji's heartfelt apology. Next, Reiji turned to Mizuki.

"I'm going to go defeat the Demon Lord. I want you to wait with Suimei, Mizuki."

It was clear on Reiji's face just how determined he was. Mizuki hung her head and trembled like she was frightened. Just what was she thinking about? After several moments of silence, she finally stopped shaking and looked back up as she declared her intentions.

"...Um, I'll go with you, Reiji-kun."

"Wha?!"

"Mizuki..."

"Wow, you too, Mizuki?"

Suimei was baffled. He hadn't expected yet another of his friends to say something so unbelievably out of touch. However, this time, Reiji was on Suimei's side.

"Mizuki, you can't. What I'm going to be taking on is a matter of life and death. That's why I can't take you with me. I don't want to put you through something so dangerous."

Even though Reiji turned her down, Mizuki vigorously shook her head from side to side in protest.

"If this world is doomed if the Demon Lord isn't defeated, then I'm in danger no matter what I do. That's why I want to go with you, Reiji-kun. Maybe I could be of a little use. I don't know what I'll be able to do, and I don't know if I have the same desire you do to save these people, but even so, I want to be by your side, Reiji-kun."

"It'll be dangerous. I may not be able to protect you, Mizuki."

"I know. And if it comes down to that, I won't be upset if you leave me behind. So..."

Even if it came down to that, there was no way she'd be okay with that. Mizuki wanted to be together with the boy she loved, and to that end, she lied about her true feelings now. It was enough to give Reiji pause before he replied.

"...I understand. If you're willing to go that far, then let's do this together. But I need to make one thing clear. I will never, no matter what happens, abandon you, Mizuki."

"Mm..."

Mizuki smiled. Perhaps it was because Reiji had accepted her. She seemed somewhat happy, but even after mustering all her courage, there were tears welling in her eyes.

"Your Majesty. Regarding the subjugation of the demons, I will indeed accept your request. Mizuki and I will do our best."

"Understood. Mizuki-dono, are you truly alright with this?"

"Yes!"

Seeing Mizuki reply so enthusiastically, the king gave her a delighted smile. He then turned his attention to Suimei.

"Suimei-dono, after all this..."

"No, I'm not going to fight against an absurdly oversized army of monsters. Indeed, I will not be going with these two."

"I see..."

The king sounded somewhat disappointed, or really, apologetic. Perhaps that was to be expected since he felt responsible for their summoning. But in stark contrast to the king's attitude, the response from the surrounding audience towards Suimei was ice cold. Whispers of exasperated disbelief and irritation could be heard from the crowd. "Even that girl decided to follow along, yet that young man..." and "It's like he has no backbone," they said.

For people who won't do anything to defend themselves, they really just say whatever the fuck they want. Well, since I'm not doing anything either, I can't really talk, but... Wait, that's not at all what's important here.

After internally griping for a moment, Suimei moved on to something he needed to ask the king no matter what.

"Your Majesty. I have a single request to make of you. Is that alright?"

The people kept whispering. Suimei could hear them hiss "How unbelievably impudent!" and "A bastard like you is not in a position to make a request of His Majesty!" Suimei, however, ignored them. And the king replied without so much as raising his voice.

"Let us hear it."

"Alright. I won't be taking part in subjugating the Demon Lord, so I want you to send me back to my world."

He had no intention of helping with the counteroffensive, so there was no need for him to stay here. He wanted them to invert the hero summoning ritual and send him home as quickly as possible. He thought it was a simple enough request, but the king made no reply.

"..."

Instead of an answer, a heavy silence fell over the room. When Suimei looked around, he saw Reiji standing there looking like he didn't have a single clue what was going on, and Mizuki looking like she at least had a faint idea. As for Titania and Felmenia, they were both pale and had sour looks on their faces. It was pretty clear something was up. They hadn't looked like that until Suimei asked to be returned home. In other words, his request was the cause. Realizing that much, a terrible hypothesis crossed Suimei's mind.

"Hey, wait a sec. Don't tell me…"

Suimei had long lost the composure to stay polite, but his behavior was understandable. If his hypothesis was correct, what he was asking was out of the question. The silence lingered in the air for another few moments before the king resolutely spoke up.

"My apologies, but I cannot return you to your own world. It is not that I do not wish to do so. It's simply that there exists no such way to do so."

Hearing those words, Suimei's temple began twitching. And then, knowing full well it was disrespectful, he decided to go all in on asking just one more time.

"I'm sorry. I didn't hear you very well. Could you please repeat that one more time?"

"There exists no method to return you to your own world. Thus, we are unable to send you home."

There it was. That was the decisive blow. Suimei spontaneously stomped his foot on the ground so hard he almost put a hole through the floor.

"Wha… DON'T FUCK WITH MEEEEEEEEEEE!"

Suimei's second shriek of the day rang out through the audience chamber.

★

After the incident in the audience chamber, an uproar broke out that was unprecedented since the founding of the Kingdom of Astel. After hearing the king tell him he couldn't be returned to his world, Suimei screamed and broke out into a royal rage. "Aren't you just a fucking idiot to summon someone when you can't send them back?!" and "No matter how you put it, that's just too selfish, you moron!" were some of the gems that left his mouth in his outburst. And after hurling all manner of verbal abuse at the king, he approached the throne. At that point, Suimei had gone completely berserk. He was no longer thinking rationally, and he didn't give so much as a second thought to where he was and what consequences his actions had—

he was that mad. However, considering the circumstances and what he'd just been told, it was perhaps a normal enough reaction.

But to those present, this was a frightening situation. They had no idea what the summoned party was capable of, and whether or not Suimei would harm the king. As he approached the throne, the leaders and soldiers present came running over to stop him by force. Things were on the verge of escalating into an irreversibly serious affair, but once Reiji and Mizuki sensed the tension in the room, they held Suimei back and somehow managed to avoid any further problems.

And then, before his rage had even cooled, Suimei was frantically carried away, just about crammed into a room that was given to him, and shut inside alone. That was where he found himself now—his emotions still unsettled and his stomach churning nonstop.

"Shit, seriously? Seriously…?"

At his wits' end, Suimei doubted the reality of it all a countless number of times. However, no matter how many times he pinched his cheeks, he just wouldn't wake up in his own bed. No matter how many times he looked out of the window, the foreign scenery remained unchanged. Being so confronted with the ugly truth of it all only multiplied his anguish. Suimei screamed out, cursing the culprits who were no longer there with him.

"Aaaaaaaargh! What the hell do I do now?! I don't know the equation for a fucking spell that can cross the boundaries between worlds!"

The summoning spell that brought them to this world was different from a normal summoning spell. The function was the same in theory, but in order for it to work across dimensions, the scale of it was nearly unthinkable. If they'd summoned him to the astral plane, it would be a different story, but to summon a target whose location couldn't even be verified in a parallel world was something Suimei had never even heard of back home.

Even assuming these two worlds were bound to one another by a causal relationship based on the fact that they'd already traveled between them once, using such a connection as the basis for teleportation magicka would be incredibly weak. It would be like sending a train out on rickety, brittle tracks and hoping to reach your destination on faith alone. It was just as likely to go flying off course and lose absolutely everything in the process.

"Ugh..."

Suimei let out a pained groan. Since he was summoned here, even if it was by accident, he knew some kind of path had to exist. Even if it was grasping at straws, if he could somehow make that work...

"Please connect, Mary..."

Communication magicka—thanks to the widespread use of cell phones, it was a fossil of magicka that was rarely ever used nowadays. But with it, Suimei tried to establish a connection with one of his acquaintances, Hydemary Alzbayne. She was the girl he had completed the most jobs for the Society with back on Earth, and if he could get through to her, it would be possible to solidify the connection. That way, even in the worst-case scenario that he really couldn't return home, he could at least let her know what had happened to him.

"Shit!"

But the attempt was fruitless. The distance between this plane and his was just too great, and he couldn't establish a connection.

"If it's come to this, I'll have to make a way back myself, huh?"

The difficult challenge weighed on his shoulders like nothing he had ever faced before, and he fired out a tremendous sigh. There was always the option of giving up, but in order to accomplish what he needed to do, he absolutely had to find a way home.

"Hahh…"

Suimei took a deep breath in, and then…

"I'M DEFINITELY GOING BACK, YOU HEAR MEEEEEEEEEEE?!"

He released his determination as a roar.

★

A few days after Suimei and the others were summoned to this strange new world, Reiji and Mizuki stood before the royal knights and court mages in the outdoor training grounds of Royal Castle Camellia.

"Finally, huh, Reiji-kun?"

"Yeah."

Mizuki was unable to contain her enthusiasm. After all, they were about to begin their magic training with Titania and the royal mages and knights. It was no surprise that Mizuki was ecstatic, but Reiji was also unable to hide the fact that his blood was pumping with excitement.

"Magic, huh? I never thought the day would come when we'd be able to use it."

In their world, something like that was completely unthinkable. It was just a dream that anybody could have, but no one could accomplish. It was merely a fictional power that only existed in fantasy. But no longer.

"I guess we really are in a different world, huh?"

Mizuki hung her head as her heart was seized with loneliness and the feelings that she was hiding within her escaped her lips. In truth, this was difficult for her. But that was perfectly understandable. Suimei certainly wasn't the only one who was shocked to hear they couldn't return home. Though Mizuki had decided to follow Reiji, she felt the same way. Even Reiji felt the weighty sadness of never being able to see his loved ones again.

"Mizuki…"

"Ah, I'm s-sorry! I just got a little gloomy."

"No, it's fine. I know how you feel…"

"Yeah…"

"But relax. I'm going to protect you, remember?"

That was right. Reiji was the one who'd made the decision to undertake all this, and he'd promised to support Mizuki in the process. But when she thought about that and what it meant, she began blushing furiously.

"R-Reiji-kun! D-Do you mean…"

"Hmm? What's wrong?"

"What I'm asking, um, is…"

"…?"

"Ah… That's right. You are Reiji-kun, after all…"

Just what was wrong with her? After realizing something, Mizuki grumbled to herself in a disappointed and somewhat exasperated voice. Reiji didn't know what drove her to behave like that, but Mizuki suddenly recalled a different anxiety and shared her thoughts with Reiji.

"I wonder if Suimei-kun's okay…"

Her thoughts had wandered to their friend who wasn't with them: her classmate Yakagi Suimei. After the scene in the audience chamber, he'd shut himself in the room given to him and wouldn't come out. Perhaps not being able to return to their world was just that much of a shock to him. Even when Reiji and Mizuki tried to talk to him through the door as concerned friends, he would only give them listless replies. They still didn't really know what condition he was in. But to alleviate Mizuki's worries, Reiji smiled at her.

"I don't really think you need to worry about him. It's Suimei we're talking about. After a few days, he'll come out of his room and act like nothing happened, you know?"

"Yeah... I hope so."

Reiji's kind words helped, but Mizuki was still anxious. The situation was just that complex and alarming. Her concern for Suimei and her concerns about what would happen from here on out fed off of each other. But those feelings were only natural, all things considered. It was just as Suimei had said in the audience chamber that day. Was it really okay for Reiji to make a decision like that on his own without consulting them?

"It seems everybody has gathered, so let us begin. Reiji-sama, are you finished with your preparations?"

While Reiji was pondering for himself whether or not he'd made the right choice, Titania looked around at the line of court mages and suggested starting their practice. Her words brought Reiji out of his thoughts.

"Yes, I'm ready at any time."

"I do apologize for keeping you waiting."

"No, it's no problem."

"You're so gracious and kind, Reiji-sama."

Titania offered a grand smile. Reiji hadn't known her for that long, but she had been courteous with them all this time. Perhaps that was just her nature. Despite being royalty, she didn't give off even a hint of arrogance, and was quite personable. While Reiji was admiring her qualities, Titania gracefully spun around on the spot.

"Then to start, I shall introduce the court mages who will be watching over your progress. First, White Flame-dono—forgive me—Lady Stingray."

Titania had to correct herself since she wasn't used to addressing Felmenia that way. Felmenia took a step forward from the line as her name was called out, and made a respectful bow before Reiji.

"This will be the third time I've introduced myself, but please allow me this formality. My name is Felmenia Stingray. I may be the most inexperienced of Astel's court mages, but please do treat me well."

"I look forward to working with you."

Reiji returned her polite greeting in kind. This first mage that Titania had introduced was none other than the mage who had summoned him to this world. That was likely why the princess had called on her first, but Felmenia Stingray stood out on her own. Her most remarkable feature was her beautiful silver hair. And though she called herself inexperienced, she was collected and came off as wise. She was no Princess Titania, but Felmenia was also an exceptional beauty. Furthermore, her pronounced chest was—Reiji gulped.

"To the left is Lord Malfous, then Lord Kran…"

"Huh?"

Mesmerized by Felmenia's body, Reiji missed Titania's introduction of the other court mages. Titania realized that he seemed lost, and read far too much into the confused sound that escaped his lips. She was worried something had happened.

"Um, Reiji-sama, is something the matter?"

"N-No, um…"

67

"Are you not feeling well?"

"I'm fine. Really, it's nothing, hahaha…"

Having difficulty smoothing this over, Reiji forced a laugh. He couldn't possibly admit that he wasn't listening to her because he was staring at Felmenia. That would be far too lame.

"Is that so? Well, that's all for the introductions, but—Oh, now that I recall, there is still something that I must inquire about, Reiji-sama."

Remembering something she wanted to ask him, Titania clapped her hands together and turned to Reiji.

"Let me see. If I remember correctly, the world you two hail from doesn't have any magic, so…"

"It's true. Instead, our world has a power known as science."

It was common knowledge—or at least commonly believed—on Earth that there was no such thing as magic. But to the people of this world, that was almost unimaginable. Mutterings like "What's science?" and "I haven't ever heard of that" could be heard here and there in the gathered crowd, but it was Felmenia that finally spoke up with a dubious expression.

"I apologize for cutting in on the conversation, but Hero-dono, is that really the truth?"

"Yes, it is, but… Is something wrong with that?"

"No, I was just a little curious… Forgive me for asking again, but there is no falsehood in what you say?"

As Felmenia asked for confirmation once more, one of the court mages in the line deliberately cleared his throat. And then, with plenty of sarcasm in his voice, he rebuked her.

"Lady Stingray, are you not being a little discourteous to the hero who has been conferred the task of saving this world?"

"My apologies."

Felmenia politely bowed her head in response to the criticism, but she looked perturbed. There seemed to be something bothering her. Reiji had no idea what she was getting at by questioning him like that, so Mizuki took it upon herself to explain things to Felmenia.

"In our world, the concept of magic exists, but it only has a place in works of fiction. Sadly, in our world, there really is no magic."

To them, magic was nothing but a product of the imagination used in literary works. Authors created it to make their stories more interesting; it was literally fiction. Like Reiji, Titania thought Felmenia's questions on the matter seemed strange, and grew curious as to her motivation.

"White Flame-dono, is something the matter?"

"No… It's nothing. I apologize for putting a damper on the conversation."

"Truly? If you insist, that's fine, but…"

As Titania tilted her head to the side, the attendant standing next to her whispered something in her ear. It seemed she was being urged to move things along, because Titania then recollected herself and continued the original conversation.

"Well, it's about time we begin. This will be Reiji-sama's first real encounter with magic, so I would like for somebody to present a simple demonstration and explanation. As such…"

Before Titania could even finish making her request, the court mage who had reprimanded Felmenia earlier stepped forward full of confidence. If Reiji recalled correctly, this was the man Titania had introduced as Lord Kran. Whoever he was, he had a distinctly thin figure and long hair. Quite bluntly, he was a gloomy-looking fellow. He seemed to be concerned about his appearance, however, as he had been persistently fidgeting with his bangs right up until he stepped forward. Reiji suspected he was either offering his opinion, or saying that he would answer Titania's request himself. His latter prediction turned out to be correct.

"Though it may be presumptuous of me, I shall gladly teach our hero the basics of magic."

"...You will?"

"I'm at your service, Your Highness."

The mage replied to Titania's perplexed question in a particularly pompous manner. His behavior was courteous on the surface, but somehow his self-satisfied smirk left Reiji with an indescribable sense of unease. And then, Titania turned towards Felmenia.

"I was thinking White Flame-dono would be most suitable for the task... What do you think, White Flame-dono?"

Both the man who'd stepped forward and Felmenia looked surprised at Titania's suggestion.

"Wha?!"

"...Is it alright for me to take such an important job?"

"Yes. You wield the greatest magic in all our kingdom, so I believe you're the ideal candidate."

"G-Greatest in the kingdom..."

Titania made her endorsement with confidence. Felmenia seemed especially moved at the use of the word "greatest" to describe her and her skills, but the court mage who'd stepped forward was unable to stomach it and voiced his objection accordingly.

"W-With all due respect, Your Highness, I do not believe that White Flame-dono is more qualified than I am to instruct the hero in magic."

He wasn't happy with having his job taken from him by a girl who could have easily been his daughter. And Felmenia certainly didn't miss the implication in what he said.

"Are you suggesting I'm an inferior mage?"

"White Flame-dono, perhaps you might know that I am also an instructor at the Mage's Guild. I might even dare to say that I have a little conceit in my teaching ability when it comes to magic. Surely you can see how my experience benefits me here, especially compared to a young lady like yourself."

Felmenia looked slighted at first, but her expression quickly changed to a daring smile.

"Oh? Then shall we have a little test to see?"

"If you so wish."

Tension filled the air. Invisible sparks were flying between Felmenia and the older court mage.

"H-Huh? Is this a fight? Are they going to fight?"

"I don't know if it's going to be a fight, but something's about to happen for sure."

Mizuki was antsy at this sudden development in what was shaping up to be a very unorthodox first lesson, so Reiji tried to calm her down. Titania, on the other hand, said nothing. She seemed perfectly content to let this continue. Contrary to Reiji's first impression of her being especially softhearted, she seemed to have quite the stubborn streak.

"Very well. We'll have a demonstration from both of you, and we'll judge which is more worthy."

After Titania declared what the rules were, both mages took their positions.

"Oh Earth! Gather and transform! Become a tremendous power to oppress my foe! Rock Ridge!"

The first to cast was the older court mage. He recited a spell that sounded like something right out of a video game. Mizuki squealed in excited anticipation. And as soon as the mage finished his incantation, ocher masses of stone gathered from thin air and took shape as a sharp rock angled into a peak that floated in midair.

"Amazing!"

"…!"

Mizuki animatedly threw both her hands in the air and cried out with joy. Reiji simply stood there with his eyes wide open in surprise. And once the spell was cast, the court mage flashed a satisfied smile and began his explanation.

"Hero-dono, this is what we call magic. As mages, we use mana to appeal to the Elements that compose our world and summon their great power. By calling to the earth and praying silently to it, you will also be able to—"

"How abstract."

"What?"

Felmenia interrupted the court mage's prideful explanation with a scornful laugh, and he immediately turned to her with an irritated scowl.

"I said, 'How abstract.' You might be able to get away with an explanation like that with someone from this world, but if you might recall, the hero is from a world with no magic at all. How could you expect him to know what you mean when you talk about mana and the Elements?"

"Th-That's…"

"You'd do well to watch and learn."

After coldly declaring that, Felmenia began chanting.

"Oh Fire. Thou art imbued with the essence of all flame, but burn unbound by the laws of nature. Now, turn everything in existence to ashes, the white calamity of truth! Truth Flare!"

Felmenia weaved her spell together swiftly. As she spoke, Reiji could feel heat welling up in his own body.

Ah...

Just a little below his navel, right where one of his meditative focus points would be, he felt a mysterious heat growing. It was like Felmenia's chant was calling to it and summoning something inside him.

"Hero-dono. The power of the Elements is the power of all creation. It is the source of anything and everything. The heat you feel when touched by fire. The cool, soothing sensation you feel when you touch water. If you can appreciate that, the Elements shall rightfully lend you their assistance. As for mana, just harnessing that incredible power you feel within you now will be enough."

"Wow..."

Mizuki was in awe. And it was no wonder. The moment Felmenia finished her chant, a flame the same pearlescent color as her robes appeared and lit up their surroundings. The shimmering white flame then consumed the small mountain created by the court mage and reduced it to cinders.

After a mere glance at her handiwork, Felmenia turned her gaze on the older court mage. She looked bored.

"Hmph. It seems your magic was all bark and no bite..."

"Wh-Wh-Wh-Wh-What?!"

"D-Did you see that, Reiji-kun?! The white flame went whoosh, then it was all ba-ba-boom!"

"Yeah, I saw..."

While Mizuki excitedly recalled the events with childlike glee, Reiji just stared at the smoldering white embers. Mizuki quickly calmed down, but she was still fascinated by what she'd seen.

"So that's real magic..."

Indeed, what they'd witnessed was real magic. And it was just as awesome as they'd imagined it would be. Seeing how mesmerized they were, the older court mage took action. Even though he'd been shown up, he didn't have any intention of admitting defeat. Unfortunately for him, however, Felmenia had anticipated that much.

"Oh White Flame, become a vortex! Tornado Flare!"

As Felmenia recited her spell, the smoldering remains of the white flame still on the ground ignited once more and swirled around the court mage. He had no time to take any countermeasures. In an instant, he was completely encircled in white fire.

"It's over."

After Felmenia declared her victory, the court mage let out a dissatisfied groan.

"Ugh... Don't think that just because you won with the sheer destructive force of your magic..."

His magic had been completely overwhelmed. He'd utterly lost in that regard, but as he was suggesting, that alone wasn't enough to determine who would make the better instructor. Everyone then turned to Titania for the final call.

"As I suspected, White Flame-dono will do quite nicely, don't you think? Between her magical prowess and her considerate quick thinking regarding Reiji-sama being from another world, I don't see any shortcomings."

"Yes, but Your Highness…"

Felmenia directed her sharp gaze at the court mage continuing to grasp at straws.

"You don't know when to give up. As one of Astel's proud court mages, you should gallantly accept what's happened."

"Wh-What are…"

"Stand down. Or are you saying that you find fault in my judgment?"

Titania interjected and voiced her displeasure. The older court mage let out two or three bitter groans as his face turned a dark red. Then, after squeezing out his assent to the princess's decree, he finally stepped back. He still wasn't satisfied, but knew it wasn't smart to earn the ire of royalty. When that was all said and done, Felmenia turned to Reiji with a confident grin.

"Now then, Hero-dono. As the foremost mage of this kingdom, I will be instructing you in the ways of magic."

"Yes, Felmenia-sensei."

"S-Sensei?"

"You're going to be my instructor from this point on, so I thought it would be appropriate to address you accordingly."

"But, Hero-dono, you are the one shouldering the burden of saving us and our world. Moreover, there's no significant difference in our age. So isn't calling me 'sensei' a bit strange?"

"Even if the circumstances are unusual, it's not wrong. I'm not putting myself on a pedestal just because I'm a hero, and I intend to treat the person teaching me magic with all due respect. So please, let me call you sensei. If you dislike it, however, I'll refrain."

"...Truly? If that's your wish, then I do not have any reason to object. Please address me as you see fit."

"Thank you very much, Sensei."

Felmenia was still a little perplexed at being addressed with such a title, but she seemed to grow a little used to it as Reiji repeated it with a cheerful tone. She nodded in response.

"V-Very well then. Are you ready for your lesson, Hero-dono?"

"You have my full attention."

With that, Felmenia whipped around and began giddily mumbling to herself.

"Sensei...? I'm an instructor... The hero's instructor... Heehee..."

Reiji couldn't hear her, but Titania urged them to begin the lesson as Felmenia recovered from her brief intoxication and collected herself.

"White Flame-dono, I leave the rest to you."

"Yes, Your Highness. Then first, Hero-dono, I would like you to bear in mind what I said when I demonstrated my magic earlier, and imagine the phenomenon you felt inside yourself again. Now try focusing that feeling... in the palm of your hand would be appropriate, I believe. With that, even without a spell or other specifics, you should be able to do something simple."

"Is that really all it takes?"

"It's not like you'll be able to do it right away. You will likely have to try focusing several times. No one gets it right on their first attempt."

Reiji nodded in response to Felmenia's explanation and prepared himself. He'd have to give it a try before anything else. He tried remembering what he'd felt in the pit of his stomach earlier when Felmenia had used her spell.

"Reiji-kun, good luck!"

With Mizuki's cheering him on from the sidelines, Reiji took a step forward.

I can do it. It's okay.

Assuming that the welling heat he'd felt in his abdomen earlier was mana, Reiji slowly closed his eyes and tried to focus that energy in the palm of his hand as he lifted it.

"Looking good. Now, just like that, find the pulse inside you that's coming from a source other than your heart."

A pulse that's not from my heart? Is... this what she's talking about here?

Following Felmenia's instructions, Reiji concentrated solely on the sensations within his body. As he did, he realized there was something pulsating inside him. It wasn't his heart, but it beat with a regular rhythm all the same. Just as he'd expected, it was coming from right below his navel—the place believed to gather one's chi in Oriental medicine.

"Once you've found that, you're almost there. All you need to do now is guide the energy of that pulse to the palm of your hand... That being said, doing so is no easy task."

It sounded like she was under the assumption Reiji wouldn't be able to do it. Attaining magic was no mean feat, and what she was asking Reiji to do was the litmus test that determined whether or not someone was capable of becoming a mage.

No, I can do it...

Reiji, on the other hand, didn't doubt himself. He could still feel the warm sensation growing inside him, and that inspired and encouraged him. Trying to conjure up its power, the first thing that came to Reiji's mind was fire. But his was different from what Felmenia had used. Reiji's was as red as the sun as it melted away at the evening hour—a dazzling and burning fire.

And then words came to Reiji like a revelation.

"Oh Fire, manifest here and now! Flare!"

Reiji's mana gathered as he shouted out his command like he was unleashing the rage in his heart, hailing the Elements. In the center of his palm, a brilliant red flame was now flickering—a magical flame. But in a split second, Reiji's concentration was broken and the flame vanished without leaving a single ember.

"I did it…"

Reiji was floored at his success on his first try, and the other mages watching seemed to share the sentiment. "Th-That was really his first time?!" and "That's our hero!" they whispered excitedly. Even Felmenia who had coached him through it step by step offered praise.

"Magnificent… You're a natural, Hero-dono. A genius."

Titania followed up after her.

"My heartfelt congratulations, Hero-sama. With this, you now have your place among the mages."

"I'm… a mage?"

Reiji was swept up in a flood of emotion at Titania's words. She turned to address Felmenia next.

"Well done, White Flame-dono. Your method of teaching must be quite effective."

"No, I hardly had anything to do with it. Hero-dono is simply gifted."

"Of course Hero-sama has talent, but there is no mistaking that you had a vital hand in his success. Hero-sama came from a world with no magic, yet he was immediately able to grasp its use with your help. Both his power and your instruction are exceptional."

"Thank you very much, Your Highness."

Felmenia respectfully bowed in response to such high praise. Yet even as she lowered her head, she was overflowing with joy. Mizuki timidly called out to her as she stood back up.

"U-Um…"

"What is the matter? Mizuki-dono."

Mizuki sucked down a deep breath to calm her nerves, and put the passionate feelings she was hiding in her heart into words.

"C-Can you teach me magic too?! I also want to learn!"

"Very well. Then…"

And so another mage was born into the world.

Chapter 2 The Place I Must Return to Is So Far Away

Two weeks had flown by since Suimei and the others were summoned to this strange new world and asked to defeat the Demon Lord. The time Reiji was set to depart was swiftly approaching. Two weeks to prepare for subjugating such a powerful foe seemed woefully insufficient, but looking to the stories of previous heroes, it seemed two weeks was historically what it took for a hero's power to fully manifest. And so Reiji had spent his days endeavoring to learn magic and master combat.

Since she'd decided to accompany him on his quest, Mizuki was training alongside him, and they were taking lessons from both the captain of the royal guard and Court Mage Felmenia. Their schedule was mind-bogglingly packed to try and fit in everything they needed to learn in two weeks. As for the results of their intense training, however... Suimei didn't even want to think about it.

Hahh...

Suimei had watched Reiji and Mizuki training from his window, and they both dropped by every day to let him know how things were going. All he could do was sigh at their progress. He was aggrieved at what they'd achieved in such a short span of time. It was downright cruel.

Since Reiji was just an ordinary citizen before all this, it was no surprise that he got thoroughly schooled in combat training. He'd never studied a martial art before and didn't even know how to defend himself—for the first two days, at least. He picked up on things so quickly that by the third day, he was able to seriously go toe to toe with the captain of the royal guard. Now there wasn't anyone that could stand up to him, so he'd taken to fighting against several men at once for training.

And if that wasn't cruel, what was it? Suimei wouldn't dare call it amazing. He knew the only way to properly describe power like that was "cruel." He didn't know if it was the divine blessing from the hero summoning or whatever else might be at work, but regardless of the reason, the progress Reiji was making was absurd.

Rather than a sponge, he was taking things in like a water pump in overdrive. He wasn't absorbing the water known as talent, but relentlessly sucking it up. Watching it happen, Suimei felt like all the hard work he'd ever put into learning anything meant nothing. It was a terrible feeling.

That's cheating. Seriously.

Even when it came to magic, Reiji's newfound talent was remarkable. It had taken Suimei two years from his first encounter with magicka to definitively get his head around the concept and hone his senses enough to be able to see the power he had. But Reiji had only needed one afternoon. He'd manifested fire on his first try, and things had only escalated from there.

It was incredible, and incredibly dispiriting to Suimei. Life was simply unfair. And unable to face it, Suimei had kept himself shut up in his room while Reiji only continued to grow stronger.

Yet even though he'd sequestered himself, he was far from idle. He spent most of his time reading books from this world. Suimei remembered King Almadious telling him he couldn't return home all too well, including the uncharacteristic temper tantrum he'd thrown afterward. It sucked, but it was reality. Suimei was stuck here.

So for the past two weeks, Suimei had amassed the knowledge he'd need to survive in this world by devouring books retrieved from the castle library. Since he was going to be living in this world now, there was plenty that he needed to relearn. And that knowledge might be the make-or-break difference in his survival here. It would be the difference between him adapting seamlessly and struggling to scrape by.

Fortunately, thanks to the benefits of the hero summoning, Suimei was able to understand the common language of this world, both spoken and written. That gave him the ability to read books here without relying on anyone's help, and he was utilizing that to the fullest.

As for the masses of knowledge he was attaining, he was breaking down information and sorting it into three categories: things he could easily remember, things that were important enough to hold on to and store in his bag, and things he could write down on his magickal memo pad. With that system, the amount of knowledge he'd acquired over the last two weeks was nothing to sneeze at.

But it still wasn't enough. There was no doubt that he'd increased his knowledge base several fold, but only harvesting information from books was insufficient. Sadly, articles on current events were scarce, and books on the magic of this world were inaccessible to him. In short, Suimei wasn't satisfied with what he'd managed to accomplish.

"Now then, setting that aside..."

But what he needed to focus on now was much more pressing.

Currently, Suimei was shut inside a gloomy stone room. It was completely devoid of furnishings, and there was no sign it had ever been lived in. In that sense, it was quite strange, but the most interesting thing of all was the enormous magicka circle at Suimei's feet. It was the teleportation circle.

Indeed, Suimei was in the ritual chamber where they'd first arrived, and he'd come here with a purpose.

"..."

What Suimei was focusing on in silence was obviously none other than the magicka circle drawn on the floor. It connected his world with this one, and as the main agent of the summoning spell that had brought him here, was an object of great disdain.

If what King Almadious had said in the audience chamber was to be believed, the spell worked by having a summoner in this world reach out to another. The target of the summoning—in the language this world used to describe magic—was hailed by the summoner. That was the problem, since the summoner had no way to reverse the process and put the target back in their original world. The magicka behind the summoning circle was essentially a worthless one-way ticket, which Suimei regarded as a giant pain.

But there was nothing that could be done about it. If no one knew of a spell to return, Suimei would simply have to come up with it himself. And he was ready to pull out all the stops to do it. To that end, analyzing the summoning circle that had brought him here seemed like the quickest possible way to get a lead.

"Just a little bit more until the analysis is complete..."

Just how many times had he already gone out of his way to try and do this? Over the past two weeks, he'd taken every opportunity he could get to sneak out of his room and come to this chamber to try and study the circle without anyone finding out.

But this wasn't a standard spell, and there was nothing standard about analyzing it. Normally analyzing magicka began with examining its roots, but information on this summoning magicka was so heavily guarded that Suimei had given up and decided to try something different. Instead, he'd adopted a top-down approach that started with investigating the circle itself.

"Alright, let's get started…"

Talking as though he meant to convince himself of what he was doing, Suimei invoked his analysis magicka.

"Correspondence of all creation…"

Acting in concert with Suimei's chant, a jade light made of mana rose up from his feet. It was an analysis circle, and it would be what he used to try and unravel the summoning circle. The spell that had actually been used to transport them here was still unknown to him. The exterior circle supplied support and kept things in balance, but there was no protection from the other side at all. The secondary circle didn't seem to play a role. The triangular shapes of the diagram were inverted, suggesting a way to control the target, and the small intermediary circles were…

★

Finishing up his business for the moment, Suimei decided to return to his room and left the ritual chamber. Sneaking, of course. As for the path back, he recalled it from memory. He'd long since memorized the way to and from his room. As he walked along, he muttered to himself.

"At any rate, the fact that nobody has found me out yet… Practically speaking, isn't that kind of troubling?"

It was true. Suimei was able to go the whole way to and from the ritual chamber multiple times now without being spotted. Since he didn't want to be seen, he was using astrology magicka to cloak himself, but even then, not a single person had suspected him or sensed that something was amiss. Security seemed lacking, to say the least. On the way over, Suimei had even walked right by someone who looked like a court mage. He'd leaned in to taunt them and test his limits, which likely looked quite silly, but they'd had zero reaction whatsoever.

"Hrmm…"

Suimei folded his arms. The fact that there wasn't any sort of alarm or detection magicka system in place struck Suimei as rather reckless of them. Perhaps the castle just didn't have any talented magicians on staff.

But nothing would come out of Suimei contemplating the castle's security issues, so he quickly put the thought out of his mind and continued on his way. In a matter of moments, however, he realized that he'd walked into a rather unexpected problem.

"Uh oh…"

The stupefied gasp that came out of his mouth perfectly matched the dumbfounded expression on his face. Thinking too hard must have distracted him enough that he'd taken a wrong turn somewhere, because he now found himself in an unfamiliar passage. Just how was he supposed to get back to his room from here? That question now dominated his thoughts. He'd only memorized the way to and from his room, and hadn't bothered learning the layout of the rest of the castle.

Oh my god, I'm an idiot.

Suimei put his hand on his forehead as he looked up at the ceiling. This was yet another blunder. He was kicking himself over it, but he knew it wouldn't help to dwell on it.

"Oooh well… I guess I'll just pop out somewhere and ask someone for directions."

Suimei dispelled his astrology magicka for the moment, and went looking for people. Surely if he said he was lost, someone would tell him where he needed to go. With a little luck and good timing, after walking down the passage for a short while, he quickly spotted someone. Approaching from behind, he called out to them.

"Um, excuse me."

The robed figure then came to a stop and gracefully turned around.

"What is the... Oh my, Suimei-dono."

"Hmm? Ah, if I remember right, you're..."

"My name is Felmenia Stingray."

Her voice and face were familiar. After politely giving him her name once more, he realized this was the young woman who'd taken part in the hero summoning—the silver-haired court mage Felmenia Stingray. He then nodded and let out a quiet "Aaah." Seeing that, Felmenia knit her brow.

"What are you doing here, Suimei-dono?"

It was a perfectly good question. After the incident in the audience chamber, Suimei had shut himself in the room he'd been given. But now that he was suddenly out and about without Reiji, it was quite reasonable for her to be a tad suspicious.

"Oh, I just thought I would take a little walk for a change of pace or something."

"I see. I do think a change of pace is a good idea, but you're still a little unfamiliar with the castle to be walking around on your own, no? On the occasion that you would like to go out, it would be better for you to call someone and have them escort you."

"You have my sincere thanks for the advice. Much obliged."

Despite appearing to be about his age, the girl took a somewhat formal and cool tone with Suimei. Perhaps it was because of her position as a court mage, but Suimei took to imitating it when he spoke back.

"It pains me to ask after you've already been so helpful, but could you perhaps introduce me to somebody who knows how to get back to my room?"

"...Have you forgotten the way?"

"It's rather embarrassing to admit."

"Understood. I know where your room is, but I have business to attend to, so I can only accompany you part of the way there. If that will suffice, then please follow me."

"My apologies for the trouble."

After bowing his head, Suimei followed behind Felmenia as she walked down the hallway. Since she was here in the castle now, she'd probably just finished her magic lessons with Reiji and Mizuki for the day. She was probably on her way to give a report to the king or something. As Suimei continued to wonder what she was up to, she suddenly came to a stop. She then turned around and spoke to him in a quiet voice.

"Suimei-dono, may I ask you something?"

"What is it?"

Suimei urged her to continue with a question of his own, but wondered why she felt such a need to stand on ceremony. Perhaps she was going to ask him about the magicka he'd used in the ritual chamber on the day they met. It was possible she'd noticed. As Suimei was making that grim supposition, Felmenia questioned him in a somewhat sharp tone.

"Suimei-dono, why do you refuse to take part in the Demon Lord's subjugation?"

"Even if you ask why..."

"The hero is your good friend. So why is it that you will not go forth and assist him? I do believe that you are in a position to do so."

As far as Suimei was concerned, these people had summoned him out of laziness and convenience, so to hear one of them talk about duty and obligation—especially to him—was comical and meaningless. Of course they wanted him to save them, but to him, even the thought of having to do that pissed him off. But he knew that he wouldn't get anywhere raising hell about it every time it came up, so he decided to be as blunt as possible.

"My answer to you will be the same as what I told His Majesty in the audience chamber. I flatly refuse to do anything so dangerous. That's why I decided not to go with them."

Felmenia's expression grew even more stern.

"Even the delicate Mizuki-dono said that she would accompany the hero, but you won't?"

"I have no intention of making an emotional decision and getting dragged along."

"...Are you suggesting that's what Mizuki-dono did?"

"Isn't it? In the heat of the moment, what other answer could she have given?"

Suimei knew he was being bitter, but what he was saying was still true. Mizuki had made the same mistake Reiji had and made a commitment without fully understanding the situation or taking the time to discuss it with her friends. They'd all been put on the spot, but Suimei felt Reiji and Mizuki had acted foolishly.

When Suimei dropped his formal manner of speech, Felmenia's attitude also changed. She'd been treating him rather courteously up until now, but her tone suddenly turned cold.

"Hmph, what a despicable man."

"What did you say?"

In response, Suimei immediately became combative. Seeing Felmenia look at him so scornfully irritated him. But despite the change in his mood, she continued to pour oil on the fire.

"I said you're despicable, you damn coward. Do you really think you're so smart for looking down on the courage your friends have mustered? No, it makes you petty and a fool. A bastard like you has no right to call himself a friend of the hero."

"Whether or not agreeing to this insanity was the right thing to do, don't you at least think it was my choice to make the call for myself? Let me remind you that we were magically kidnapped— 'summoned,' you call it—and asked to go to war to save the people who kidnapped us. Forget me. Don't you think any sane person would say no to that?"

It was a nearly unthinkable situation to be in. Suimei found it hard to believe that anyone, even from this world, would actually agree to a request like that. Felmenia, however, seemed completely unmoved by his argument.

"Even though you were brought here by the hero summoning, however imperfect you may be?"

"So what? It's not like I came here to help you guys out. All you did was arbitrarily summon me. I was dragged into an accident that you caused. Kidnapping, remember? Don't you see that I'm a victim here too? I don't know what kind of ideals you hold that hero summoning or whatever it is to, but I have absolutely no obligation to you people. I don't owe you anything."

After Suimei further drove that in, Felmenia reluctantly conceded that he had a point.

"...I understand what you're saying."

"Good."

"But regardless, Suimei Yakagi, isn't what you've done dishonorable compared to Hero-dono and Mizuki-dono?"

"Ugh…"

Suimei had no intention of arguing with her there. He wasn't the only victim in all this. He had no reason to be nice to the people who had summoned him, but as Felmenia was saying, they weren't the only people he should be thinking about. While Reiji and Mizuki had selflessly stepped forward despite knowing the danger that lay ahead of them, Suimei was still keeping his true identity a secret for personal reasons. It was dishonorable. Selfish, even. And he knew it. He wasn't going to make excuses.

"Yeah, okay… You got me there. The fact that I care more about myself than this world may very well be because I have no honor whatsoever."

"You can admit that, but you still won't help them? What a bastard. You're beyond salvation."

Hearing Suimei cop to being dishonorable, Felmenia exploded. When it came to matters of morality, it seemed she felt quite strongly.

Tch… This damn…

However, to Suimei, Felmenia's anger was quite unexpected. He didn't enjoy being told he was beyond salvation, but she was mad for Reiji and Mizuki's sake. After watching them work so hard, she just couldn't stand Suimei's cavalier attitude on the matter. When he realized that much, despite her role in the miserable summoning that had brought him here, he started to think she was actually a good person.

But while what she was calling him out for was quite valid, he had no intention of opening up to her and telling her the real truth. His thesis was something close to his reason for living, but it was private. And so instead, he frivolously shrugged his shoulders and replied like he didn't care in the slightest.

"Yeah, yeah. Sorry 'bout that."

"You bastard!"

Felmenia was visibly displeased with Suimei's insolent attitude, and glared daggers at him. More importantly, Suimei could see the mana inside her body growing agitated.

"Hey now... just what're you planning to do in this kind of place?"

A strong wave of bloodlust swept down the stone corridor. While keeping his focus on Felmenia as her rage only grew, Suimei put his hands on either side of his head. It looked like a gesture of exasperation, but he was at the ready if worse came to worst. Not a moment later, Felmenia fluently began weaving a spell together.

"Silence, you damned fool. I, Felmenia the White Flame, shall beat some sense into you!"

"Oh come on... Why did it have to come to this?"

"You should take a good look in the mirror and ask yourself that!"

"I mean, you can say whatever you want, but..."

Seeing that Felmenia had taken excessive offense to it all, Suimei let out a somewhat perplexed groan. Her getting fired up for no good reason would only make things more difficult for him. Suimei himself couldn't have been more disinterested in a fight, but when Felmenia realized that he wasn't taking her seriously, she only grew more infuriated.

"Bastard... Are you even listening to me?!"

"Yes, and I can hear you just fine without the yelling. If you keep shouting like that, you're just going to start bothering other people, get it?"

"H-How rude of... No, you bastard! You need to pay serious attention when—"

"My god, just calm down a little... Hmm?"

As Felmenia grew more and more indignant, Suimei scratched his head with a vexed expression on his face. Starting to think there wasn't any way to keep this from breaking out into a fight, he took a moment to size up his opponent. His narrowed eyes looked her up and down, and it was then that he realized the hem of her robe was caught between the sole of her shoe and the floor. In other words, she was stepping on it.

"H-Hey, wait a sec. You're gonna..."

Fall. And dramatically. She would magnificently trip herself on her own robe. He could distinctly envision that future.

"What?! I'm going to what?!"

"I just meant that if you keep this up, well... You see, your foot..."

"Did you think that I would fall for such a transparent ruse, you bastard?! Don't insult me!"

"No, I'm not insulting you or anything. But good grief, calm down already. Seriously..."

In the end, it was tragic. Consumed by anger, Felmenia failed to heed Suimei's warning. She never looked down at her feet, and Suimei's moment of clairvoyance came to fruition.

"Hmm? KYAH!"

Trying to take a step forward with her robe still underfoot, Felmenia pitched forward violently enough that her robe flipped up in the back. Not only did she fall over, but she looked like she was trying to moon someone while doing it.

"Wha?! What did you do, you bastard?! M-My robe, m-my robe is..."

With the back of her robe now flipped up over her head, Felmenia couldn't see anything.

"I didn't do a single thing. I've been standing right here in front of you the whole time."

"What did you say...?! Huh? Huh?"

As she angrily thrashed about, Felmenia ended up strangely wrapping herself up in her robe like a net. That she managed to tie herself up so neatly on her own was actually impressive in its own right. Suimei waited for her to get back up, but contrary to his expectation, all that rose from the lump of cloth on the floor was a tearful whine.

"It won't come off... It won't come oooooff..."

"Good grief. I guess I don't have a choice..."

His face tinged slightly red, Suimei put his hand against his brow in exasperation. The sight of Felmenia with her underwear completely exposed and her curvy backside sticking out as she wriggled around on the floor was unequivocally pitiful.

He couldn't just leave her like that. She hadn't exactly done anything wrong, so he didn't see the harm in helping her. Averting his gaze from her exposed underwear as best he could help it, Suimei untangled the robe that had wound itself up in her incessant struggle to free herself, and then wrapped his arms around her as he pulled her up.

"FUWAH?! Wh-Wh-What are you doing?!"

"That's enough. Just keep still... Hup."

Suimei ignored her protests and got her back on her feet. Once she was standing again, he even fixed the disheveled portions of her robes.

"Ah..."

"There. Are you alright?"

Felmenia was still in a daze and had no answer for him. She simply stared blankly, and Suimei couldn't help noticing the dirt she had on her face. It was most unladylike; she must have collected it rolling around on the floor. Even though she'd been furious with him just moments ago, he felt sorry for her now and took pity on her. He retrieved his handkerchief from his pocket and began wiping the dirt off of Felmenia's face.

Seriously, how troublesome...

And when he did...

"Ah... Huh...?"

Looking like she still barely understood what was going on, Felmenia's eyes darted around as if she were assessing the situation.

"AAAAAAAAAAAH!"

She then shrieked.

"Whoa, now what...?"

Suimei jumped back in surprise. Felmenia was glaring at him, her face bright red.

"Wh-Wh-Wh-what are you doing, you bastard?!"

"What am I doing? You can tell without asking, can't you?"

"Not that! I mean, I mean... Why are you doing that kind of..."

"You looked like you needed a hand."

"I-I didn't really need any help, you bastard! I was ready to take you down, I'll have you know! But then my face..."

"This and that are two different things. Besides, letting you walk around like that would have been a waste of your cute face. I at least had to wipe the dirt off."

"?!"

The moment Suimei casually said those words, Felmenia suddenly straightened out like a rod had been jammed down her back and went completely stiff.

"Hmm? What's wrong?"

"C-Cute…"

"Come again?"

"Saying I'm cute is a little…"

"Hellooooo?"

Before Suimei knew it, Felmenia had gone somewhere else. He waved his hand in front of her vacant eyes, and it took a good few moments before she snapped back to reality.

"Huh? Eek! Th-Th-That's enough! I have business to attend to, so if you'll excuse me…!"

Felmenia's face went from bright red to deep crimson. It really wasn't going too far to compare her face to an apple or tomato. However, after storming off a ways, she came to a stop and turned around with tremendous zeal.

"I-I will w-w-withdraw what I said earlier!"

"Whazzat?"

"About calling a bastard like you foolish! A-A-A-A-And you can get to your stupid room by following this passage around the bend, and… Argh, after that, just catch someone else and ask them! But remember this, Suimei Yakagi! One day, I will repay this disgrace a million times over, you hear?! Don't forget! Don't you dare forget—FUGYAH?!"

Though she was standing still, she was flailing her arms so violently as she yelled that she pitched forward like a fish on a hook. Indeed, Felmenia fell over once more. It seemed tripping was her signature move.

"What the hell's going on…?"

While watching her unsteadily pick herself up and dash down the hallway, Suimei muttered to himself. Felmenia, however, was still screaming her lungs out even as she disappeared into the distance.

His image of Felmenia Stingray, a cool girl with a just and resolute heart, was shattered. In the back of his mind, he now filed her away under the klutz category.

"…Whatever. It's about time I get going."

And with that, Suimei's quest for his room resumed.

★

Aside from his unexpected encounter with Felmenia, Suimei managed to safely return to his room from the ritual chamber without any fuss. But he didn't have long to catch his breath.

"Hmm…"

Suimei detected the sound of footsteps and the presence of mana approaching his room. After his last run-in, Suimei was thinking of just relaxing in his room for the time being, but this put him on edge. He focused his mind and shifted his attention to the approaching presence.

It was likely a visitor to his room. Whoever it was was headed straight towards his door with no hesitation. Concentrating on their mana presence, Suimei could break it down into three wavelengths he recognized. It was his friend who had been growing more powerful by the day, Reiji, and two other people. One of them, enamored with him and serving as his advisor around the clock, was Titania. The other was Mizuki, who clung to Reiji even more than before thanks to Titania.

The moment he sensed them, Suimei gathered the books and magickal items on his desk and used magicka to cloak them without leaving a single trace.

After the incident in the audience chamber, the people of the castle believed that Suimei had locked himself away in his room and was merely sulking in his bed. Felmenia had demonstrated she was under that impression too, and of course Reiji and the others were no exception.

If Suimei came into contact with people, the possibility of his identity being discovered would only increase. To prevent that, he'd pretended to seclude himself and made sure not to interact with anyone when it wasn't strictly necessary. He'd gone to such lengths all to conceal the fact that he was a magician.

As a guest of the castle, all his meals were brought to his room. The only times he left his room were to check on Reiji and Mizuki, to go to the castle's library, or to investigate the ritual chamber, and those activities were all conducted in secret. Apart from that and going to use the bathroom, he stayed in his room.

That would reduce the chances of him being found out. He didn't want to be taken advantage of by those who would have their eyes on his power, and he was still resistant to the idea of Reiji and Mizuki learning his secret. In addition to that, hiding in his room gave him the privacy and the free time to study and investigate things.

But for every day he spent locked away in his room, the people of the castle thought less of him. Whether it was for his cowardice in refusing the mission with the hero, his pettiness in locking himself up in his room, or his uncouthness for the scene he caused in the audience chamber, no one had anything nice to say about him. Other than the king and Titania, the entire castle staff was quick with a vicious word about his behavior.

To Suimei, this was all a cover, so he didn't really care what they thought. In fact, the less they wanted to do with him, the better. Contemplating that, Suimei slipped into his bed like he was sulking.

A few moments later, he heard a reserved knock at the door and Reiji's voice.

"Morning, Suimei. Are you up?"

"...Yeah, come in."

"Sorry to intrude."

"Pardon me. I'm coming in too."

Waiting until they entered the room, Suimei slowly got out of the bed. Waiting for everyone to take their seats like usual, Suimei struck up a conversation with Reiji.

"So? What happened today?"

"Oh? Th-That's awfully sudden of you, Suimei."

"The atmosphere around you is a little different from usual today. You're getting restless, aren't you?"

"Ahaha, so you can tell?"

"Well, yeah."

Reiji laughed as if to hide his embarrassment, and Suimei replied with a nod. When Reiji entered the room, Suimei had noticed something was off. Though Reiji looked fine, he was anxious. It was as if both something good and something questionable had happened—that kind of feeling. Reiji put on a brave smile as he began explaining.

"I learned body enhancement magic today. Wanna see?"

"Yeah? Show me."

So was that it? Reiji was just excited that he'd learned some new magic? Suimei could relate to that pretty well. Weaving together new magicka and then putting it to use for the first time was a thrill like no other.

Reiji began stretching his joints and loosening up his muscles. This was body strengthening magic. If it wasn't used together with magic to stabilize the body, it could be dangerous. Such preparations were a serious matter.

"Here I go."

With that, Reiji spread his mana throughout his entire body. The spell took shape in the blink of an eye, and he activated the stabilizing magic without a chant.

"Burn Boost!"

Reiji then spoke the name of his true spell, and flames born from those words coiled around his body. Thanks to his invocation, Reiji's physical abilities had been enhanced. Right now, his body was overflowing with an intense power on top of the strength he'd been granted by the hero summoning.

"Oooh!"

Yakagi Suimei, a magician at heart, couldn't help admiring Reiji's performance. His use of magic just now was splendid. From the optimization of the mana to the way he'd prepared the spell, right down to the details of its activation, it was a grand display. To sum it up in one word, it was masterful. Of course, it wasn't a particularly complicated or high-level spell, but for someone who had only been studying magic for two weeks, his exemplary demonstration of the basics was truly praiseworthy. Suimei found no fault in it.

He'd cast body enhancement magic with a fire attribute, so in addition to improving his physical abilities overall, it granted him an explosive increase in strength. In a similar fashion, using the wind attribute would have dramatically increased his speed, the water attribute his agility, and the earth attribute his constitution. While Suimei thought about Reiji's body enhancement and began to analyze the potential effects of other attributes, Titania drew nearer to Reiji with an entranced look in her eyes.

"That's Reiji-sama for you. Truly exquisite…"

"Ahaha, thank you, Tia."

Reiji thanked Titania, who was cheerfully smiling at him. He was apparently close enough with her now to have a nickname for her. Hearing it, Mizuki looked at Titania with a somewhat sulky expression.

"Hey, Tia, aren't you a little too close?"

"Is that a problem, Mizuki? You're usually the one who's this close, so surely you can manage to share a little with me."

"Wh-What? I'm never that close!"

"That's simply not true, Mizuki. You're always unnecessarily close to Reiji-sama. It's unfair."

Even though Reiji's body enhancement was supposed to be the star of the show, the girls were apparently more concerned about his attention. Sparks were flying between them as they glared at each other. Suimei had had more than enough of it already.

"Guys like you should just... I mean... That's some pretty cool magic, huh, Reiji?"

"Hmm? Oh, yeah. Sure is, isn't it? It's pretty easy to use too, so I quite like it."

"Yeah. It looks good. Surprisingly, it doesn't give off any evil or ominous vibes, either."

That was what Suimei honestly thought. If nothing else, it got high marks for style. Fire was wrapped around Reiji's body like a coiled dragon. It was quite cool. It had impact, and that was worth something. It could go a long way towards intimidating and overcoming an opponent. With magic, looks were a surprisingly important matter.

Mizuki finally interjected her part too, but she turned to Reiji instead of Suimei, the boy she'd come to visit.

"I-I'm also able to do it now!"

"I see. You really are working hard too, aren't you, Mizuki?"

"Huh? Oh, yeah…"

Mizuki nearly seemed startled that Suimei was the one who replied to her. Because of her quarrel with Titania, it seemed that Mizuki was solely focused on Reiji and had completely forgotten Suimei was even there. Really, she'd wanted Reiji to praise her, and to use that as ammunition to antagonize Titania. At any rate, the friend who was watching them from the sidelines was half ready to kill Reiji, and half charmed by the amusement of it all.

"Heh…"

"Wh-What is it, Suimei-kun?"

"Nothing. Give it your best."

"Mm! I won't lose!"

Just who was it she was determined not to lose against, exactly? If anyone had been listening in on their conversation, they would have probably assumed she meant the Demon Lord, but that was the wrong answer. And Suimei only fanned the flames by cheering her on. But then he turned his attention back to Reiji.

"So, what else?"

"Huh? Well, all sorts of stuff…"

Reiji gave an evasive answer. Something had clearly happened, but he was apparently reluctant to talk about it. Whatever it was was likely the cause for his strange state of agitation today.

"What is the matter, Reiji-sama?"

"Huh? Oh, nothing…"

"Princess, did something strange happen?"

"Nothing strange, no. But we did witness something beyond amazing from Reiji-sama."

Titania spoke in both excitement and happiness. Suimei didn't think that she was lying, but if what she said was true, why was Reiji trying to brush it off?

"So what was it?"

"Th-That's, um…"

Reiji tried to shoot down Suimei's question, but Titania paid no mind to his hesitant answer. As if she was proud of something she herself had accomplished, she explained what happened in a boastful tone.

"You see, today, specialists from every branch of the Mage's Guild affiliated with the Kingdom of Astel came to have magic bouts with Reiji-sama."

"Hmm, the Mage's Guild, huh?"

The Mage's Guild. That was something Suimei had yet to investigate thoroughly, but if he remembered correctly, it was more or less a coalition of most of the country's mages.

"Indeed. We've consulted with them about this for quite some time, and everyone managed to gather for the event today."

"Is that strange?"

"Yes. They're all dignitaries and they keep quite busy. Normally they'd be running all around the country performing their various duties."

That did make it sound like it would be hard to get them all in one place at the same time. But Suimei was more interested in what she'd said about "specialists from every branch," so he decided to ask her more about that.

"So what do you mean by 'specialists?'"

"They are the most skilled mages in the eight schools of fire, water, wind, earth, lightning, wood, light, and darkness. Each one of them is talented enough to go toe to toe with the court mages, and they have each been granted the honorary title of elemental emperor for their talents. The emperor of the school of fire is known as the Flame Emperor, the emperor of the school of light is the Brilliant Emperor, and so on."

Really?

The word "emperor" was supposed to imply something exceptionally exalted, and there were eight of them? Even in modern Japan, that title was exclusively reserved for the most esteemed man in the country. Suimei wondered if something was being lost in translation there since the language Titania was speaking was being magically translated in his head, but be that as it may, it still left him a bit puzzled.

"Suimei-sama, is something the matter?"

"Ah, no, it's nothing. So, what was the result of the bouts?"

"Naturally, Reiji-sama won."

Titania puffed out her chest with pride as if she'd been the real victor. But then she said something that really got Suimei's attention.

"And on that occasion, Reiji-sama was given his own title by the master of the Mage's Guild."

"A title?"

A title was an honorary name used to celebrate the achievements or characteristics of the person it was bestowed upon. Naturally, they were an indispensable part of a fantasy world. Reiji, however, tried to change the topic in a somewhat awkward tone.

"D-Do we have to talk about that?"

Apparently finding Reiji's discomfort amusing, Mizuki let out a stifled laugh.

"Pfft…"

"What's up, Mizuki?"

"Heehee, nothing. Just wait 'til you hear it."

105

"Oh yeah? So, Your Highness, what was the title given to Reiji by the guild master?"

"Listen, Suimei, that's—"

"The guild master bestowed Reiji-sama, the miraculous prodigy who controls all attributes, with the title of Attribute Master!"

Titania thrust a triumphant fist in the air and passionately declared Reiji's title. The room completely froze for an instant. But when Suimei couldn't take it anymore, he burst into hearty laughter.

"Pffffft!"

"What…? Suimei-sama!"

"A-Attribute Master? Haha. Ah crap, I can't, pfft… Aha… AHAHAHAHA!"

Titania was utterly shocked at Suimei's sudden fit of laughter. She looked around in a fluster, but Reiji had his face planted in both hands as he shook his head, looking utterly disappointed it had come to this. Mizuki, on the other hand, was fondly looking at Reiji's blushing face like they were talking about her favorite food. After letting Suimei have a good laugh, Reiji finally spoke up in a pout.

"…Look, that's why I didn't want to say it."

"I… I don't understand. Receiving a title is a great honor for a mage, so why is Suimei-sama…?"

Titania just couldn't get her head around Suimei's reaction. She looked dumbfounded, but she had no way of knowing that standards for what was considered cool could differ between worlds. Mizuki already knew, but that was exactly why Reiji wanted to avoid bringing this up altogether in front of Suimei.

"Seriously? Attribute Master? Oh crap, guys! Look out, it's Reiji the Attribute Master! Pffffft! What kind of guild master would pick a title like that? One with no style, that's for sure! Absolutely none! Oh god, my sides… Pfft! AHAHAHAHAHAHAHAHA!"

"Suimei, I'm begging you… don't say it."

Reiji sounded utterly disheartened, but the rest of their conversation that day was in high spirits at his expense.

★

A few days later, Court Mage Felmenia Stingray was on her way to lessons with the hero and his good friend Mizuki Anou to teach them the ways of magic.

"To think I would become the hero's instructor…"

Felmenia's inner thoughts escaped her lips as she walked down the hall. What was swirling around within her chest at the moment was a mixture of delight and exaltation. After all, out of the dozens of court mages, Felmenia—the youngest among them—had been charged with the responsibility of teaching magic to the boy who would save their world. That's right, Felmenia was the hero's magic instructor. To a mage of this world, there could be no greater honor. She could hardly contain herself.

"Heehee…"

Felmenia was a fair beauty who was always dignified, but for the moment, that was superseded by her childish smile. When she realized she was giggling to herself, she panicked for a moment, but was unable to stop herself. She was grateful there was no one else around. Such a girlish laugh from a court mage like herself, who should always be stately and proud, was wholly inappropriate. She would have been devastated if someone had heard her.

The honor of teaching the hero magic had actually come rather unexpectedly to her. She was certain that in order to train a hero, the greatest masters of both sword and sorcery would have to be called in. In reality, she was stiff competition for that title, but that wasn't the point.

As it turned out, the hero came from a world that had no magic whatsoever, so he needed to be taught the basics from the very beginning. On the day the summoning was carried out—the day that Reiji and his friends arrived in Castle Camellia—they witnessed magic for the first time. The surprise on their faces as they watched the great doors to the audience chamber open was etched into Felmenia's memory. Just like when she had first witnessed magic, their eyes were sparkling.

When she later inquired how their civilization advanced despite not having magic, she was told that they used science instead of magic to develop technology and mechanisms that used steel and a controlled form of lightning. From what she heard of it, it sounded quite interesting. So—

"Is that… Suimei Yakagi?"

While Felmenia was pleasantly ruminating over the honor of her duty as she rushed to meet the hero, she caught a glimpse of one of the hero's friends at the end of the corridor.

Suimei Yakagi was a good friend of Reiji's, and an extremely commonplace man. Other than his neatly kept black hair and gentle eyes, he had no notable features. His appearance was unremarkable, and when he stood next to Reiji, he was completely drowned out by Reiji's extraordinary aura.

Felmenia recognized him even from a distance because of her last run-in with him, and she was keenly aware she needed to keep her guard up around him.

No, that was…

That was wrong. At that time, she had been completely overcome by rage. But he never laughed at what she said, or at the complete embarrassment she'd made of herself. She knew he was a kind person beneath it all. She couldn't bring herself to hurl insults at him for refusing to take part in the Demon Lord's subjugation anymore. Moreover...

"Cute, huh...?"

She remembered the choice word Suimei used to describe her that day. Just how long had it been since somebody had called her cute? When she thought back on it, it was something that was only said about her when she was a small child. But when she recalled Suimei saying it, her cheeks burned.

"N-N-No, what am I thinking?! It's not like I'm particularly happy about hearing that kind of... that kind of..."

She couldn't actually say she wasn't happy to hear it. The words and actions of that kind young man had truly touched her heart. And for that alone...

"I should at least apologize to him..."

If he was taking a stroll, then he was probably on his way to meet up with Reiji and Mizuki. Since she didn't see him that often, she couldn't pass up a chance encounter like this. It was only proper for her to apologize for getting carried away and saying too much last time. Even if they didn't get along any better for it, she wanted to clear the air between them.

So with the intent to apologize, Felmenia marched straight down the hall towards him. Before she could catch up to him, however, Suimei vanished around a bend.

"Huh...?"

The direction he was heading was the opposite of where she was. Seeing him go that way surprised her, and she stopped to think for a moment. Why would he have taken that turn? He was headed to the north side of Royal Castle Camellia. Not the kitchen, the toilet, or even Reiji were in that direction. The only thing of any significance down that way would be the ritual chamber. He shouldn't have any interest in that, so just what was he up to?

Actually, if I'm remembering right, people have been saying that Suimei-dono has been keeping himself confined to his room ever since the incident in the audience chamber...

Squinting her eyes, Felmenia's expression turned serious. She hadn't been involved with Suimei, so she didn't know exactly what his circumstances were, but it was true she'd heard the rumors that he'd kept himself locked up in his room practically since he'd arrived. People said he only ever left to use the bathroom or go see Reiji and Mizuki, but just recently, Felmenia had run into him while he was out taking a stroll.

And the castle staff loved to talk about him. She'd heard all kinds of things. That he was locked in his room because he was terrified of being brought to an unfamiliar land, that he was sulking like a child because he couldn't get what he wanted. It all seemed reasonable, really, yet everything she'd heard came from the mouths of the same people who all too readily ridiculed him as a coward and a churl. But either way...

"Just what..."

Just what was he doing here in the sparse north wing of the castle? The moment that question crossed her mind, Felmenia could no longer suppress her curiosity over such a mystery. She gave it a moment's consideration.

It's not like the hour for the hero's magic lesson was precisely arranged beforehand. I still have some time before I need to be there, so let's see where this leads for a bit...

And so Felmenia quickly made up her mind and followed after Suimei. And she wasn't just motivated by curiosity or her desire to apologize. As a servant of the castle, this was her duty as a court mage. If by some chance he was out for revenge over the summoning and planning to do something dangerous, she was obligated to stop him. That said, Felmenia wanted to believe that wasn't the case.

No...

But that wasn't the only thing on her mind. Suimei knew of her arrangement with the hero, including their schedule. That meant that he had to have known that he likely wouldn't encounter her if he went sneaking around at this hour.

That's right. When we went to greet them on the day they arrived, Suimei-dono was most certainly...

He had been trying to use some sort of magic. When they opened the door to the special room constructed in the secluded north wing of the castle explicitly for the purpose of the hero summoning, they'd walked in on him preparing to utilize a spell. Felmenia was the only one who had noticed. The princess possessed great talent as a mage, but not even she had picked up on it.

He'd released the spell on sight, however, and had conducted himself like nothing had happened at all since then. But there was no mistaking it. Felmenia was quite sure of what she'd seen and sensed. It wasn't her imagination. Without a doubt, the young man known as Suimei Yakagi was a mage.

But Reiji and Mizuki had said that there was no magic in their world. They had described the world they were from in great detail, including science and its countless milestones and achievements. They had structures many times the size of even Royal Castle Camellia that could illuminate the darkness of the night like it was daytime. They had devices to allow men to fly into the sky and beyond to the moon. Overall, their quality of life thanks to science was so high that this world hardly held a candle to it.

And it certainly didn't seem like Reiji was lying. His straightforward gaze belied no falsehood, and there wasn't a hint of dishonesty in his character or behavior. So how was it that Suimei could use magic? Did even his close friends not realize he could?

Pondering those questions as she walked along, Felmenia caught sight of Suimei once more. She'd finally caught up to him, but it seemed Suimei had yet to notice her. He was walking forward at a regular gait and without looking back. He had no idea anyone was following him. She watched as he disappeared around another corner. She hurried along after him, but when she took the same turn...

"Oops!"

"Kyah!"

Felmenia reacted instinctively when she heard a yelp. Just as she was about to collide with somebody, she took an evasive step to the side. When she composed herself and looked back, she saw one of the castle maids was standing there in a fluster. She must have been the one who yelped.

"My apologies. Are you alright?"

"N-No, I should be the one to apologize! Stingray-sama, is your face injured?"

"Huh? No, why? Does it look like it?"

"Th-Then are you hurt somewhere else?! Aaah! What do I do?!"

"No, I'm completely unharmed. Since I moved out of the way, I have not even a single speck of dust on me to show for it all."

What was the big deal? They had narrowly avoided each other, but the maid was making an exaggerated fuss like she had personally offended Felmenia somehow. There wasn't a soul in the castle who would punish her over such a minor blunder. Felmenia tried to reassure her with a gentle smile. Seeing that, the maid took a deep breath and looked a little relieved.

"Really...? I'm so glad..."

"Sorry for the fuss."

"N-Not at all!"

"Very well."

Felmenia gave a dignified nod. It was polite, but not in the austere fashion that court manners sometimes called for. It was a gesture that emulated the behavior of the sage who had been her mentor. She believed that carrying herself that way, even though she was young, would convey her dignity without being too imposing with formality.

In response, the maid simply beheld her with an entranced gaze. It took her a few seconds to realize she was staring, and when she did, she embarrassedly bowed her head.

"M-My apologies!"

"No, that's quite alright."

After telling her not to worry, and after the maid bowed one more time, Felmenia was about to take her leave when she realized something.

"Sorry, but could I trouble you over something?"

"Oh? Ah, of course. Is something the matter?"

"Just before we bumped into each other, you should have passed by a young man. Did you happen to see where he went?"

"...No? I'm afraid until I ran into you just now, Stingray-sama, I haven't seen anyone here..."

"What?!"

Quite out of character for herself, Felmenia raised her voice. She simply couldn't believe what the maid had just said.

"U-Um, did something bad...?"

"I shall ask you once more: did you truly not meet anyone in this hall?"

"T-Truly."

"You're not lying?"

"No. I swear by the Goddess Alshuna. I would never lie to you, Stingray-sama."

Shrinking under Felmenia's intimidating stare, the maid swore in the name of the sole deity that the Church of Salvation worshipped, Alshuna, that she was telling the truth. But that couldn't be right. There was no way that the two of them hadn't crossed paths. While that was spinning around in Felmenia's head, she began questioning the maid again.

"It's simply impossible that you didn't see him. Just before I turned this corner, Suimei-dono, a friend of the hero, should have come around it."

"One of the hero's friends? But I didn't…"

The bewildered maid's eyes darted around frantically like she was looking for the right answer. Seeing her genuine confusion only confused Felmenia more.

"Just what does this…"

"U-Um, Stingray-sama, I'm expected in the south wing, so… um…"

"A-Ah, sorry. My apologies for holding you up over such a strange matter."

"Think nothing of it. If you'll excuse me…"

The maid took her leave after shyly bowing to Felmenia.

Then…

Felmenia saw the maid off, but her eyes narrowed as she turned this bizarre situation over in her head. Just what had happened?

It seemed that right after she saw him last, Suimei had simply disappeared.

I still have time. Let's look around some more.

Felmenia proceeded further into the north wing. But just as the maid had said, there didn't appear to be anyone else around. Finally, she arrived at the last room in the north wing, the ritual chamber. And she was in for quite a surprise.

Wha—?!

What she was seeing should be impossible. She had to look twice to believe her own eyes, but the door to the ritual chamber, which nobody could open except in an emergency when the leader of the court mages commanded it, was ajar.

Not only was it a directive that the door never be opened unless required, it should have been sealed with special magic to keep it shut. Unless someone knew how to dispel that, no one should ever be able to enter. But sure enough, the door was open even though only the king and the court mages should have the ability to do that.

But if neither the king nor any court mages were present aside from Felmenia, then who exactly had done this? She gulped and suppressed her presence as she approached. Rather than muscles, bone, and skin, it was pure tension that was keeping her together right now.

Who could possibly be inside the room? She could hazard a guess based on the string of events that had brought her here, but she couldn't stop her heart from pounding. When she peered through the slight gap in the door, she could see a pure white notebook—a true rarity in Astel—as well as a long, narrow glass cylinder, and Suimei Yakagi, who was holding both objects while scowling over the summoning circle. It seemed he was grumbling to himself and concentrating quite intently on the notebook and thin cylinder.

As I suspected...

Just what kind of magic and wiles had he used to open the door? Felmenia was surprised, but she couldn't deny what was right in front of her. She now had irrefutable proof that Suimei was a mage.

But... what do I do? Should I reveal myself?

Felmenia was torn between the mystery before her eyes and the laws of the land as she racked her brain over the matter. This was a restricted area. Normally she would immediately barge in to stop him. That was what her duty as a court mage demanded. But this young man was the hero's friend. Not only that, but he was a mage.

Certainly, even if her opponent was also a mage, Felmenia had full confidence that she could still subdue him. Her main concern was his status as the hero's friend. If there was another scene involving Suimei, the hero might get involved. And Felmenia couldn't risk doing anything that might ultimately lead to the hero changing his mind about subjugating the Demon Lord. That would be a serious crisis for both Astel and the world.

But this man... What is he doing? He's likely analyzing the summoning circle, but...

Looking at it from the perspective of a mage, his actions were completely baffling. He appeared to be investigating the summoning circle, but in the most amateur way possible. He was just randomly walking in circles with a notebook and cylinder in hand. It was difficult to even call it analyzing.

To analyze a spell, a second magic circle had to be drawn around the original. From there, you would use that to expose the spell and read it. That was standard practice when it came to analyzing magic, but it wasn't anything close to what Suimei was doing. To Felmenia, he looked less like a mage and more like a normal person who knew nothing of magic and was arbitrarily grasping at straws through trial and error.

At any rate, this summoning circle was something that had been passed down without knowledge of the laws behind the spell itself. No one had ever truly been able to analyze and comprehend it, but...

In the end, Felmenia couldn't make a move or call out to him. She did nothing but observe Suimei's mysterious actions until it was time for her to go meet the hero.

★

Later that evening, a visitor had come to Felmenia's private quarters in Royal Castle Camellia.

"What...? Is that truly the case?"

Felmenia questioned the court mage who'd come to deliver information to her. She received an affirmative but unconvincing answer.

"Yes. It is just as I said."

"..."

Hearing her colleague's tone, Felmenia narrowed her eyes and ruminated over what she had just been told. This fellow court mage had come to see Felmenia privately, saying it was an urgent and important matter. While she wondered what had happened for him to arrange such a meeting, it seemed that for the last few days, Suimei Yakagi had been spotted walking in and out of all sorts of places around the castle.

Gripped with anxiety that he was plotting some kind of mischief, yet unable to do anything for fear of Suimei's status as a friend of the hero, this court mage hadn't gotten anywhere on the matter and had decided to come to another court mage to discuss it. Her apparent disbelief made him worry that she thought he was lying to her.

"Do you not believe me?"

"I do. In truth, I have also caught a glimpse of him walking around."

"Truly? Are you certain?"

"Yes. It was just today, in fact."

"Then there can be no doubt. By any chance, if Suimei-dono is plotting something…"

When it sounded like her colleague was starting to imply that Felmenia might know what Suimei was up to, she shook her head.

"No, we cannot be sure. It's far too hasty to decide he is plotting something before we even investigate, is it not?"

It was certain that Suimei's actions were suspicious, but from what Felmenia had witnessed to date, all he had done was go in and out of the ritual chamber. That in and of itself was worth a reprimand, but not a witch hunt. The court mage visiting Felmenia seemed to come around quite quickly.

"You're right. Your wisdom never fails, White Flame."

"Ah, no…"

Felmenia was glad he was on her side, but she was slightly conscious of his flattery.

"I am in full agreement. I will begin an investigation on my end."

"I will leave it to you."

"Then I shall excuse myself for now."

Saying that, the court mage swiftly made his exit. Felmenia closed the door to her private quarters, and making sure there was no longer anyone nearby, muttered to herself.

"Suimei-dono, just what are you doing…?"

It was a question that would go unanswered for now.

★

"About the hero's good friend, you say?"

It was now a few days after Felmenia had witnessed Suimei's mysterious behavior. Currently, she was in Royal Castle Camellia's audience chamber before the king. The reason for their meeting, quite naturally, was Suimei. After seeing him in the ritual chamber, Felmenia had thoroughly observed him and was now reporting her findings to the king. She was bowed before him on one knee, but the king looked puzzled.

"Yes, Your Majesty."

"Do you mean Mizuki Anou?"

"No, sire. What I wish to tell you concerns the other one, Suimei Yakagi."

When Felmenia said his name, the king frowned.

"Hmph. So far as I have been informed, he still hasn't left his room after the scene he caused."

"I'm afraid that's not so, Your Majesty. In truth, Suimei-dono has been seen walking around the castle on many occasions."

Felmenia had determined this from her investigations over the past few days. After witnessing him sneak around for herself, she'd used all of her free time to dig deeper into what he was doing around the castle. From there, she'd discovered that sequestering himself was a complete farce. In reality, he was quite active and likely had been this whole time. Hearing this news, the king gave Felmenia a probing gaze and his tone grew stern.

"I have not heard any such reports prior to this."

"He is maintaining the facade that he's locked away in his room, and moving about behind the scenes."

"Without being spotted by anyone?"

"Yes, Your Majesty. It seems that only a handful of people, myself included, actually know about this."

The king managed a perplexed frown at Felmenia's explanation.

"This makes no sense to me. How can he be going around the castle, yet so few people have noticed?"

"That I happened upon him walking around was complete coincidence. My theory is that in order to avoid the eyes of others, he is using some sort of magic."

"Magic, you say? Did you teach him?"

"No, sire. I have taught him nothing."

"Then what? Did another court mage?"

"No, sire. I believe that Suimei-dono was somehow able to use magic from the very beginning."

The king had been hesitant and puzzled so far, but with those words, he now looked outright baffled. Felmenia had expected as much.

"Felmenia, I have been told that magic does not exist in the world the hero hails from. The hero himself said that they had technology in its place, and that magic was a mere fantasy to them."

"I understand, Your Majesty. I have personally spoken to the hero on that matter, but nevertheless, I can say with certainty that Suimei-dono can use magic."

"Are you saying that the hero lied?"

"No, there is absolutely nothing to suggest that, Your Majesty."

Reiji hadn't lied. She could say that definitively. Reiji's aptitude as a mage was quite high, but when it came to the fundamental knowledge of magic, it could be said that he had absolutely none at all. The king also seemed ready to trust in Reiji's honesty.

"Yes, I believe in him myself. However..."

"You wish to know why there is an inconsistency with Reiji-dono's statement and Suimei-dono's ability, correct?"

"Indeed. Either that young man personally requested that his power be concealed beforehand, or the hero is not even cognizant of the fact that magic does actually exist in the world he's from. How mysterious."

Even the king was puzzled over this. Magic was a technology in its own right. Even here in this world, it was able to protect people and improve their quality of life. Magic was inherent to the universe, and therefore to all intelligent life that inhabited it. Humans were unable to sever their bond with it any more than they could with their own history.

So how was it really that the hero's world—one of such advanced technology—was without magic? No matter how developed and superior their science may be, it wasn't the same thing as magic. It was simply impossible for magic to be rendered completely obsolete. How then had Reiji been able to declare so honestly that his world thought it was just make-believe?

"Your Majesty, I'm sure the world the hero comes from is a complicated one indeed. But for now, the pressing matter at hand..."

"Is the young man who is skulking about the castle, right?"

"Yes, Your Majesty."

"Despite them being new to this world and outsiders, I placed no restrictions on their movements within the castle. There's no issue with him walking the grounds freely, so he should have no reason to hide it..."

Suimei was a guest, the same as the hero. Concerning their stay in the castle, the king had decreed that they were free to roam and do as they pleased, and the castle staff was to assist them if there was anything they needed or wanted. In a demonstration of his hospitality and consideration, the king had placed no restrictions on them whatsoever. And after pondering this strange situation for a moment, the king gave his answer concerning Suimei's movements.

"Ultimately, I don't believe there to be a problem."

"I'm afraid, Your Majesty, that the places that Suimei-dono has been visiting do indeed make it a major problem."

"The places he's been visiting, you say? Just where has he been?"

"First would be the library. He goes every day to retrieve several books and take them back to his room."

"You don't say... I thought he had been spending his time idly, but I am quite impressed that he has been visiting the library. Since he cannot return to his world, he is likely trying to amass knowledge on ours."

The king had a surprised look on his face and a twinkle in his eye as he voiced his approval of this piece of news. He nodded repeatedly, seemingly touched by the story of the young man who was summoned against his will, but refused to be defeated by it and immersed himself in studying. And he wasn't wrong about that part, but there was more to the story yet.

"That may be, Your Majesty, but there is evidence he's gone into the forbidden archives as well."

"Wh-What did you say?! No, that can't be. Not just anyone could waltz into there..."

As the name indicated, the forbidden archives were off limits to most people. Since historic and important documents were stored there, entry to the archives was strictly regulated with magic.

The king was rightfully startled to hear Suimei had gained access somehow.

"It appears he did so with ease, Your Majesty."

"My goodness... So, is that the only place that young man has been visiting?"

When the king asked her that, Felmenia paused for a moment and shook her head. Digesting just how grave the situation was, she hesitantly gave her answer.

"Suimei-dono has also been going in and out of the ritual chamber, Your Majesty."

"Preposterous... The only ones who should know the spell to enter are myself, you, and the other court mages."

"I understand, Your Majesty, but I believe Suimei-dono was able to open the door through some kind of wile."

With those words, an oppressive silence fell over the audience chamber. It was no wonder. The ritual chamber was specifically designed and built to prevent unauthorized access to it. That door had been sealed with such complex earth magic that not even a specialist in that attribute would be able to grasp it. To a degree, that in and of itself gave them a glimpse of Suimei's abilities as a mage. And in that case, it went without saying what significance that had.

"What was he doing... is a foolish question, I suppose... That young man was investigating the summoning circle, was he not?"

"It did not look that way at all to me, but considering the circumstances, I do believe that was his goal, Your Majesty."

"He wants to return so badly that he would go to these lengths...?"

The king's expression as he uttered those anguished words appeared to be melancholic at a glance. As expected, this weighed heavily on the king since he felt responsible for having summoned

Suimei to this world. As a kind, considerate king, his heart went out to the poor boy who felt trapped here.

Even during the summit between all the nations, Felmenia had heard that the king was opposed to using the hero summoning ritual. He thought it was cruel to call on people who had no relation to this world at all and push such an outrageous task on them. Even if they succeeded, they would never properly be able to repay them for their service. They weren't even able to return them home after calling them here.

Moreover, if the people of this world relied too heavily on the strength of others, they would never have the power to deal with a dangerous crisis on their own. And the weaker they grew, the more situations like this would present themselves in the future. Eventually this world would be brought to ruin that way too, the king had said.

And even though he'd declared that much, his voice would never be loud enough to reach the leaders of each nation cowering in fear of the Demon Lord. In the end, he was forced to agree to performing the hero summoning by an overwhelming majority vote.

As Felmenia recalled the bitter sense of powerlessness the king must have tasted as his noble heart was trampled on, he began speaking in a heavy tone.

"And so, Felmenia… Why is it that you've remained silent and waited until now to inform me of all this?"

"I judged that it was not a good plan to make contact with him by my own will and risk complications, Your Majesty. If it ended up becoming a scene and it reached Reiji-dono's ears…"

"Certainly, we cannot ignore the potential threat of discord between us and the hero."

"And the reason that I did not deliver this news to Your Majesty sooner is because I had not yet gathered enough information to make a full report."

An incomplete report—or what amounted to speculation on the matter—was a dangerous prospect. Something like that was bound to produce misunderstandings and lead to mistakes being made. It was Felmenia's wish to avoid that, which was why she hadn't spoken up sooner.

"Naturally, if anything were to happen, you were planning to take action, I presume?"

"Yes, of course, Your Majesty."

That much was obvious. That was why she was constantly keeping tabs on him.

"And so, have you discussed this with any others?"

"Aside from myself and Your Majesty, only a few of my colleagues are aware of this matter. Regarding Reiji-dono and Mizuki-dono, they seem to know nothing of it either."

"Understood. Then see to it that word of this doesn't reach anyone else's ears. I shall speak with the other court mages myself. Also, you may not inform the hero of any of this. Understood?"

Felmenia respectfully acknowledged the king's order. She didn't understand his intentions in trying to keep this information from spreading, but she trusted him and had faith in his decision. She would obediently follow his lead. The only question on her mind now was how to proceed in the future.

"Your Majesty, what should I do from here on out?"

What exactly should she do with regards to Suimei? How should she deal with him? Felmenia was certain he shouldn't be left to his own devices, even knowing he was the hero's good friend. However, the king frowned at this unexpected question.

"Hmm? There is nothing for you to do. Are things not fine as they are? If that young man has no ill intentions, then there is no need to forcibly get ourselves involved. He's been moving in stealth and clearly does not want us involved, so we shall respect that for now."

"But Your Majesty, the forbidden archives…"

"If he has already entered them, then so be it. All that is stored there are records of historical significance and maps. Nothing will come of him learning their contents."

That much was true. Felmenia wouldn't be so trusting of someone from a foreign country having access to them, but Suimei was from another world and had no connections here. Even if he stole a document, he wouldn't know what to do with it. She understood that much, but even then, she thought the king was being naive.

Is that why His Majesty doesn't want word of this to get out?

The king intended to continue to let Suimei do as he pleased. But letting someone off the hook after breaking the rules would set a bad example. It was an insidious poison to public order. But if the public didn't know of the offense, there was no need to hand down a punishment for it for the sake of making an example. So was that why the king wanted to keep Suimei's behavior hush-hush? Because he knew he was going to look the other way? As long as the only people who knew about it were in the palm of the king's hand, he would have nothing to worry about.

Impartiality was required to be a king. Felmenia's master had taught her of decorum, and she had always lived by her morals. She believed stoutly in the king and the proper way he should behave. And that's why she grew irritated at this lax lapse in his judgment.

"Then… does Your Majesty intend to do nothing about this?"

"Are you opposed to that?"

"Suimei-dono is a mage, Your Majesty. I think that we should take some measures against him. It is true that we must be careful about this in regards to Reiji-dono, but if we let him run amok within Castle Camellia, then it will reflect poorly on Your Majesty's good name. And in the unlikely event that something does happen…"

"…Personally, I am not concerned."

The king flashed a completely disinterested expression at Felmenia's proposal. Based on that, she could see his intention to put an immediate end to all talk of taking measures against Suimei. However, if she stepped down here, how could she call herself a court mage?

"Your Majesty, a light punishment… Yes, at least something *like* a punishment. I shall do nothing that would cause injury to his body. And if Suimei-dono informs Reiji-dono of it and something happens, then I shall persuade Reiji-dono."

"Oh? It's rather confident of you to suggest you could persuade him like that, is it not?"

"Though I may not look it, Your Majesty, I am still his instructor. I know that he will take my words to heart."

Felmenia was indeed confident she could persuade Reiji if something were to happen. After all, she was the court mage who'd taught the hero magic. Reiji even called her "sensei." And if his sensei told him that his good friend was doing something wrong, even if that friend had to be strongly reprimanded, she thought that things would work out. Even from their daily casual conversations over magic lessons, Felmenia could tell that Reiji had a just heart and believed in doing the right thing. There should be no issue there, meaning there was only one thing left to handle.

"All that is left is for Your Majesty to give the command. Please give me your wise sanction."

As she made that royal request, the king shut his eyes for a moment in consideration, and before long, he spoke in a solemn tone.

"…You mustn't."

"Your Majesty! But…!"

"Felmenia, I have said that you mustn't. Suimei-dono is, just like the hero, an important guest of my castle. I cannot allow you to think of doing him harm."

"I would never think of doing that…! I would merely dress him down appropriately for having such a flagrant disregard for the rules. I-It is true that I do not think Suimei-dono is planning any mischief, but… Before he does something and it becomes a serious matter, we should put a stop to this. That is, um… I believe it to be my duty, so…"

Seeing Felmenia cling so obstinately to the idea, the king made a curious expression. This was somewhat strange to him.

"You seem quite fixated on this."

"Your Majesty?! Ah, no… That's, um…"

"Is Suimei-dono that much on your mind?"

"N-No, sire! I am not particularly… It's just, because of him… I thought it would be bad if he causes trouble for Reiji-dono…"

Having her unusual behavior pointed out to her, Felmenia's thoughts scattered hither and thither as she tried to stay on track. Certainly if she said that she wasn't fixated on this, it would be a lie. Seeing her like that, the king suddenly became quiet. She once more requested his consent, but…

"What mustn't be simply mustn't be, Felmenia. Understood?"

"…"

"Understood?"

"Yes, Your Majesty…"

When the king pressed her for compliance, Felmenia relented. She had no choice. Swallowing her chagrin, she bowed her head down deeply. Just how long had it been since she was so utterly shot down? Since the day she became a court mage, it had happened once or twice, but nothing in recent memory. The opponent she was focused on was a mage, and that only amplified her frustration at not being able to take him to task. She was unhappy with the king for not granting her permission to do so, but in the end, her anger was focused on Suimei. He was right in the crosshairs of her rage, which was now easily increased fivefold.

How had things gotten like this? Why did she feel so strongly about it? If Suimei had just kept quiet and stayed obedient, that would have been the end of it. But sneaking around the castle like some common thief was unacceptable. It was like he was mocking her. Taunting her. Felmenia knew that Suimei wasn't a bad person, but knowing that only made her angrier over his present behavior.

No, not yet...

Though the king hadn't granted her request, she had no intention of blindly obeying his order. This was the royal court, the king's garden. Even cutting her personal feelings out of the matter, as a court mage, there was no way she could stand for some mage running amok in the castle.

And that being the case, the time to act was now. While there were still only a few people who knew of the matter, she would be able to act without scrutiny. This would be her only chance. Suimei still didn't know that she was following him. And if no one else was involved, she would probably be able to bring the matter to an end without anyone ever knowing.

That's right. I am a glorious court mage of Astel.

Felmenia assured herself of her pride in her identity. The king's dignity, order in Castle Camellia, and her self-respect as a court mage all had to be protected. And she would be the one to protect them. That was exactly why she'd become a court mage in the first place.

So no matter what that insolent young man was up to, Felmenia was going to put her foot down. She didn't know what the magic and mages from his world were like, but he had to learn his place here. Regardless of his origins, if he got a taste of the greatness of this world's magic, he would surely fall into line.

Just you wait, Suimei Yakagi! I'll show you. I, the White Flame, will put an end to your damn foolishness.

Felmenia was a court mage, the mage known as White Flame, and the hero's instructor. She was without peer in that regard. No other mage held all three of those honored titles. And a mage of her caliber should be able to handle a meager problem like this with ease. She was more than qualified.

★

"My goodness, you are still so young, Felmenia…"

After watching Felmenia exit the audience chamber, King Almadious muttered to himself. He could tell just by looking at her that her youth would lead her astray. Indeed, her eyes were not the eyes of a girl who had given up. Surely she was intent on acting in secret from here on out.

But perhaps there was nothing that could be done about it. The king felt a bit sorry for that young man, but it could also be said that he was merely reaping what he'd sown. But after Felmenia acted on her own, what would be a suitable punishment?

"It is also a difficult thing to have talent, I see…"

Recently, Felmenia's self-conceit had grown considerably. It was the flipside of her strong sense of responsibility, but it was also a problem when it manifested like this. King Almadious sighed once more.

★

"North wing, all clear… Huh?"

The sound of military boots tapping against the stone floor rang out in the hall as a soldier wearing the standard equipment given to him by the kingdom marched down his patrol route. An open door had caught his attention, but after peering into it with a torch, he shut it and moved on.

It was the last room in the north wing, and since there seemed to be nothing out of the ordinary, that marked the end of this section of his patrol. Tonight, this soldier was in the middle of doing his evening rounds around the castle. The daily patrol was divided among the soldiers, and didn't just take place during daylight hours. There was an additional check once everyone had gone to bed for the evening.

Camellia at night was very different from Camellia during the day. Naturally, the firelights didn't illuminate the entire castle. Candlesticks were stationed in the darker areas so that it was relatively easy to get around, but between the candlelight and the pale moonlight, the castle could be rather dreary at night.

Thus, the nighttime patrol wasn't a particularly popular job. Not only did it mean missing out on a good night's sleep, but it took quite a bit of backbone to navigate the vast and complex castle in the dark. Add to that the somewhat spooky atmosphere, and the whole task seemed rather daunting and ominous. No one enjoyed the job, so it was inevitably pushed onto the younger soldiers by the older ones. They would justify it by saying it was important to learn their way around the castle inside and out.

"Hahh, will this ever end…?"

This soldier in particular was one who'd had the night shift pushed on him. Fed some line by his senior and more domineering colleagues, it was a task he'd been forced to take on often quite recently. But night after night, it was all the same. No matter how you cut it, no idiot would dare attack or invade the castle where the hero was staying.

The soldier muttered to himself in the darkness as he proceeded along, quite understandably. Ever since the hero had been summoned, there had been a directive to strengthen security around the castle. However, after having seen the hero training, anyone would realize that such measures were unnecessary.

This soldier had happened to witness it by chance, and it was honestly a terrifying sight. He'd seen Reiji holding his ground and squaring off with the most idolized and feared knight in all of Astel, the esteemed captain of the royal guard. And nowadays, Reiji was regularly taking on the captain in addition to ten or so other men all at the same time.

Reiji was the hero who would be protecting the whole world, so did he really need protecting himself? It made sense on a certain level as a courtesy, but this slightly selfish soldier could hardly see the value in that as he wandered the halls at night. And just about the time he was grumbling about his discontent with the higher-ups…

"…Hmm?"

He heard a clang behind him, a sound like metal slamming against something. The soldier immediately turned around and held out his torch.

"Is somebody there?"

The soldier called out, but no reply came. He couldn't see anyone where his light was shining. The only thing in that direction was the hall to the room the court mages allegedly used for their special rituals. The door to that weird room was at the end of the hall, and nothing more. The soldier had just patrolled that hall as well, and there was nothing out of the ordinary. The only thing of note was that, unlike the previous day, some ornamental armor had been placed in front of the door.

"Harris, is that you? Cut it out with the bad jokes."

Hiding the anxiety sprouting in his heart, the soldier called out to his comrade who had also been stuck with the night shift. This part of the north wing was the place none of the soldiers wanted to come, especially on evening patrol. There was a possibility that, knowing this, his comrade had come to play a prank on him and get a rise out of him.

It was irritating, but he was also hoping that was the case. As the soldier suppressed the desire to curl up and hide, he stared down the dark passage before him. The only answer to his call was the blackness that was so dark it seemed to absorb his very voice. There was no sign of his smiling comrade lying in wait for him. Then once again, a little louder than before, a clang rang out.

A chill ran down the soldier's spine. Was it an intruder? Even his joking comrade wouldn't go this far just to play a prank. And if it wasn't him, the soldier didn't know where they might have gotten the information from, but it might be a demon pawn who had come for the hero.

The soldier was skeptical that any intruder could get through the magical security systems put in place by the lauded White Flame, but the soldier drew his sword, took a deep breath, and slowly moved closer to where the sounds were coming from. Worst-case scenario, he had his emergency whistle. Even if something happened to him, he could use that to inform his allies of the danger.

"Hmph. What's this? There's nothing here. Seriously, fucking scaring me like that..."

In the end, the soldier's fears all turned out to be groundless. When he went back down the hallway, all he saw was the ornamental armor that had been placed in front of the door. Everything was as it had been. There were no intruders, and certainly no demons. But that was good news, and all was well. The only person who could possibly be prowling around Royal Castle Camellia in the dead of the night like this was the young man right before his eyes, after all.

It turned out that there was never a need to draw his sword in the first place. He had wasted his energy getting worked up over nothing, which was a crying shame. After getting stuck with the evening patrol, he was tired enough as it was already. All he really wanted to do was get some rest. In fact, a sudden wave of drowsiness overcame him, and the boy in front of him smiled and bid him goodnight with a wave. Raising one hand up to respond, the soldier turned around and headed back down the hall once more. His shift had finally come to an end.

★

"Pheeew, holy crap. By the skin of my teeth..."

As Suimei waved goodbye to him, the sleepy soldier vanished around the corner. Suimei then let out a sigh of relief. He hadn't thought that soldier was still on patrol.

He'd been a little negligent in just assuming that there wasn't anyone around, so this risky encounter was the fault of his own carelessness. But everything had turned out fine. The soldier was no magician, just an ordinary person with no magic training. He was caught by Suimei's magicka immediately, and was none the wiser to what was going on. That soldier would go immediately to the barracks to sleep, and would wake up without a single memory of what had happened.

It was an unexpected encounter, but that soldier was the least of Suimei's worries. More important was the matter of the suit of armor standing in front of him.

"To think they'd put an automaton here... There was nothing here last time. That woman is really getting spiteful..."

Suimei passed a cold gaze over the ornamental armor. Was he mad at the suit, or the person he believed to be responsible for it?

Automata. Generally classified under alchemy, they were the products of one of the techniques used to manufacture golems. Earthen and wooden figures and puppets, or sometimes even armored suits like this one, were stitched together with mana to imitate a living being using a core and a spell. They were given a predetermined condition that would activate them, and they would take specified action accordingly. In modern terms, they were something like programmable androids.

In Suimei's world, it was one of the techniques that stemmed from the Judaic secret art of Kabbalah. Since this was a different world entirely, the spell behind it was probably completely unrelated, but that didn't matter.

135

When Suimei touched the ornamental armor, it collapsed into a neat pile of scrap on the floor as if it had been completely disassembled. It was loud, but there was now no longer anyone around to hear it. Suimei then let out a sigh. The first clang had rung out when the automaton attacked him, and the second when Suimei broke it.

But in all seriousness, it's quite well made. It doesn't look new, though, so it isn't likely that someone here was the one who made it...

Just where had they gotten a relic like this? Suimei had sensed its presence and the danger it posed on the way over, so it hadn't caught him off guard. But nevertheless, he couldn't help admiring it.

Just as he'd suspected, the automaton was programmed to activate when an intruder endowed with mana entered a certain range. It would automatically start sucking up the mana in its surroundings. Its anti-magicka and physical defenses were quite high, and it was aggressive. When it had detected Suimei, it came at him with its sword raised high and the intent to kill. It was vicious, but impressive.

"...Seriously, just what the hell was that woman thinking? No matter how much I've been sneaking around the castle, arranging for my murder is a little over the top. I'm not even her enemy, damn it. Is she just that much of a goody two-shoes?"

Suimei griped about Court Mage Felmenia in a tizzy. He was pretty pissed about the whole thing. Even as someone else walking down the path of magicka, just how much value did she put in her pride and her service to the royal court to be so calculating as to set up a trap that could have easily gotten him killed? This seemed like a pretty blunt way of saying she'd have no mercy to any potential threats in the garden that was Castle Camellia, and she would act without hesitation to nip any danger in the bud.

"I guess… That's normal for a magician, right? Right…? Surely."

That was just the law of the magical jungle. He didn't need to read into it so much. Even if this was another world, magicians were still magicians. It was perfectly normal to use lethal force against other magicians who dared to trespass or tried to steal research. That kind of behavior may not be quite as pronounced in this other world where magic was as common as saying hello, but Suimei couldn't overlook that possibility.

But still, how violent… Is that it? Is this what she meant by paying me back a million times over?

Suimei knit his brow as he remembered what had happened between them last time. He didn't have a problem if she didn't want to be indebted to him over even a small act of kindness, but this was extreme, to say the least. She was totally trying to kill him.

"…Well, whatever. If that's her intention, I just have to respond in kind."

There was no way he could let this slide after she'd gone so far. He scoffed as he muttered to himself and began thinking of what he might do. And it wasn't just the boasting of a teenage boy; it was a declaration by a trained magician.

Suimei then casually shifted his attention to the collapsed armor at his feet. He couldn't just leave it this way. He didn't really care if Felmenia found it, but it wouldn't make him happy if somebody else found it in the morning and raised a fuss over it. After all, it would only be a pain for him if they increased patrols because of something like that.

"I guess I'll fix it…"

With that, Suimei optimized his mana and began invoking a spell. At his feet and centered on him, a small magicka circle giving off a red light slowly spread out and became bigger. It rotated while it expanded, and after a fixed amount of numbers and characters were set within it, it stabilized where it was, and then...

"Renovato, atque restituito."

[Restore, and then reconstruct.]

It was fundamental restoration magicka. It was a technique that didn't repair anything per se, it simply returned something to its previous condition. And he put that to good use.

Two magicka circles appeared below the automaton and split apart. They were both rotating, and one steadily rose up into the air. As it did, the broken parts began stacking themselves together in the reverse of the order they'd fallen in. It was like watching a tape rewind, and by the time the magicka circle reached its peak, the automaton looked just like it had when Suimei first arrived.

"Okay. Not good and not bad, just as usual."

Suimei praised himself for his smooth, practiced use of magicka with no abnormalities. The automaton stood before him in good condition. It could no longer move, however. Since Suimei had completely destroyed not only its body and core, but also the spell that was engraved into it, it was now just a mere shell in the shape of an automaton.

★

Leaving behind the restored automaton, Suimei snuck into the room it was guarding. This was quite a casual affair for him by now.

The ritual chamber where he was originally summoned was one of the few rooms that Suimei visited aside from the library. His objective, of course, was to continue to investigate and decipher the summoning circle drawn on the floor with the ultimate goal of figuring out how to return home. To that end, Suimei had read every book that he could get his hands on and had been coming here to research the summoning circle whenever he had the chance.

He wanted to get home no matter what. Suimei had the magicka thesis that his father entrusted him to take care of. To complete it, it would be fastest to return to where his research results, research materials, and various magickal items were. Certainly, given the time, it may have been something that he could accomplish in this world, but he wasn't even sure if he had enough time to do it in his own world. Time was of the essence, and he couldn't afford to waste any of it.

That's why he was so desperate to return home. Yes, that was certainly his primary reason for it, but...

"Surely those two want to go back too, don't they?"

Suimei looked up at the ceiling of the stone room illuminated by the glow of mana and muttered to himself. Suimei knew. He would catch Reiji looking up into the empty sky every now and then. Beyond that void, beyond the horizon he couldn't see, was a vision of his hometown. It was a sign of longing, and a sign of regret that he hadn't been able to say goodbye to his loved ones.

Suimei knew. He knew that Mizuki would sob all alone in her room. She mustered her courage to be with the boy she loved, but the price for that was all-consuming fear and loneliness.

And when Suimei thought about the two of them, he could feel something bubbling up in the depths of his heart. It was difficult to describe and he didn't know how to express it, but it was a heavy feeling.

He didn't want his friends to remember leaving for school that morning as their final farewells with their families. He didn't want them to wallow in the regret and sorrow of never being able to see them again. He didn't want them to struggle with that weight in their everyday lives. Tragedy may strike, and they may even be separated from each other, but Suimei didn't want his friends to suffer. As long as there was hope, he didn't want them to give up.

That's why on the day his father had asked him to become a magician, he'd accepted. It was so that he could stand up in the face of unfairness. To prove conclusively that there wasn't a single person in the world who couldn't be saved, and that no one should have to feel that way.

"…It's not like me, but I just thought I'd give it my best shot too."

Suimei put that feeling into words, and once he did, it could no longer be denied. He'd said it himself. Those words were a manifestation of his determination. They were proof. Even though he wasn't accompanying his friends on their foolhardy quest, he would do his part to help them here. He wanted them to have a choice too.

Yet as he spoke those words to himself, as if to pour cold water on his noble determination, a mana presence appeared nearby. It was being skillfully concealed, but Suimei recognized it. Indeed, there was no doubt in his mind who it might be. It was the court mage called the White Flame, Felmenia Stingray.

Felmenia drew closer to the room, and after stopping for a moment near the automaton, she leaned against the door. It seemed she was using the gap in the ajar door to peek at what was going on inside.

Just how many times had they gone through this song and dance before? She'd been shadowing him for a while now. Naturally, he pretended not to notice and left her to her own devices, but this was getting to be incessant. She would spy on what Suimei was doing for a time, but then eventually withdraw without making a sound.

"The stage is almost set, I believe would be the expression. It's about time I think about the timing and the venue…"

Yes, this had gone on long enough. Felmenia was determined to set straight this boy who'd been sneaking around and sticking his nose where it didn't belong. She was intent on punishing him at first, but perhaps just embarrassing him would be enough.

★

A little after Suimei entered the ritual chamber, the innermost room of King Almadious's Royal Castle Camellia's north wing, Felmenia was standing in front of it stock still and completely dumbfounded.

What... in the world...?

Her mind was overflowing with such expressions of bewilderment. But her state of confusion would be perfectly understandable to anyone who knew what that armor was and what it could really do.

The armor she'd stationed at the ritual chamber door was called the Slamas Armor. It was something created by a celebrated heroic mage famous throughout the history of the Kingdom of Astel. It was an autonomous mobile golem hailed as the greatest of its kind.

Slamas was a great sage known for his use of earth magic, and he himself had heavily contributed to the construction of Castle Camellia. This automaton was the crowning jewel of his life's work. How it had ended up in front of the ritual chamber was a simple question with a simple answer: Felmenia had done it.

The reason was to chastise the mage Suimei Yakagi who didn't know when to stop. She'd asked a favor from an influential former court mage, and had had the automaton dragged out of the treasury for her. She'd set it up in this spot exactly, predicting that Suimei was likely to come again today. She'd come to check on it after she knew the evening patrol would be over, and at first glance, it appeared it hadn't been activated.

That meant that either Suimei hadn't come, or that he'd come and turned back when he saw the armor. But then her sharp gaze spotted the door, which, yet again, was slightly ajar.

How?

Shaking her head to try and rid her thoughts of that question, she moved closer to inspect the golem. When she did, she discovered that the kingdom's greatest golem was reduced to nothing more than a wreck in the likeness of a golem.

For this golem to be so cruelly...

Felmenia was truly dumbfounded. There was no mistaking that the golem had been activated. Before setting it up, she had personally run an activation experiment on it. Though it was an antique, it had functioned perfectly, so there was no way it hadn't worked when Suimei approached it.

But if it had activated, that meant that Suimei must have fought it. Contrary to all expectation, however, there wasn't a single hint anywhere that suggested a fight had taken place. That should have been impossible. This golem was specifically created for localized defense. This was its designed purpose. She'd tested it out herself, too, so she knew that it wasn't easy to defeat.

So how in the world had it ended up so utterly and thoroughly destroyed? The spell engraved within the golem was entirely annihilated, yet the exterior looked exactly the same as it had before. It was even standing upright just as she'd left it.

Just what kind of divine skill would it take to render a golem like this into such a tragic state? If someone had defeated it by using brute force to tear it to pieces, it wouldn't still be standing. Moreover, all traces of the magic holding it together were erased. Felmenia had no idea what kind of power it would take to do something like this.

But one thing was clear. The person responsible for it was in the ritual chamber with a light, glaring at the summoning circle as he always did. It was as if he was saying that he thought nothing of her.

Shit...

As she imagined that, her anger roiled and she spat out a vulgar word that she hadn't used once since the day she was born. The thought of her, Felmenia Stingray, the genius who became the youngest court mage ever, being completely ignored pissed her off to no end. She knew that Suimei didn't actually realize that she was there, but she was still unable to stop her anger.

She couldn't tolerate the magic wiles he used to insult her and the other court mages. She couldn't tolerate the way he behaved himself with no consideration for her whatsoever. The golem had been set up as an indirect way of making a move on Suimei so Felmenia wouldn't have to get her hands dirty. It was supposed to be a dependable method of keeping him in check, so how was it that he was still being so rude?

"Suimei-dono... Tch."

Felmenia stewed on the matter, but it wasn't like she could do anything. Judging she'd done more than enough for one day, she silently returned to her room to seethe.

★

Departing the ritual chamber in the north wing, Felmenia headed back to her private quarters. She'd had enough sneaking around the castle and decided to turn in for the night. When she put her hand on the doorknob to her room, however...

"Hmm…?"

What was this? She could suddenly sense the faint presence of mana. Felmenia didn't recall using any magic when she'd left. And as she investigated using her own magic, it seemed it had just been her imagination. There were no traces of any magic around.

It was likely the remnants of mana that she was unintentionally leaking out. It was the magical equivalent of jumping at your own shadow. For her to react to such a thing, she knew she must be quite tired. And it was all Suimei Yakagi's fault.

"Tch, just you wait…"

One day, she would teach him a lesson or two. She went into her room grumbling. She knew she should get some sleep, but she was a bit distracted by planning her revenge. But then…

"I apologize for coming in the middle of the night. Is Lady Stingray present?"

Along with a reserved knock, a courteous voice came from the other side of the door. Felmenia recognized it. It was the same court mage who'd come to report Suimei's activities to her the other day. She was in the middle of preparing for bed, but she couldn't just ignore him. Felmenia put her white robe back on and called for the court mage to enter. He opened the door and cautiously stepped inside.

"Dear me, please excuse the intrusion."

"What brings you here at this hour?"

The time being what it was, Felmenia had no intention of starting with idle chatter. She cut straight to the chase, but the court mage replied politely without indicating at all that he felt somewhat slighted by her curtness.

"I had something to relay with all haste…"

"With all haste? What is it?"

"Naturally, it is about Suimei Yakagi."

So it had come. Really, it was unlikely the court mage had come to talk to her of anything else. If Suimei did anything, he was to notify her immediately. Since there was also the incident with the golem, Felmenia braced herself for what he was about to report to her.

"So, what has that man done now?"

"Well, this is hard to say, but…"

"What is the matter?"

"I only caught hold of this information just now, but it seems that he's no longer satisfied with merely sneaking around the castle. I fear he has plans to harm His Majesty."

"What did you say?!"

The court mage relayed all this to Felmenia with a grave countenance, and it was quite a shock to her. It was so outrageous, in fact, that she couldn't hide her surprise at what she'd heard. However, thinking about it rationally, she knew that there was no way it could be true.

"…Oh, come now. That's a bit incredible, don't you think? For starters, Suimei-dono has no reason to target His Majesty."

"I agree with you, but it seems that Suimei-dono bears quite the grudge against the king. One of the castle maids reported him saying something treacherous along the lines of, 'It's the king's fault I can't return. Just you wait.'"

"What…"

"It also seems he's been having violent outbursts in his room and striking furniture. It appears there may be more to this than we think."

Felmenia was at a loss for words. Certainly, what he was saying wasn't unthinkable. Even if the hero summoning had been the result

145

of an international accord, the one who'd actually signed off on it in Astel was the king. That gave Suimei one very big reason to hold a grudge against the king, and Felmenia couldn't deny that.

"There are other reasons for us to suspect him as well. Several magic tools that were installed today to deal with intruders were destroyed, predominantly near His Majesty's quarters."

If it had gone that far, she could predict the rest of what he had to say. But even so, Felmenia had to hear it for herself.

"So then..."

"Yes. They were put in place during the day, and there were several witnesses who spotted Suimei-dono in the area that night. I believe the evidence speaks for itself."

"Suimei-dono, you would really go that far...?"

Casting her gaze downward, Felmenia muttered to herself. She wasn't expecting this. The shock was too great. Not satisfied with skulking around the castle, he was now planning on resorting to violence. Felmenia didn't even want to think about it. She didn't want to believe he would do such a thing. The kind boy she'd met that day suddenly seemed very far away.

"Hngh..."

And just then, Felmenia's vision suddenly became shaky. Was it dizziness? She could see the worried face of her colleague, but it was distorted like ripples across the reflection on the surface of a pond.

"Is something the matter?"

"No, I'm just a little dizzy."

"You must be tired, White Flame-dono. I know how busy you are."

"Hahh... My apologies."

Her colleague spoke with a sociable smile and a concerned tone, though Felmenia's dizziness had mostly settled down by the time she answered him. She could tell she had worried him, but that struck her as odd.

This colleague was one she had quarreled with previously. Up until recently, they hadn't gotten along well. It seemed with the passage of time, however, that there were no hard feelings, and perhaps they made a good team after all.

It was a nice thought, but right now Felmenia's focus was on Suimei Yakagi. She couldn't forgive him if he really was planning on bringing harm to the king. And now that her dizzy spell had passed, that was the only thing on her mind. Plagued with questions, she turned to her fellow court mage for answers.

"…Have you spoken of this matter to anybody else?"

"No, I came to you first."

"Understood. Then please keep this matter private from the other court mages. If it is reported to His Majesty, it will affect what happens next."

The court mage looked puzzled at Felmenia's statement, which carried a profound implication.

"Lady Stingray?"

"I will settle this matter personally. I would like you to leave everything regarding that man to me."

Felmenia made a simple but weighty request. Just like after she'd made her request of the king, she was planning on taking matters into her own hands. The most qualified person to put an end to this was the one with the most information on it, and she knew that was her.

"As you wish. I'll take my leave then."

"Thank you for going out of your way to inform me."

"It was nothing. Goodnight, Lady Stingray."

They exchanged farewells as the court mage exited the room. Shortly after he left, the frustration Felmenia could no longer contain escaped her lips in a mumble.

"To think he was that kind of man after all…"

Giving words to her disappointment, anger swelled up deep in her heart. Without a care for his friends, he moved only to satisfy his own revenge. Worse yet, he was targeting the compassionate king who'd been nothing but kind and considerate to him. Was he truly that dishonorable? Was the kindness he'd shown her that day just a conjured ruse? Was he the type of calculating mage that only used magic as a means to his own selfish ends?

The more Felmenia thought about it, the more righteous indignation stirred in her heart for that unseemly man of a mage.

"Ugh…"

Felmenia suddenly felt dizzy again, but once the sensation passed, her anger immediately returned.

"A mage who can do nothing but sneak around in the shadows without a shred of pride is…"

Gripped with emotion, she spoke as though he were there in the room with her.

"Very well. I'd be happy to show you how this works. If a bastard like you thinks you can continue to act so foolishly with impunity, then just you wait…"

A dark fire began to burn in the young woman known as the White Flame. A proud, consuming fire that threatened to burn so brightly that she lost sight of herself. Indeed, that was the moment that Felmenia stopped acting out of a sense of duty and began acting out of self-conceit.

The image of the young man from another world immersing himself in what was at his feet as he ignored her was burned in the back of Felmenia's eyelids, and she declared her own personal war on him with irrepressible anger.

"Suimei Yakagi, say your prayers and wait for me. I shall fully and thoroughly demonstrate to a bastard like you the power of the one known as the White Flame."

That was her intention, not knowing the despair it would bring her in the future.

★

After Felmenia made that dark pact with herself, a contemptuous insult was quietly hurled her way.

"How naive…"

The ridicule was directed at the proud words she'd uttered, audible even from outside her room. It was the court mage who'd come to deliver information to Felmenia, who was still standing outside the door to her private quarters.

"And so the stage is set."

With those words, he pulled up the hood to his robe and vanished into the darkness.

Chapter 3 The One Who Seeks Mysteries

A few days had passed since the night the golem was destroyed. In the dead of the night in Royal Castle Camellia where everyone had gone to sleep, Felmenia was tailing a single young man.

She chose this evening to confront him while he was secretly walking around. To put this boy—who wasn't just prowling around the castle, but now allegedly had designs on the king's life—in his place, she would maintain her distance for a while until she had a chance to corner him.

As usual, Suimei hadn't noticed her. There was no way he could. Whenever she tailed him, she was using wind magic so that her footsteps, body heat, and even her slight exhalations would not reach him. When she used this concealment spell, even if the cleverest guard searched for signs of someone present, they would never find her. Suimei didn't stand a chance.

There were no lights around, yet the young man walked straight down the passage cloaked in utter darkness with no hesitation. He seemed to be headed somewhere different than normal, but just like usual, he was dressed in the strange article of clothing Reiji had called "a blazer." She wasn't sure where he was going, but she fully intended to confront him tonight.

"...Huh?!"

Felmenia spied a moving shadow out of the corner of her eye. She was quite surprised by it and whipped around to see what it was.

She didn't think that there would be anybody else walking around at this hour. The most likely suspect would have been a guard on the night shift, but knowing that she was going to be going after Suimei tonight, Felmenia had put a stop to their patrol for the time being. Not even the guards should be out and about right now, so then just who was it?

Felmenia scanned the hallway for the shadow again, but no one appeared. It seemed she was imagining things, but that was only natural in the dead of night. Even the plants were asleep at this hour, and without another soul around, Felmenia was left alone in the darkness. So what if her eyes were playing tricks on her? She turned her determined gaze forward again to give chase after Suimei, but...

"He... vanished?"

Suimei wasn't there. She had only looked away for a moment, but he was gone. It was baffling to Felmenia. At the pace he was walking, he shouldn't have made it to any of the intersecting passages. She glanced down them anyway just to be sure, but there was still no one to be seen.

Felmenia, however, wasn't going to let that stop her. If she'd lost sight of him, she'd just have to find him again. With an iron will, Felmenia gathered the mana within her body and wove together a spell using wind magic.

"Oh Wind. Thou art my servant. Inform me of that which I desire. Wind Search."

What she invoked was a sort of detection magic. Using it, she could use the wind to perceive the area around her. Before long, Suimei's footsteps were carried to Felmenia's ears by the wind. Tap, tap... She knew the sound of his rhythmic steps well. He hadn't gotten far, so she stayed calm and pursued him.

"This way... Hmm?"

Following the sound of his footsteps as she hurried along, Felmenia was suddenly struck by something.

Wait, this way is...

When she realized where Suimei was going, her anger flared. He was headed straight towards the Garden of the White Wall. It was one of the gardens within Royal Castle Camellia, and it sat right next to the audience chamber.

It was a private area and entry was limited to those who had special permission. It was one of the few sanctuaries where the king could spend his private time. How dare this rude mage try and trespass there? It was unforgivable. The anger in her heart intensified into fury, and it spurred her forward. Felmenia gave chase with heavy steps.

Stomping through the stone passageway and passing a small courtyard after that, Felmenia continued onward. She swore to herself over and over that she would strike that impudent mage down with her wrath as she finally came to the last gate. The light from the stars and the moon overhead shone down in dazzling beams as she ran into the garden, her entire body overflowing with mana.

She was met with the sight of a single mage cloaked in jet black from head to toe.

The Garden of the White Wall. Next to the obelisk that rose out of its center, Suimei Yakagi stood still with his back to Felmenia, gazing up at the starry night sky that looked like a downpour of twinkling gems. The bluish black of night extended from the earth to the heavens, and from the heavens to the earth. It seemed to stretch forever, but it was lit with the magnificent glow of the moon, which practically animated the stillness of the breathtaking scene. That moon and Suimei were all Felmenia could focus on right now.

But… when had he changed? Earlier he was wearing that blazer of his, but now he was wearing a black coat. He was so well dressed and put together that she had to wonder for a moment if she had mistaken him for someone else.

"My goodness… Surely it's in poor taste to stalk someone like this. That's behavior befitting the pitiful and foolish stray sheep who know nothing of the truth and providence of the world, you know?"

Suimei's mouth curved into a broad, daring grin as he spoke snidely. He then turned around casually, like he'd known she'd been there all along. Yes, he looked like he was sneering at a lost child who didn't know where they were going.

"It couldn't be… You noticed me?"

"But of course. After darting around behind me like that, it would have been stranger for me *not* to notice."

"…!"

Suimei replied in a composed fashion, as if the answer were only obvious. He already knew she was shadowing him. Felmenia was stunned that he had the capability to see through her perfect concealment.

The situation was rather suddenly turned on its head for her. She'd gone from being the cat to the mouse, and she'd played right into the palm of his hand by following him here. Felmenia ground her teeth to the point they were audibly creaking. To think that being made to dance in the palm of someone's hand was this vexing… It was the first time she tasted such humiliation, and it only fanned the flames of her rage more.

She had been lured in, sure, but she wouldn't let that be the end of it. She boldly stepped forward and began to question the man in front of her.

"If that is so, you bastard, what are your intentions here?"

"There's no need to ask such a thing. I'm just taking an evening stroll. I don't have a curfew, do I? And this time around, I simply thought I would go somewhere I hadn't been before, you see."

"Do you honestly think an excuse like that would work on me? If you realized I was following you, then you came here full well knowing that, did you not?"

She didn't know exactly what or why, but she knew he was playing games with her. She didn't hesitate to call him out for that, and she didn't bother hiding her irritation at doing so. When she did, Suimei let out a shameless laugh like a naughty child whose prank had been exposed.

"No dice, huh? I was afraid of that."

"I'll ask you again. Why did you come here?"

"Why, you ask? That's…"

Suimei let out a laugh like a gentle spring breeze was brushing by him. He seemed to be taking exceptional delight in whatever he believed would come next. And then, with eyes that looked like they saw right through Felmenia's true motive…

"It's the same reason you came here, isn't it?"

"…"

"The silent treatment, hmm? I was sure that was the reason, though. Was I wrong?"

With that, Suimei slipped on a pair of black gloves with well accustomed movements. When Felmenia showed no reaction, he spoke up again in a seemingly disappointed tone.

"I never thought that I would be stuck having to do this kind of thing with you. Honestly speaking, I would've liked to settle this in a more peaceful manner…"

"How shameless of you to speak of handling matters peacefully…"

That's right. Suimei was after the king. There was no way he had any intention of handling things peacefully. And when Felmenia pointed that out, Suimei flashed a somewhat self-deprecating smile. Rather than objecting to what she said, he admitted to it.

"Perhaps I shouldn't speak that way after setting this stage. Thinking about it, there were several other methods that could have settled this peacefully by now."

"Hmph."

Did he think it would be alright if he simply confessed? Completely clueless as to what Suimei was thinking, Felmenia scoffed at him. Suimei then looked up at the sky like he was recalling something.

"Is this the second time we've talked?"

"It is."

After she curtly replied to Suimei's question, he grimaced as he continued.

"My, you're a tough one to love…"

"What of it?"

"Aah, nothing. It's just some idle chatter. There's no deeper meaning in it, but… My, my, you *really* hate me, don't you? Is it that? Are you still holding a grudge over what happened last time?"

"…"

"Again with the silent treatment."

Suimei let out a somewhat disappointed sigh, but he wasn't the only one feeling that way. Indeed, Felmenia had thought him to be a rather upright man. He'd refused to participate in the Demon Lord's subjugation, but when it really came down to it, he was good-natured and did truly care about his friends. Reiji and Mizuki never had an unkind thing to say about him. Hesitation still lurked in a corner of Felmenia's heart, but…

"Honestly speaking, I too wished it wouldn't come to this."

"You wanted to settle it a while back, you mean? Certainly it would've been much quicker with what you cooked up, huh?"

"...?"

Just how had he interpreted what she said? He was nodding as if he'd come to some sort of understanding. She wasn't sure what he was talking about, but as she looked at him now, something else piqued her interest.

"Be that as it may, you bastard, where did you come up with those clothes?"

She had never seen him in the outfit he was wearing before. In fact, she had never seen anything like it. He was wearing a pitch-black coat with long coattails and an embroidered blue rose on its lapel. A piece of cloth shaped like an inverted sword hung down from the collar of his tightly knit, pure white shirt. He was also wearing trousers the same pitch black as his coat. It was a truly unusual ensemble.

"Hmm? Ah, you mean the suit? I always carry my combat clothing around so I have it whenever I need it."

"You carry it around? But you had no clothes with you other than what you were wearing the day you were summoned."

"This was in my bag. You saw that I was carrying that, didn't you?"

Felmenia heard what Suimei's tone was really implying: "Try and remember." He gestured with his hands, indicating the size and shape of the bag to try and jog her memory. Thinking back on it, it was true all three friends had arrived with bags of personal belongings, but...

"There is no way such bulky clothes could fit inside such a small container."

"...Really? Regardless of how you come at this, isn't that a little narrow-minded of you?"

The way Suimei shrugged his shoulders in astonishment annoyed Felmenia, but he had a point. He was a mage, so if what he was saying was true, there seemed to be an obvious answer.

"I see... A magic tool?"

"Magic tool, huh? That's quite a plain way of putting it, but you're not wrong. It's a bag that can hold several times its apparent size—it's one of my favorites."

Suimei spoke in a slightly boastful tone. Magic tools were objects given some sort of power that would ordinarily be impossible. She knew such things existed, but Felmenia had never heard of an enchantment that could increase the capacity of a container without increasing its size. She couldn't think of which of the eight attributes would even allow for such a thing. If Suimei did truly have his hands on an exceptional magical tool like that, she could understand why he would boast of it.

While Felmenia was admiring the effects of his bag, Suimei fastened his gloves, fixed the collar of his coat, and boldly cut to the chase.

"Now then, the hour is already quite late. Shall we begin?"

Felmenia responded arrogantly.

"Do not say such stupid things, you damned fool. Where do you think this is? This is the Garden of the White Wall, a favorite of His Majesty the King. Do you think for a minute that fighting is permitted in a place like this?"

Yes, this was the Garden of the White Wall. The king's garden. Laying it to waste with a battle would be a terrible indiscretion. Condemning him for the suggestion, Felmenia challenged Suimei with a sharp glare. Suimei, however, only seemed amused. He answered her with a bold smile as he sneered.

"Hmmmmm? The Garden of the White Wall, huh? It's a perfectly pompous name for such a gaudy garden, but… are you sure that's really where we are?"

"What kind of incomprehensible thing are you suggesting? The Garden of the White Wall is identifiable above all else by its signature white obelisk in the center—the very structure you're standing right next to. The colorful flowers which decorate the garden come from every manner of seed, ordered from all over the entire kingdom. This is His Majesty's favorite place, and the spire that you can see on my left is—Huh…?"

Not there. She emphatically raised her left hand to point it out, but the grand spire which housed the king's private quarters wasn't where it was supposed to be. It was gone without a trace.

Felmenia's mind instantly plunged into the depths of chaos. Perhaps aware of her inner turmoil, and as if sneering at her inability to say anything further, Suimei made a declaration.

"What's up? There's nothing where your left hand is pointing, you know? The spire that houses the king's quarters and commands a view of the Garden of the White Wall—the one I assume you're talking about—is over there on your right, isn't it?"

Suimei exuded an ominous aura. His bangs concealed his eyes as he hung his head, and Felmenia could feel her heart being sucked in by this black devil. His lips peeled back into a foreboding smile that revealed his canines. Felmenia whipped around to see the spire she'd been looking for… right where he said it would be.

"Preposterous… His Majesty's personal quarters should be on the left side. Why… How is it on the right…?"

Felmenia was aghast at this baffling phenomenon. She could think of no explanation. It was impossible, but she couldn't deny what she was seeing with her own eyes. The spire was on her right instead of her left.

Just what happened? Doubts swirled in Felmenia's head, threatening to drown her. The royal family's spire should have been on the left side of the garden. She hadn't been invited into the garden but so many times, but she was quite sure that she distinctly remembered that much. She would have sworn to it. So how was it now that it was on the wrong side? And why?

Suimei closed his eyes with a knowing look and explained the mystery.

"Let's see. There are two answers that come to mind. It's simple, really. The spire is on your right because either you were simply mistaken in the first place, or perhaps this is not the Garden of the White Wall as you know it."

"Absurd. Those are both impossible."

"Are they really? Then how is the spire on your right instead of your left as you remember it? Why is the moon that we're seeing rising on your right as well? Why are the colorful flowers planted here in the reverse order you might recall? Try answering that for me."

"Th-That's…"

Suimei kept talking as if he intended to pry the answer out of her, but she still didn't know it. It was just as he said. The Garden of the White Wall they were standing in appeared to be entirely reversed, as if its existence was reflected in a mirror.

Even the moon and the constellations… Everything Felmenia could see was inverted. It was as if, without her knowing it, she had lost her way and stumbled into another world.

"Phantom road…"

"Fan tum… Rode?"

Suimei began speaking a foreign language of some kind, which wasn't automatically converted into the one Felmenia spoke. It must have been something extraordinarily unusual. Felmenia did her best to repeat what he said, sounding it out in words she knew in her own tongue.

"That's right. This is the inside of a barrier I created. It's a confined phantom world where anything and everything in the present world is reversed as though reflected in a mirror. Weaving in numbers that do not exist in the world, I created a place that does not exist. In other words, this is a complex number space, so to speak."

"Wh-What is that? Numbers that do not exist? A c-complex numb-her space, you say? What the hell are you talking about? What did you do?"

Suimei's explanation only served to fan Felmenia's impatience. The words she'd never heard before were bad enough, but she had never seen nor heard of such magic before either. Never. Not once. And she was a court mage.

To her, magic was the mysterious power of the Elements: fire, water, wind, earth, lightning, wood, light, and darkness. Since mages borrowed the power of those eight Elements, magic always held one of those eight attributes. That Elemental power gave way to great miracles. Mana was the driving force, the chant called to the Elements, and their power came to the mage in the form of a spell.

But what Suimei had done didn't play by those rules. It had no Elemental power whatsoever.

"My goodness, it's that bad…? Well, I said what I did knowing that much. The magicka here is some Dark Ages level nonsense. And the theory seems to be several centuries behind even that… Well, that's why the language and concepts of it are completely unknown to you, right?"

"This is… You mean to say this is magic? Magic that can change the appearance of the world? Such a thing exists? Without even using an attribute… How could you reflect the entire…"

"It's not just the looks that have changed, you know… Is it really that confusing? This is just slightly more intricate barrier magicka."

That was yet another phrase she had never heard. Maybe this mysterious thing he spoke of was some kind of unknown attribute.

"Bury-her magic-ah?"

"What?! We have to go that far back?! Don't tell me the concept of barriers doesn't even exist here…"

"Like I've been saying, just what are you—"

"Barriers! Barrier magicka! Have you seriously never heard of it?!"

"I-I haven't! I don't know what you're talking about, but that kind of suspicious magic does not exist in this world!"

"N-No… Seriously? I feel like I'm suddenly peerless in this world."

Suimei looked floored. He held his head up with his hands like it felt heavy. Was the magic of this world that shocking to him? Had he come to the conclusion that it wasn't even worth his time to try and explain anymore? Suimei let out a grand sigh of resignation.

"Well, whatever… Let's leave the discussion for later. All that matters right now is that this isn't the Garden of the White Wall as you know it. It's a mirror world I created with magicka based on the Garden of the White Wall. This way, even if we sling spells and make a ruckus, nobody will ever notice. It'll be like it was all a dream."

"…"

Felmenia still didn't understand half of what he was saying. The magic he used was a complete mystery to her, but she understood the situation she'd gotten herself in. She'd been lured into a cage. An arena, even. Suimei took her silence as understanding.

"I know it's above your head, but it seems you've at least gotten that much down. Well, it's important to be able to calmly come to grips with any situation. Now then, it's about time... Shall we begin?"

"Cut it out. You seem to be quite full of yourself after dragging me into this incomprehensible place, but do you seriously think a bastard with your level of mana could defeat me? I am a court mage of the Kingdom of Astel, Felmenia the White Flame. I will not lose to a man who cannot face his opponents unless he uses this kind of cowardly, petty trick!"

Suimei tried to lord some perceived advantage over Felmenia, and she roared back at him. She wouldn't be spoken to like that. She was the White Flame. The mage who arrived at the truth of the flame. There was no need for her to shrink in the face of this man. If it came to a fight, her position was absolute. She'd reduced countless beasts and monsters to ashes before this day.

There was no way she would lose to this young man who barely even had mana. Even if he'd lured her into this strange place, what real advantage did it give him? He was the kind of disgraceful mage who couldn't fight without such wiles. She had nothing to fear from him.

"Hmph. You insist on prattling nonstop about utter nonsense, but the outcome of this fight has already been determined."

"Oh me, oh my. You sound awfully confident. But can you really defeat me with your power, I wonder?"

"How admirably spoken. Allow me to demonstrate. I shall show you why I am called the White Flame here in Astel. I shall show you the truth at the summit of the ways of magic, my flame!"

"Huh? The truth?"

Felmenia loudly sang her own praises, and she heard Suimei's voice turn quite serious at the last bit of what she said. He'd looked like was leisurely basking in the breeze this whole time, but his countenance turned grave now as well. But Felmenia was unsurprised. What she had threatened to use on him was the truth of the flame. There was no way a degenerate mage like him could maintain his smug facade hearing that. And so she began chanting. She was going to manifest that very magic right before his eyes.

"Oh Fire. Thou art imbued with the essence of all flame, but burn unbound by the laws of nature. Now, turn everything in existence to ashes, the white calamity of truth! Truth Flare!"

The moment she recited the final words that served as the key to her spell, a shining white flame swirled around her. It sucked in the wind in the surrounding area, and it gave off heat several times that of any red flame. It was fire that could reduce anything and everything to ashes, the true flame.

"Wha—Huh?"

Suimei let out a confused stammer as the white flame wrapped around him. Bewilderment was written across his face, and unable to do anything else, he simply stood there dumbfounded.

But that reaction was to be expected. The white flame that all coveted and revered threatened to engulf him. Before such power, it was perfectly normal to give up without any resistance.

Yes, that was how things normally went. It was how things should go, but for some reason, after Suimei spun around with a bewildered look on his face, he timidly snapped his fingers. Then it happened in the blink of an eye. The white flame lost its color and became a plain red flame.

"Wh-What?!"

And in the brief moment that Felmenia was astonished by this phenomenon, the flames surrounding Suimei quickly lost their fury. They died down and vanished as if nothing had happened at all.

After casting a sidelong glance at the surprised Felmenia, Suimei took a good long look at where the once white flame had just been burning brightly. He eventually sluggishly turned back to her.

"So… is that it?"

He sounded as though he had been expecting something extraordinarily violent, but those expectations had been disappointingly betrayed. It was what someone might say at the turn of an anticlimax.

His tension and worry lost all purpose and merely hung over him, aimless and with nowhere to go. But Suimei's nonchalant words triggered a whole new firestorm of their own—a conflagration of confusion from Felmenia's mouth.

"Wh-Wh-Wh-Wh-What?! HOW?! Why did my white flame disappear?! It's the summit of all flame that only those who have arrived at its truth can use! How did it… with only a snap of your fingers…"

"Wow… No, are you serious right now? You said 'the truth,' so I was wondering what kind of dangerous magicka you were about to whip out on me, but then all you did was mix in oxygen to slightly accelerate the combustion…"

"I-I won't stand for that attitude! M-My flame is…!"

Seeing Suimei's striking disappointment, Felmenia was unable to choose her words properly. Why did her white flame vanish? Why was he so disappointed? Those thoughts dominated her mind and were hindering her ability to make any sort of meaningful retort. But Suimei wasn't done. He moved from outright disbelief to offering candid advice.

"No curse, no meaning given to the flame… If there isn't even a single thread tied in from legend, you can barely call that magicka. If I were your teacher, I'd be yelling at you to go back to the basics right now."

"Wh-What?! Just where do you get off saying my magic is so lacking?!"

"Everywhere! Anywhere! It's got nothing of what I just said. You're nothing but a glorified flamethrower! And a crappy one, at that!"

"What?!"

"Hahh, that's enough, damn it… Seriously…"

Suimei spoke like a professor who had abandoned all hope of trying to explain something to a student. He had gone well past exasperation and his eyes were now swaying more towards pity, all of which infuriated Felmenia. And that was on top of her initial confusion. What had actually just happened? What had he done? Suimei let out another grand sigh, and then suddenly… a magic circle manifested at his feet.

"What?!"

"…What is it now?"

His reproachful tone conveyed how over this he was. But Felmenia didn't care. She was still reeling from seeing the impossible just happen before her very eyes.

"A magic circle drew itself on the ground… Impossible…"

"…Hmm?"

"Hmm, my ass! Why… Why did a magic circle suddenly manifest at your feet?! Such a thing shouldn't be possible! S-Suimei Yakagi, what the hell did you do?!"

While Felmenia was shouting over the strange phenomenon, Suimei furrowed his brow. He was starting to look a little pale, but Felmenia felt like she was the only one who had the right to be making that kind of face right now.

A magic circle had to be drawn, but it didn't necessarily have to be on the ground or the floor. They could be drawn on walls, rock surfaces, paper—largely anything that could be written on could be used to construct the magic either in whole or in part. These circles served as a way to simplify the course one had to follow to invoke a magic spell.

In short, a circle contained the letters or numbers that comprised a spell's equation and combined them with precise shapes. Since it required a fair amount of effort to draw one carefully, it was needless to say that it wasn't something that could be done in the middle of combat. Creating one was far more complex than any one single gesture or motion, but this man…

"That's normal, isn't it?"

"How is that normal?! Just how exactly do you manipulate mana to get a magic circle to just draw itself?!"

"That kinda thing is just done using liturgy on the spell beforehand to…"

In the middle of explaining, Suimei seemed to realize something else and once more put his hand to his head.

"Man, this too? This world is even further behind than I imagined. Do you guys even take magic seriously?"

Suimei paid no mind to Felmenia as he vented his anguish. But after racking his brain for a long few moments, he came back to her question. He repeatedly traced a circle with his finger on his forehead, and spoke in a much different tone than before.

"Um, you know… This is all set up in advance. By interfering with the world beforehand so that when a portion of the spell is constructed, the magicka circle which supports it automatically forms, it then gets inserted into the infrastructure of the magicka being cast. So by doing that, when the magicka is used, the magicka circle automatically manifests, and the magicka can be invoked at a high speed. Got it?"

"Eh, ah…?"

"Don't just fucking chirp like what I'm saying doesn't make any sense. This is totally legitimate. You just saw me do it right in front of you. I'll say it before you start ranting and raving again, and this also applies to the magicka before, but if you're gonna deny the mysteries that happen before your very eyes, I can't acknowledge you as a scholar of the mysteries. Got it?"

"…"

Hearing Suimei reprimand her so, Felmenia was at a loss for words. There was no room for her to object in the slightest. He had a good point, but this was the very first she'd ever heard of a technique that could automatically manifest a magic circle even existing. Nobody had ever used a magic circle like that before. Even the sage had never talked of such things.

"Simplifying the process of invoking magicka is essential in the middle of combat, isn't it? I thought this was a world of swords and sorcery? If you guys are this inept, then the world I came from is more fantastical than this one…"

"W-We do have a way of simplifying the process to invoke magic! Magic without chanting is the extreme pinnacle of that!"

"Huh, oh yeah? You think not having a chant is some kinda sophisticated technique?"

"O-Of course."

"Well, I guess for some grand magicka it would be, but... Well, let me ask you this. Is this kinda thing really some amazing technique to you people?"

With those vexed words, Suimei snapped his fingers. When he did, with a profound snap—in complete concert with the sound created by snapping his thumb and index finger—the air right in front of Felmenia's eyes burst with violent vigor.

She had no time to take a breath or even gulp. It was as if the air in front of her eyes exploded in all directions. Its destructive force surpassed that of wind, and rattled everything in the area with a shockwave.

"Huh, ah... What... was that? No chant, and not only that, but no keyword..."

"'Amaaaaazing, Suimei-kun! You invoked magicka without a chant! From today on, I hereby acknowledge you as one of the great magicians...!' Hahh, how stupid..."

Suimei's chest, which had been proudly puffed out, now deflated. After pouring cold water all over his own joke, Suimei was no longer in a good mood.

"I'm tired of explaining things. I can't keep up with all these questions. That's why..."

Suimei trailed off, and then switched tracks.

"Archiatius overload!"

Arc hiatus over-lode?

Was it a magic chant? It was far too short to differentiate between the spell and the keyword. She didn't even have a single clue what he was even calling out to. Yet all the same, the magic circle at his feet began shining brightly. It then filled with a corona of a rainbow's brilliance and unleashed something within the young man.

"Huh?!"

Immediately following that, an enormous amount of mana blew against Felmenia. She reflexively closed her eyes against such dazzling power, but when she reopened them after the torrent had calmed down, she could see the form of something standing there with tranquil mana filling it to the brim and covering it in an overpowering aura.

"Y-Your mana increased?! What did—"

"What did I do? I said I was done with questions, remember? I'm not gonna explain any more. Oh, wait, I get it. You're surprised that my mana was amplified just now. I suppose you can't even get your head around that, huh?"

Suimei spoke in a somewhat irritated voice. He'd lost all interest in answering her questions, to the point he didn't even want to hear her ask them anymore. Taking a moment to return to his normally calm disposition, he brought the conversation back around.

"Hmph. Ever since saying that we should begin, we've wasted quite a lot of time, so… now then, little miss mage, is it my turn yet?"

Suimei scoffed like he wasn't amused at all.

Felmenia was taken aback. Just what was happening right before her eyes? She'd lost count of how many times she'd wondered that after wandering into the garden now. The amplification of his mana was one thing, but the circle he used to activate it was genuinely mind-blowing.

Going out of your way to construct a magic circle to simplify the process of invoking magic seemed contradictory. Drawing the magic circle would only increase the effort, and in the end, increase the overall time that went into casting the spell. Yet this man had turned all logic on its head and invoked magic in far less than what should have been the bare minimum amount of time required to do so.

It was no trick. Nothing she'd seen was just for show. And acknowledging that, she could no longer treat this young man as someone inferior to her. Things that she couldn't do, things that she couldn't understand... He did it all with ease. Surely this young man wasn't overestimating himself when he proclaimed his power. He'd walked down a magical path she knew nothing about in a world she knew nothing about. His knowledge towered over hers.

Felmenia took a moment to ponder what that meant. Surely this young man was stronger than her. Surely he was stronger than the sage who taught her. Surely he was even stronger than the hero Reiji. Surely this young man, even before the Demon Lord who was guiding the world to ruin...

"...Who are you?"

"Now that you mention it, I guess I haven't properly introduced myself since coming here, huh? Well, fine. Just for you, why don't I do that now?"

Suimei looked like he'd remembered something long forgotten, and then looked right at Felmenia.

"I am the magician Yakagi Suimei. One who aspires to unravel all the truth in the world using the mysteries, and a scholar of the mysteries from modern Japan."

Magician Yakagi Suimei.

That was the name of the man who would, shortly after this, bring the mage extolled as the greatest in all Astel to the ground for the first time. The name of the mage she could never catch up to.

★

"Hmph…"

Impudently and quietly, Suimei scoffed. Just as he had planned, Felmenia Stingray was lured into his barrier, and at present, he had just transitioned to demonstrating his utmost power as a magician by activating his archiatius, his mana furnace.

Having finally come to grips with the overwhelming difference in power between them, Felmenia was bound in place by unease and fear. Suimei stood before her, making the most of his knowledge and skills, with his mana overflowing from within him. If anybody with a proper understanding of the situation had been present, they likely would have thought that using the full extent of his power was going too far.

Felmenia Stingray—no, the magicians of this world were just that far behind magicians of Suimei's world. He knew that, and it would have been prudent to hold back in order to suppress any needless mana consumption. That would be the smartest, most efficient, and most gentlemanly way of carrying things out.

But Suimei had no such intentions. Even if this world's magicians knew nothing of the varied systems of magicka, even if they knew nothing of the effective usage of magicka circles, even if they didn't dedicate themselves to improving their chants, and even if they didn't do something as fundamental as forging mana furnaces within themselves, to Suimei, a magician was a magician.

And so he prepared the stage for battle. As the host who beckoned her to battle, no matter how lowly the conflict would be, Suimei couldn't ignore etiquette as a magician of the Society by not demonstrating his full powers. A magician should act like a magician, and that meant using magicka with all their heart and soul to mesmerize their opponent and force them to yield. Regardless of what his intentions were after the fight, as the host, he had to stand tall in battle and put on a good show. That was Yakagi Suimei's pride as a magician.

Suimei squared off with Felmenia. Naturally, this battle had no starting signal. Really, it had already begun. All that was left was for one side to make their move. And unable to bear the tension anymore, the first to act was Felmenia.

"Tch! Oh Fire! Thou art imbued with the essence of all flame, but burn unbound by the laws of nature! Now, turn everything in existence to ashes, the white calamity of truth! Truth Flare!"

It was the same magicka that she used before—the one she said demonstrated the truth of flame, the white flame. Though she claimed it revealed the true nature of fire, it was really just magicka that caused a flash of fire at a higher temperature than normal. But it seemed her attack from before was just a warmup. This one was on a remarkably larger scale. The amount of mana she poured into it was also considerably increased.

The flame that was suddenly given birth undulated like a wave and twisted like a vortex as it clashed against itself. As it spread out, it focused on Suimei in an instant and converged at his location.

In that moment, Suimei's heart completely changed gears.

This was a flood of fire that could burn him to death. He held nothing against it, but he wouldn't let that just happen. Certainly not. Sucking in a nimble breath, he focused his gaze. Then, optimizing his mana, he invoked his magicka.

"Secundum, tertium, quartum moenia, expansio localis."

[Second, third, fourth rampart, local expansion.]

This was Suimei's defensive magicka.

The ramparts from the brilliant golden fortress—what he'd nearly used in the ritual chamber the day he was summoned—spread out within a limited area. Suimei stuck out his arm as if catching something with his palm, and three golden magicka circles piled atop each other to become his shield

A flame that was only hot would never get to him now. The fortress's walls were sturdy. Mere flame wouldn't be able to bring them down. The worst it could do would be getting caught up in the threefold rampart shield and extinguishing itself in vain.

The white flame roared thunderously along its trajectory as it tapered to a point and crashed into the golden magicka circles. The obstructed white flame let fly pure white sparks upon contact and fanned out. It burned so brightly and furiously that the whole area was bathed in a blinding white light. With a thunderous roar like an excavation machine, the collision hurled white sparks every which way, showering the area around Suimei. One second, two seconds, three seconds, four seconds passed. But the white flame couldn't pierce through the shield. Caught up on the second rampart which served as a barrier against spells, the rotating third rampart unraveled the spell behind the incoming attack. Thanks to that, the dazzling white light faded as it regressed to red. Then by the fourth and final rampart's reflective power, what was left of the magicka exploded and was scattered.

"I-I'm not done yet!"

Suimei could hear Felmenia's panicked but brave voice. That was likely her declaration of intent to follow up. He managed to ward off her attack straight from the front, but as she implied, there were still white flames burning in the air around her.

Issuing the command, she sent them flying. The white flame rushed for Suimei once more, but this time it wound around and came at his side. It continued to shift and change directions as it closed in. It seemed Felmenia's title as a court mage wasn't for show. The mana to manipulate the flames, the quick thinking to manage their movements, and the strength to handle them—she was showcasing her skills masterfully. That unhindered magicka control could be called first class and was certainly worthy of admiration.

However, in the end, no matter how flashy the fire was, it wouldn't amount to anything without substance behind it. Magicka that couldn't penetrate his ramparts and had no special destructive effects would never even scratch the golden fortress. But Suimei released his defenses and took evasive action instead. The flame chased after him without missing a beat as he charged off in a straight line, his coattails not so much as singed.

Casting a glance back at the white flame that couldn't keep up with him, Suimei shifted to his counterattack. The distance between himself and his opponent was quite large, so he conjured some acceleration magicka.

"Gravitas residito, massa reducito."

[Abate gravity, reduce mass.]

With that quiet murmur, Suimei's body was lightly released from the shackles of gravity. It was now as though he weighed nothing at all. He then ran—no, he flew. With his black coattails whipping through the air behind him, he tore away from the white flame that was chasing him, and then closed in on Felmenia at the speed of a darting swallow.

"Too fa—"

Was she trying to complain? She likely mistook his acceleration as he closed in on her as instantaneous movement. By the time she realized it, he was only three meters away from her, after all.

But before she could even finish voicing her complaint, he snapped his fingers at her. In an instant, his cold eyes met her shocked gaze.

Strike magicka. As a modern magician, Suimei could invoke magicka that could compress air and then release it in a burst without a chant just by snapping his fingers. While it was simple magicka, its power was easy to guess. Precisely because it was simple, its speed was excellent. And since its effect was purely physical, it was easy to understand.

Snap!

As if a transparent bomb had triggered a transparent explosion, a shockwave burst forth right at Felmenia's feet. It was so close that she only managed to evade it by a hair when she rolled away.

"Ugh, ah…!"

As if blocking off her path of retreat, Suimei snapped his fingers once more. Felmenia seemed to sense the impending danger and changed her course. She ran for dear life from the shockwaves, evading left and right almost like a dance. Unhappy with this turn of events, she screamed at Suimei.

"Th-This is absurd! How can you just continuously fire off magic so easily?!"

"Hahh. You're a third-rate magician precisely because you can't do it. Did you think that I was going to shoot once and let you have another go at me? We're not playing an RPG here, you know?"

That's right. This was no game. It was a competition with their lives at risk. Suimei came from a world where a single second's hesitation could bring a merciless end to things. It was incomparable to the mysteries Felmenia knew.

While Felmenia was scurrying about trying to dodge his attacks, Suimei pulled a reagent vial from his pocket and opened it quickly. Inside was mercury, the only metal in the world which was naturally a liquid at room temperature. Alchemists nicknamed it quicksilver, but when magicka was cast on it, that name took on its true meaning.

With great force, Suimei swept his arm from left to right as if to scatter the contents of the vial, then focused on the mercury that was waiting for him in a line in midair.

"Permutato, coagulato, vis existito."

[Transform, coagulate, become power.]

Grabbing the mercury while it was still in a liquid state, he swung it back as if flicking blood off of a katana. By the time he followed through on the swing, the mercury had taken shape. Since he'd been using it like a sword, it naturally imitated that shape. That was what he'd intended. What he held was a weapon, a mercury katana. Using magicka, he could give it any shape. It was a weapon with no form—a Mercurial Arm.

"Oh Earth! Turn thy body into obstinate stone and smash my enemy! Stone Raid!"

The moment before Suimei's mercury solidified, Felmenia completed her magicka. She called out to the earth, and small stones took shape and flew at Suimei along planned trajectories. Just before they reached him, they finished tapering to sharp points and became vicious projectiles.

"Eat th—"

"Too naive!"

Suimei cleared the incoming stones out of the air with his newly-formed sword. Not even a bullet could get past a trained magician's eye. Flying rocks posed no threat. Suimei's blade smashed through one stone fired off with mana after another. The flow of his swordsmanship was elegant. He was unfazed, his face never revealing even a single hint of panic.

"You can use a sword even as a mage?!"

"Is there something wrong with that? Close combat techniques are essential to magicians where I come from, I'll have you know. But whether up close and personal or at a distance, it isn't a hindrance to using magicka though—"

Slash!

"Shit! Shitshitshitshithsitshiiiiiiiiiiit!"

Felmenia began to fire off stones blindly in an act of desperation. But they would never hit Suimei. Not even a speck of sand would reach his coat. As he cut down the last rock, it shattered into crumbling lumps of earth. They could no longer maintain their form.

"Oh Fire! Become my will to pierce through and—"

"Permutato, fluctuato, acutum flagellum exisistito."

[Transform, flow, become a sharp whip.]

Suimei and Felmenia started their chants at the same time, but his was shorter and he finished sooner. The thought that longer chants were better was old fashioned. Chants were meant to be short, and they were far more functional that way. It was smart to only pull power from words with meaning.

By trimming away the excess, word for word, and thoroughly considering the vocabulary used for every single verse, the chant would eventually become faster. The answer was obvious and clear.

And with Suimei's expedient chant, a magicka circle formed centered on his mercury katana like the sword was piercing through it. Suimei then deftly flicked his wrist. The mercury, which was in the shape of a sharp and stiff blade, then transformed into a whip like a leather cord. Just like his chant implied, he now had a mercury whip that flowed freely through the air. He used it to lash at the ground by Felmenia's feet and interrupt her chant.

"Huh?!"

The mercury whip surpassed the speed of sound, and a violent boom rang out like a gun firing a blank. The ground where it struck was deeply gouged. The metal whip possessed destructive power that far surpassed one made of leather. Its weight, its hardness, its sharpness, and even its length were free for Suimei to control. It could penetrate iron plating like it was paper, so the effect it would have on flesh and bone need not be said. Its destructive power could be glimpsed just by looking at what it had done to the ground.

"Ugh... This can't be..."

With a single swing of his arm, Suimei could reap her life. Staring down that cold realization, Felmenia was frozen. She couldn't take a single step from where she stood, and her lips simply refused to chant anymore. She could hardly articulate herself, but the mortified look on her face said it all.

Suimei could see her grow pale. He knew this was the endgame, but he couldn't stop yet. The curtain wouldn't fall until his opponent was on their knees. If she was merely mortified, then she had not yet given up. She was still wondering how to recover, still looking for an opening. And until all such thoughts were purged from her mind, Suimei wouldn't relent. He would carve utter defeat in the depths of her heart.

With that intent, Suimei fed his passion to his mana furnace like kindling, and his mana suddenly exploded. With a roar that sounded like an earthquake, the whole castle shook. The erupting torrent of Suimei's excited mana unleashed a surge of ultramarine light with a thunderous cry like a dragon.

And right before Suimei's eyes, Felmenia lost the ability to even tremble in the face of his true identity. Seeing the truly overwhelming difference between them, she fell to her knees in a daze and simply stared up at him in awe.

Suimei then sang out another chant.

"Intra velum. Noctis lacrimarum potestas."

[Beneath the curtain. The majesty of the tears shed by the night.]

At his feet, an enormous magicka circle expanded to cover the entire garden. It shone with an ultramarine light made of mana that was deeper than even the hue of the starry sky. Its remarkable brilliance was dazzlingly bright, and the illusionary world they were in grew even more fantastical.

"Insigne Olympus et terrae pingito."

[Colored by the symbol of heaven and earth.]

With every verse of his chant, something new happened. This spell was not built up all at once, unlike the magicka of this world that required an entire recitation to manifest. Each line of this chant was an embodiment of power. With each line, the world was changing, already transitioning toward the mystery that would occur.

Like fireflies dotting the air, golden particles of power rose from the earth and soared heavenward as they were sucked in by the vast emptiness of the starry sky.

"Infestato ad irrationabilis veritas."

[Infest towards the irrational truth.]

Next, a massive magicka circle appeared directly overhead and covered everything below. As if projecting the stars that lit up the sky, countless smaller magicka circles took shape within it.

"Caecato, pluvia incessabilis."

[Dazzle, incessant rain.]

179

The magicka circle which covered the heavens was categorized as a wide area expansion type. Its attribute was the void, modelled after ether. Its system was a combination of Kabbalah numerology and astrology. It was a fusion of styles, which could be said to be the representative style of modern magicka.

All that was left was the final verse. A bold grin crept across Suimei's lips as he pronounced her execution.

"Court Mage-dono. Get ready to defend with everything you've got."

Felmenia didn't even protest. She deployed her best defensive magic as she clung to dear life.

And then...

"Enth, Astrarle—"

[Oh starry sky, fall—]

With those keywords as a signal, pillars of light shot down from every single magicka circle covering the starry sky. Those countless pillars of mana and starlight held directionality, and came down like a rain of meteoric tears.

All sound above ground was blown away by the thunderous roar of the grim reaper's approach. Death bared its fangs at all the earth within its range in a magnificent spectacle. Those rays, which looked like they could consign even enormous beasts to oblivion with a single strike, hailed incessantly from the countless magicka circles overhead.

Everything directly below naturally had no way to defend against such destruction, and the ground rumbled like it was letting out a death knell as it crumbled under the merciless light. This was the star magicka Starfall.

Using the power of the stars themselves and the dormant seed of power sleeping within humans, it manifested in concert with the words left behind by Pericles, "Enth Astrarle." It was one of Yakagi Suimei's grand magickas.

Eventually, the rain of stars calmed down. And all that was left, as if that destructive scene was nothing but a dream, was the original Garden of the White Wall in complete tranquility, Yakagi Suimei wearing his black suit, and Felmenia in her pure white robe, reduced to such tatters it could be mistaken for rags.

"No way…"

The first one to speak was Felmenia. She was still on her knees, completely devoid of her usual dignity and unable to move as Suimei held his mercury katana to the nape of her neck.

"I'm calling this my win. Any objections?"

As he inquired about his victory, a trembling voice came back to him.

"A-Are you a damn monster…? Just whose mouth was spouting bullshit about how they couldn't fight…? Why did you refuse to take part in the Demon Lord's subjugation? If you went, even that damn Demon Lord…"

"Could be defeated? That's bullshit and you know it. I said it back in the audience chamber, but fights are about numbers. History has proven that much. No matter how strong the individual, they cannot win against overwhelming numbers. There is no precedent for a single person attaining victory. Even if someone's remarkable, talented, and tough, they'll still drown in a sea of violence big enough. An individual is no match against the united will of many."

Suimei felt like he had made his point, but he didn't stop there.

"You're not just asking us to defeat the Demon Lord you call Nakshatra or something, right? There are the legions of demons under this guy. That barcode baldy said that the army that toppled the country called Noshias or whatever numbered in the millions, but just think about it. Surely that wasn't their whole force. If they gathered their reserve soldiers, who knows how much bigger it could be? Is it double? Triple? How were you going to suggest I take on one million demons, much less three? Even with a solid plan to take out a few elite demons to turn the tables and shake up morale, there's no guarantee you'd even make it through the rabble. No matter what you do, you can't fucking beat that."

"What the hell are you talking about? It is said that battle is where one's individual valor means everything. With that much power, our victory would be certain and defeat would be impossible."

"Are you an idiot? I'm saying that quantity and quality are in different categories when it comes to war. There's no way that quality equals quantity, right?"

"You bastard of a... How could a man of your strength say such a cowardly thing?"

"What? Me? Stop it. I'm no first-rate magician. Well, I've been told I've got a bit of talent, but back home, I'm only a magician in about the lower-middle class at best... I guess you're right in that if we actually had the best of the best here, they might be able to do it with one hand tied behind their back. Sure. But that kinda talk doesn't have a single iota of relevance to what we're talking about."

"..."

Felmenia was unable to say anything. Whether it was because she was terrified of the people of Suimei's world, or of him as he laughed and bragged about them wasn't entirely clear. But nevertheless, her speechlessness only reasserted the difference in power between them.

"Well, I knew it before we started, but the magicka here is pretty outdated, huh? Frankly speaking, this wasn't even all that fun. Granted, that may be a bit harsh to you."

Suimei spoke honestly. The joy of witnessing mysteries not known to him and working out techniques to deal with them, giving birth to new magicka… That was what Suimei desired from battle as a magician. He'd gotten none of that out of the fight just now.

There was nothing surprising, unexpected, or praiseworthy in what had just transpired. Suimei's victory was inevitable, negating all pleasure he should have taken in winning. All he'd gotten out of it was throwing it in Felmenia's face.

"Alright then, it's about time we bring the curtain down on this stage, mage."

Suimei took a tone so cruel that it would send shivers down the spine of anyone who heard it. He froze his heart. His gaze was subzero. He was ready to end this. Felmenia was on her knees and wasn't trying to stand back up. This was it for her. As if she was facing the end of the world all on her own, her face was pale as a sheet.

"A-Are you going to kill me…?"

"I wonder. How do you think I'll bring this score to an end?"

"I-I'm a court mage…"

"Oh, so if you're a court mage, then it's no biggie?"

Whenever Felmenia asserted her title, it was an attempt to stoke her bravery and steel herself, but her nerves failed her here. With

Suimei's mercury katana to her throat, she could no longer pretend to be bold.

"Ah, ngh…"

Hearing the fear overcome Felmenia, Suimei showered her with rebuke.

"Don't fucking seize up with fear this late into it, you damn good for nothing. All I did was answer your request in kind."

"S-Silence! You're the bastard who… to His Majesty…"

"What about the king?"

When he sharply questioned her, Felmenia's tone wavered. Why did that come up all of a sudden? Did King Almadious have anything to do with their quarrel?

"You were planning to harm… His Majesty the King…"

"What? Are we just making up excuses now? Just when, exactly, was I going to hurt your good-natured king? I don't have a single reason to do that kinda crap, do I?"

"Huh…? But you…"

"Hmph. I've had enough of your shit."

"—!"

When Suimei viciously cut her off, a shiver ran down Felmenia's spine. And then, scoffing with a cold stare, he asked her a grim question.

"A magician is always prepared to pay for their actions with their body, isn't that right, court mage?"

A magician must head into all things prepared for the consequences. In the world Suimei came from, that was common knowledge. But the young Felmenia had no such resolve.

"P-Please! Anything but that!"

Felmenia cast her pride to the wind and fell prostrate before Suimei. She silently pleaded for him to spare her and show mercy without a care for her appearance. She would have even sworn never to defy him again. But Suimei was unamused. He scoffed and began to mean-spiritedly interrogate her.

"Hey now. You couldn't wait to knock me off, but now you're begging for me to go easy on you?"

"Y-You're wrong! I never had any intention of killing you! I just... wanted to chastise you a little..."

Felmenia shook her head vigorously to the sides, and Suimei threw a suspicious gaze over her like a wet blanket. Even though she had nothing to stake her life on, her lack of resolve was pitiful. She had the backbone to try and take out her opponent, but clearly hadn't considered what the worst-case scenario might be like for her. Suimei considered this her punishment.

He recalled hearing that she was some important noble, and for better or worse, that seemed to have had an effect on her personality. But putting that aside, Suimei went back to interrogating her.

"Is it true that you had no intent to kill me?"

"It is! I swear to the Goddess Alshuna, I'm not lying!"

"I don't know what her name means to you people, but as a Japanese person from another world, it means nothing to me."

Suimei adjusted the katana, and it chinked as though it had a guard on it. Since Felmenia wasn't Japanese, she likely didn't know what that sound signified, but she instinctively seemed to sense she was that much closer to losing her life. She then resorted to sorrowful supplication.

"P-Please! I don't want to die yet! I don't want to die... Please..."

Anyone would have been able to see he'd bullied her too much. But now that she was this much of a mess, Suimei thought it was about time to move on to the main subject. Maintaining the malicious act, he began speaking in a decidedly bored tone.

"Then let's see… In exchange for sparing you, shall I have you accept my conditions?"

"…C-Conditions?"

"That's right. First, you will never speak of what has happened here tonight to anyone. Second, you will never tell anyone that I am a magician. Especially not Reiji or Mizuki. Got it?"

As Suimei pressed her for consent, Felmenia shook her head from side to side with all her might as she trembled in fear.

"N-No, please wait! Reiji-dono and Mizuki-dono is one thing, but I have already informed His Majesty that you're a mage. In that case, what do I…?"

"Hmm, how unexpected. I'm surprised someone as overconfident as you would have bothered talking to someone about it. I thought you would deem someone like me to be insignificant, and being sure that you could deal with me at any time on your own, wouldn't even set up any insurance in the event that you lost against me… Well, I don't really mind that much. In any case, you must never speak of the details of this encounter to anyone ever."

Dodging the bullet of having violated his request before he'd ever even asked it, Felmenia let out a sigh of relief. Suimei then moved on to the final and most important condition.

"And third, based on the two previous conditions, I'll have you sign this document."

With a gesture like he was reaching into thin air, a single piece of paper and a pen appeared in Suimei's left hand. The pen was the one he always used, and the paper had some sort of agreement written out on it in a foreign language. Naturally, Felmenia couldn't understand any of it.

"What is that?"

"It's nothing. Just a contract. It says that you will absolutely keep your word if you agree to these conditions. A binding agreement, if you will. You don't mind just signing something like this, right?"

"...Understood. I will sign it."

Felmenia seemed to find it just a little suspicious, but she was quick to agree to it. She hardly knew what to make of this strange document presented to her, but considering the duress she was under, she hardly had a choice about signing it.

After writing her name, she sealed it with a thumbprint in blood. After overseeing this, Suimei shamelessly informed her of what it all meant.

"Also, I forgot to mention this, but now that you've signed this, in the event that you break your promise, you'll die."

"Wh-What?"

"Hmph, you were probably planning on just spilling everything to the king after this, so this was a little insurance to keep that from happening, you know? I also don't want things to get complicated by having you make some kinda weird report to anyone."

"Wait, there's no way that you can do something like that with just—"

"To a magician, a master of manipulating the mysteries of the universe, nothing is impossible."

It wasn't like Felmenia was making light of what he said, but she stared at Suimei with a skeptical expression. He decided to demonstrate its effect in the simplest way possible. He let go of his mercury katana for the moment, then poked the signed document with his finger clad in mana. As he did, Felmenia's chest was seized with pain.

"Don't be ri... Hngh... UAAAAAAAAH!"

"It works a little something like that. It's quite hard to endure the feeling of having your heart crushed, isn't it?"

Suimei pulled his finger away from the document. When he did, Felmenia was released from the pain that was crushing her heart, and began gasping for air as she voiced a complaint without any strength behind it.

"Ack, aha... You didn't say anything about this..."

"Whether or not I said anything, we have an agreement now. And I said you'd never speak of this, right? That's all there is to it. It's not all that complicated, really. All you have to do is keep your mouth shut. About what happened today, and about how I'm a magician. As long as you pretend to forget all that, no harm will come to you. Isn't that far more fair a deal than being sold or going to pick a fight with the Demon Lord?"

Suimei turned around as he spoke, and asked his last question over his shoulder. But no answer came. Finding that to be quite puzzling, he took a careful look at Felmenia, who was hanging her head.

"Hngh... Hic, hic... You're... so mean... Waaah... Uwaaaaaaaah..."

It seemed every last bit of pride she had was gone. All Suimei could hear now was Felmenia's sobbing.

Hrm... Did I kinda overdo it a little here?

It seemed he'd done an exquisite job of breaking her. Used to facing off against magicians in his own world, he couldn't imagine taking anything other than a severe, hardline attitude against anyone who would come after him like she had... but he couldn't hide his bewilderment now.

It wasn't just about magicka. There seemed to be an impassable gap between his world and this one when it came to maturity. Having realized that, could he really continue to back her into a corner? He momentarily considered it, but then relented. Suimei wasn't a cruel person, after all, and he was actually starting to panic a little.

"W-Well, that's how it is, so keep your promise, alright? It'd also be bad for my heart if I needlessly killed someone."

He spoke with a far more casual tone than before. Sympathy had taken hold of him. He never thought she would cry like this. And since she continued to do nothing but sob, Suimei couldn't even tell if she was listening to him. He scratched his head in a fluster, and then deviated from his plans.

"Renovato, atque restituito... There."

[Restore, and then reconstruct.]

At the very least, he thought he could fix up her clothes, so he cast his restoration magicka for her. As the magicka circle rose up from the ground below the despondent Felmenia, her robe was flawlessly restored. By the time the circle reached the top of her head, there was not a single hole, frayed thread, burn mark, or speck of dirt to be seen on it.

And then, with nothing else to do, Suimei left Felmenia alone and exited the garden. In the end, he settled everything by letting her go. Leaving the consequences for later, Suimei quickened his pace as he walked away.

A fight between magicians wasn't the same as a death match. Really, it was quite rare for a magician to take the life of another magician. Certainly, mercy was never shown to those who arbitrarily intruded in the workshops of others, but aside from those cases, magicians inherently carried a mutual amount of respect for each other. They were brothers and sisters in their pursuits.

Nowadays, magicka had fallen by the wayside thanks to science, and its development had come to a halt because of its decline. With things as they were, the life of each and every person who aspired to further magicka was important. So to ensure that the art known as magicka was never fully wiped from the face of the earth, there was an implicit understanding that magicians were not to needlessly kill other magicians, even if they used different styles. To that end, the contract Suimei had just used was employed quite frequently instead.

In exchange for not killing someone, a magician could use the contract to ensure that no further harm could be inflicted upon them. And with a power like that, there was no real need to kill anyone in the first place. It kept magicians from killing themselves off, and helped maintain the ratio of those studying mysteries in the modern era.

There were exceptions, of course, but it was worth bearing in mind that a duel between magicians was more of a competition than a fight. It was a chance to show off how well they understood the mysteries. In other words, it was a contest of the precision of their magicka, the strength and the complexity of their spells, their knowledge of theory, and any special characteristics they could use. In a way, it was a chance to study and learn from each other, mutually furthering the goals of their craft.

Thinking about it like that, what about the fight just now? There was no magicka that made him unintentionally ooh and aah in admiration. There was nothing for him to linger on after his victory. No, only one thought came to mind on the subject.

"They're really too far behind, huh?"

He'd said something similar to Felmenia earlier, but it was really bothering him now. From here on, after all, he had to live in this world. He was worried whether or not there were any mysteries here that would make his heart dance. With nothing to stimulate and inspire him, he—or any magician, for that matter—would become a fossil. To Suimei, who was pursuing his thesis, this was a huge setback. In any case…

No intention to kill, right…

The next thing he remembered was what Felmenia said earlier. How could she say something like that after setting up that violent golem? But even so, she hadn't appeared to be lying when she said it.

"I guess I'll look into it a bit."

Felmenia had also said something about Suimei planning on harming the king. Thinking back on it, it didn't seem like an excuse. If he assumed that she was under some kind of misunderstanding, there was probably more to what was going on. Realizing that the curtain had yet to actually fall, Suimei grumbled to himself.

Felmenia was left completely defeated. Things had gone slightly out of order, but his original objective had been accomplished, and that reduced the potential risks for him. That being the case, it seemed like as good a time as any to make a move. And so Suimei quietly flipped open his black coat, and melted away into the matching darkness.

★

A few days after the incident in the Garden of the White Wall, King Almadious Root Astel called Felmenia Stingray to the audience chamber. The reason for this summons was naturally to receive an update on the status of Reiji's magic lessons straight from his instructor's mouth.

He'd made inquiries from others, but their reports only ever said things like "a bundle of talent," "a magic genius," and "the greatest in the world." Nothing but abstract praise. The important parts were all glossed over, and in short, all the king really knew about Reiji's magical ability was that he was talented. Since the king had the responsibility of sending him off, he wanted to know more in-depth details.

So he'd called on Felmenia to report as his instructor. Her pure white robe quietly fluttered behind her as she knelt down before the king, and attentively reported on both Reiji and Mizuki's progress. According to her, Reiji's talent for magic was indeed extraordinary. His capacity for mana was over ten times that of the castle's court mages, and while he still had some small shortcomings when it came to minute control of spells and mana, he was exceptionally quick on the uptake when it came to understanding magic.

In regards to Mizuki Anou, though she wasn't on Reiji's level, she also held a fair amount of power. Her ability to understand and conceptualize magic seemed to have no limits, and she often left her peers wondering just how she was able to arrive at such notions. It was to the point where it was regrettable that she hadn't also received divine protection from the hero summoning.

"That is all, Your Majesty. The speed at which Reiji-dono and Mizuki-dono are learning magic is incredible. Someday, I am sure they will be comparable to the great mages from around the world."

Injecting one last compliment, Felmenia brought her report to an end. The king then added on one more question as a light joke.

"Does it seem they will surpass even you?"

"With Reiji-dono's power, perhaps."

"I see. That is reassuring. If Reiji-dono has that much talent with magic, then my concerns are likely just needless worry."

"I certainly hope so, Your Majesty. I was also surprised. They've only been introduced to magic for some two weeks now, and to already be a match for intermediate level mages just goes to show that Reiji-dono was not chosen to be a hero for nothing. If you will allow me to say this as a single mage, my envy is irrepressible."

Felmenia said that last part quietly. With her head bowed, the king couldn't see her expression clearly, but if she was jealous enough to admit it to him, he had no doubt that it was showing on her face. But there was no helping it. From what he had heard, Reiji was acquiring magical knowledge from her at a rate that could no longer be described by just the word "exceptional."

"I am certain it is. However, if he did not have at least that much power…"

"It is just as Your Majesty says; he would not be able to defeat the Demon Lord."

"Indeed."

The king nodded back as their opinions lined up. Having heard everything he wanted to about the hero, he hung his hopes on Felmenia's efforts and hard work to continue training him.

"Court Mage Felmenia Stingray, your report has been received. There are still three days until Reiji-dono's departure, so make full use of that time."

"All is as you will, Your Majesty. Then, I will excuse myself here…"

After respectfully accepting the king's order, Felmenia bowed down and then turned to leave. However, the king had not dismissed her yet. He still had business with her, and he stopped her from going.

"Felmenia, I have something else that I would like to hear from you."

"Huh? O-Of course, Your Majesty."

"That young man… It's about Reiji-dono's good friend Suimei-dono."

The king wanted to talk about Suimei Yakagi. Ever since Felmenia's previous report on him, the king had been worrying about Suimei almost as much as he had been about the hero Reiji. He was mostly concerned about the potential clash between Suimei and Felmenia, and he wanted to know if anything had come of it in the several days it had been since they'd talked on the matter.

"S-Suimei-dono, Your Majesty…?"

Felmenia felt blindsided, and the dumbfounded look plastered on her face said it all. Her voice slightly cracked, but even so, the king pressed her on the matter.

"Indeed. After we last spoke, what kind of movements has that young man made? You have continued your surveillance, have you not?"

"R-Regarding that… Um…"

"Felmenia?"

She was avoiding his gaze for some reason, and hesitated to speak as if it were something difficult to talk about. In utter contrast to her report about the hero, it was like she had completely lost her composure.

It seemed that she had done something, otherwise she would be speaking loudly and with dignity as normal. Despite being quite young, no matter the situation and no matter the opponent, she never lost her composure. That was all out the window right now.

"Ah, uh…"

"What is the matter? Could it be that something happened?"

"No, sire, that's, um…"

Even when he asked a second time, Felmenia could only answer evasively. When the king looked closely, he could see that she was sweating slightly. He then asked her a third time, this time in a strict tone.

"Answer me, Felmenia. If you do not speak, we will be unable to progress, will we not? Tell me everything that has happened and everything you have witnessed. Conceal nothing."

However, Felmenia would still not answer. Instead, she bowed down so deeply that she appeared to be rubbing her forehead on the floor.

"Y-Your Majesty! Please, I beg of you! In regards to this matter, please allow me silence!"

"Are you saying you cannot speak of it?"

"Yes, sire. Though it is foolish of me, it is just as you say."

"Why?"

"The answer Your Majesty seeks is an undesirable state of affairs brought on by my lack of virtue. I cannot speak of it…"

"Hmm…"

Seeing her continue to behave so unlike herself, the king unintentionally groaned. Prostrating herself, she refused to speak of the matter. She was being unusually obstinate.

The question was why she was going to such great lengths to conceal what had happened, but the answer was obvious enough. After being told not to do something, she'd naturally be reluctant to admit it if she'd defied that order. Even if she tried to skirt the issue, one wrong word might reveal her, and then she would be punished accordingly for defying the king.

Then was this silence some form of self-defense against that punishment? If that was the case, she'd already given herself away.

"…I told you that you mustn't act, did I not, Felmenia? And it seems you've done something to Suimei-dono after all. Am I wrong?"

As the king raised his voice, Felmenia's shoulders trembled like a small animal that had been discovered by a predator. Seeing her like that, it appeared she truly feared being found out and reprimanded. The fact that she was unable to expect such a thing despite her wisdom was both unexpected and disappointing, but no matter how much she trembled, responsibility was responsibility.

But before all else, he actually needed to know what was going on, and that would mean getting the details out of her.

"Speak. Before I pass down your punishment, I must hear what you have to say. Until then, nothing can begin."

"P-Please, Your Majesty. I beg of you… I beg for your mercy."

"There is no need to be so obstinate. I already expected you to disobey my orders. Resign yourself and hold nothing back."

"Y-Your Majesty…"

"I have had enough of this, Felme…?"

When he looked closely, the king saw that this dignified young woman had tears coming from the corners of her eyes. Just how long had it been since he last saw her cry? It must have been when she was still a small child, the night she'd visited the castle for the first time for an evening party and had gotten separated from her parents, the countess and Earl Stingray. This was most perplexing.

"Why will you not speak?"

"…"

Felmenia would not answer. All she would do was bow her head down. King Almadious took a long, silent moment to think to himself. Just why wouldn't she speak? Why was she being so obstinate over this? The answer to those questions didn't come to him, but he eventually thought of a plan and changed his line of questioning.

"Felmenia. From here, I shall ask you questions."

"But Your Majesty…"

"Listen to me, Felmenia. If the answer to my question is correct, then remain silent as you are now in response. If it is incorrect, then just shake your head. Understood?"

The king made himself quite clear, and Felmenia kept silent without objecting. He then proceeded to pose the questions that had come to him, one at a time.

"Within the last few days, did you take some sort of action against Suimei-dono?"

"…"

Silence. Thus, a hit. But he had expected that much. This wasn't news to him.

"Was it a verbal warning?"

This time, Felmenia shook her head.

"Did you use force?"

"…"

Another hit, though it was likely no more than overawing him as a punishment. Felmenia should have known full well not to do anything more than that. He didn't think it was possible, but he still had to ask.

"At the time, did you injure Suimei-dono?"

The king was worried he may have phrased that a little strongly, but…

Felmenia adamantly shook her head. With that, one more question came to mind.

"…Wait, did you *try* to injure him?"

"…"

In response to Felmenia's silence, the king was also stunned into silence for a time. This was far too surprising. Not the fact that Felmenia had actually used force, but that she, despite being considered the most prominent mage in the entire country, had failed to injure Suimei when that's what she'd had the express intent of doing. That was what shocked him. Just what did it mean? Had the boy who was not given the divine protection from the hero summoning, a mere mage who had no strength imparted on him by the Goddess or the Elements, truly walked away unscathed from an encounter with the White Flame?

While listening to the sound of his own gulping, the king resolved himself and asked one more question.

"Then let me ask you this, Felmenia. Were you defeated?"

"..."

Affirmative silence. There was nothing more to doubt. Felmenia had acted on her own, disobeying the king's order and confronting Suimei, and as a result, she had tasted a crushing defeat.

"And at that time, Suimei-dono took hold of some kind of weakness of yours. And because of that, you are unable to say anything to me. Is that correct?"

"..."

A hit. As expected, Felmenia couldn't speak freely on the matter because of some sort of weakness, despite the fact that she could not be seen or heard by the one exploiting that weakness at the moment. The king had his doubts as to why she was honoring whatever arrangement she had with Suimei, but...

Felmenia, and also the one who laid her low, Suimei, were both people walking the dark, winding path of magic. For the king who had only dabbled in the magic arts, it was difficult for him to comprehend what kind of agreement the two of them may have come to.

"Hic... Hic... Your Majesty, my deepest apologies... In addition to going against your orders, I am being disloyal only to protect myself. I, Felmenia Stingray, shall accept any… any punishment that you deem appro… appropriate…"

"It is fine. You have already received your punishment from Suimei-dono, have you not? There is no point in lashing the dead. I have no punishment to bestow on you."

"Your Majesty…"

Repenting for her mistakes, Felmenia's tears flowed freely and she became excessively despondent. For her to be in such low spirits was likely because her fight against Suimei had been that devastating. In that case, the king could see that she'd already been punished enough. If the situation had rendered her so humbled, her self-conceit and pride were likely no longer an issue, and that was a relief to him, honestly. But it wasn't all good news. One worry quickly replaced another.

"Felmenia. I cannot leave this matter unaddressed. After this, I am thinking of summoning Suimei-dono to the audience chamber."

"Your Majesty, calling Suimei-dono here… But why…?"

As Felmenia raised her head in bewilderment, the king answered her without holding anything back.

"Is it not obvious? Since I cannot hear it from you, I shall ask Suimei-dono. Besides, there is the matter of the summoning as well as your weakness. I ought to diffuse any potential discord between that man and us."

"You mustn't, Your Majesty! Suimei-dono is not that kind of halfhea—GUAAAAAAAAH!"

When she tried to object, Felmenia was strangely afflicted. Suddenly, right in the middle of her sentence, a shriek came from her mouth and she was grasping at a terrible pain in her chest.

"Felmenia?! What happened?! Felmenia!"

At this strange, sudden occurrence, the king reflexively rose to his feet. Felmenia's fit was that alarming. But the pain that rendered her writhing on the ground did not seem to last for long. In a few moments, her screaming stopped and she righted her posture.

"Hahh, hahh... I apologize for showing such a disgraceful display before... Hrm, ahem..."

"Just what is the matter? Is it some sort of sickness?"

"No..."

She denied that much, but the king knew this was no coincidence. A veritable fountain of cold sweat was running down her beautiful, wise face. She was as pale as a corpse. It was only reasonable to assume the cause was illness, but the king had never heard of her suffering from any such thing.

The king reviewed the events in his head. Moments ago, Felmenia had been on the floor grasping at her chest, seemingly at her heart. And she was afflicted with this pain suddenly. Objecting to the king's idea, she had started to say something about Suimei, the very boy she'd refused to talk about otherwise. It was moments after mentioning his name that she began screaming. Following that logic...

"Could it be that pain is the weakness...?"

"..."

"Is it magic?"

"..."

Felmenia would not answer. No, because of her weakness, she likely could not answer. The king could only barely see her downcast face, but it was a vortex of bitter feelings. It was part self-condemnation and part remorse. Seeing her in that state, the king had nothing more to ask of her.

"Understood, Felmenia. You may leave everything to me."

"Your Majesty?"

"As I said before, I shall call Suimei-dono here."

"B-But…!"

"It is fine. I shall take all responsibility. You shall—"

And from there, King Almadious sent a messenger to retrieve the magician who had cursed one of his mages.

★

Night had fallen since the king concluded his business with Felmenia. He sat in the audience chamber of Castle Camellia, and was eventually greeted by the sound of the door opening. The one who entered was none other than Suimei Yakagi. He was a good friend of Reiji's, and according to Felmenia, a mage from the other world.

At first glance, this young man looked completely plain. He bowed at the door, and then approached the king with an unhurried gait. The atmosphere around him was just the same as it had been the first time he visited the audience chamber, but he was dressed differently this time. His new monochrome outfit gave him a certain sense of refinement. Perhaps because he was not used to such situations, Suimei knelt down before the king in a somewhat clumsy manner.

"At your messenger's request, I have come to see Your Majesty."

"I must apologize for summoning you so late into the night. Forgive me for saying so after you have already been so courteous, but today it will only be the two of us here. Please be at ease."

"…"

"Would that be alright, Suimei-dono?"

"…Yes, Your Majesty."

After a long pause, Suimei consented and raised his face. His expression was still a little stiff. Seeing him like that, the king deferred moving on to the main topic and inquired about his clothing instead.

"I am unfamiliar with that outfit. Just what is it?"

"It's clothing that I brought from my home world. It was inside the bag that I had on hand, and part of the few personal belongings I was able to bring here."

"It has a different sense of refinement from the clothing the hero wears."

"In our world, this clothing would be part of what is considered to be full dress. It's more appropriate for a place like this."

Hearing Suimei's words, the king passed his gaze over Suimei's outfit again. The black cloth had not one wrinkle in it. The piece of cloth fastened around his neck that hung down like a sword was a nice contrast on top of the stark white shirt he wore underneath it. And paired together with the black trousers he was wearing, the whole ensemble had an indescribable sense of refinement.

"I see. It suits you well."

"Thank you very much, Your Majesty."

As Suimei responded, though still kneeling, he deftly smoothed down his coat, straightened his sleeves, and corrected his posture. In that brief moment, it seemed as though the awkwardness had vanished. But Suimei suddenly bowed down his head when he seemed to recall something.

"Though it is quite overdue, You Majesty, I apologize for making such an unsightly scene the other day."

Suimei humbly offered an apology for what had happened on the day they met. When Suimei had heard he could not return home straight from the king's mouth, though it was a completely natural reaction, Suimei had completely lost sight of himself.

The moment he'd heard those words, he rudely stood up and started shouting. "Don't fuck with me. I can't believe it. If you can't return us, then you shouldn't have summoned us." Something to that effect. He'd completely unloaded on the king. His insolent behavior had offended and enraged the audience who witnessed it, but such was the situation. With the king's mediation, everything had calmed down since, but he never thought that he would receive an apology after the fact.

"...Ah, yes, that. It's quite fine. Your feelings were justified. After arbitrarily summoning you three to this world, we made things worse and said that you could not return. Truly, there is no reason you should have to apologize. I would have you raise your head."

"Then..."

As the king frankly declared that no offense had been taken at his outburst, Suimei obliged and once more raised his head. From his expression, the king could see that regardless of who was at fault during the commotion on that day, Suimei was concerned about it. There was still a sense of awkwardness about him. But with that out of the way, Suimei cut to the chase.

"You said that you had something to discuss with me, Your Majesty?"

"Indeed. There is something that I must know, Suimei-dono."

"...Your Majesty?"

What the king heard now was a troubled voice. Was this bewildered face and furrowed brow a glimpse into who this young man really was?

"It is about Felmenia, Suimei-dono. There is something that I would like to hear from you."

"Felmenia-san, is it…? If I remember correctly, I have heard she is the one who has been instructing Reiji and Mizuki in magic. But what of her, Your Majesty?"

"She has told me before that she has seen you outside of your room and loitering around the castle."

As Suimei shamelessly claimed that Felmenia was someone he was only casually acquainted with, the king confronted him with what he'd heard about his behavior. Suimei then smiled with a weak and bitter expression like he'd been embarrassed somehow.

"Ah, ahaha… I was under the impression that I was free to look around the inside of the castle, so I have been taking walks to keep myself occupied. Have I caused some sort of inconvenience?"

"No, that's not a problem. It was my intention that you should be able to do that, after all. You have committed no offense in that regard."

"Then is something else the matter, Your Majesty?"

"You don't know?"

"…"

Suimei wore a bewildered expression to hide his inner thoughts. The king had brought up Felmenia, but Suimei had said nothing. In fact, he was playing dumb precisely because he knew what the king was really getting at.

In a way, this was an extension of the tension between them from their first encounter. Being summoned was likely enough to put anyone on edge. If the king were Suimei, he could only imagine he would have taken some measures himself. Specifically, using force as a threat. The king had no means of controlling a mage who could defeat Felmenia. That much was simple.

However, for Suimei to be so powerful and not have acted on it all this time, he seemed to be implicitly telling the king that he would like to end things peacefully with everyone pretending that they were none the wiser. "If you keep quiet, I won't do anything, so just don't touch on it." Something like that. The king knew the hornets' nest he was potentially poking, but he had to get to the heart of the matter.

"What, exactly, did you do to Felmenia?"

"I do not understand, Your Majesty."

"Suimei-dono, there is no way that you do not know what I speak of, is there not? Speak hon—"

And just then, the moment he tried to say more, terror and goosebumps ran down Almadious's back. Just what kind of expression was this boy hiding under the hair that covered his face? Through the small gap in Suimei's bangs, the king could see a deep crimson glow. It inspired an indescribable dread in him. And then…

"With all due respect, Your Majesty, are you sure you want to ask that question?"

Almadious felt like he had lost his voice. Like it had been stolen. Suimei reproached the king in a sharp tone that made him seem like a completely different person. As a little test of the king's resolve, Suimei had silenced him for a moment and taken his breath away. However…

"…S-Suimei-dono. Yes, I wish to have an answer."

Seeing that the king would still speak of it after that, Suimei ceased kneeling and abruptly stood up. He then swung his arm backwards, and a coat appeared over his shoulders with a flutter from nowhere. The king had no idea what he'd done, but, if he had to guess, it was likely magic. It was the magic Suimei used that the mages here could barely comprehend.

As for Suimei himself, there was no sign of the awkwardness and stiffness from before. His gentle gaze had turned sharp, and his eyes were alive with a deep crimson glow that could pierce darkness. His expression was tinged with the pride that the king had seen from mages countless times before.

If there had been a proper audience in the chamber, people would be whispering about Suimei's insolence again. But this time there was no one to comment on his behavior. While the king was captivated seeing this mage-like attitude from Suimei for the first time, Suimei spoke as if letting out a sigh.

"Good grief. I haven't heard anything about that woman eating it, so how do you know that much?"

"As expected, you…"

"Yeah, it's exactly that. When I was first summoned here, that woman found out I was a magician, and the result of somehow or other sealing her mouth took on that kinda shape. But seeing as how she can't talk about it now, how is it that Your Majesty is so informed about what I've done?"

"I asked her about it. If she could not speak of it, I told her to remain silent."

After the king concisely explained what had happened, Suimei spoke quietly as though he'd come to some kind of understanding.

"I see. I didn't consider that. Certainly the covenant that binds that woman only forbids her from speaking."

In stark contrast to his gentle voice as he recalled that, Suimei shot a sharp glance the king's way.

"However, why have you called me here? I'm the man who holds that woman's life in my hand. If you understand that much, I do believe that you fully grasp the dangers of summoning me without a single guard present."

He was right. The king understood just how dangerous it was to call Suimei here privately. Yet even knowing full well how dangerous it was, he'd summoned him without preparing any sort of countermeasures. Suimei's question was only natural. However, the king had his reasons.

"That is certainly a concern. However, both you and the hero are guests that I have called to this world. No matter what happens, that remains unchanged. To have pushed our problems forcefully on those of you from a different world with a different set of principles was my sin, and I will accept that much."

That's why the king refused to bare his fangs against them, no matter the reason. The moment he did that, he would become nothing more than a beast who concealed his true nature behind a mask of kindness. It would be too much to his own convenience. As if carefully scrutinizing what the king had said, Suimei remained silent.

"..."

"Suimei-dono. After summoning you to this unfamiliar place and shutting my eyes to the misconduct of my subordinates, it is presumptuous of me to ask more of you, but would you please speak of it to me?"

"Why do you want to hear it so badly? Even if I say nothing, my silence won't harm Your Majesty, will it?"

"That certainly may be the true. But if I look the other way and she were to lose her life by some chance, my regret would be endless."

"Even over that kind of conceited woman?"

"That is right. She is my retainer, and I must protect her."

Suimei let out a sigh as he replied.

"As long as she doesn't talk, there is no threat to her life. That is absolute. I also don't want to needlessly take the life of another. That should conclude our talk, right?"

"No, not yet."

"I don't believe there is anything else for us to talk about, is there?"

Suimei questioned the king with a dubious expression. But even if their real business had been settled, the king still had things that he wanted to learn.

"Suimei-dono, I know nothing about you. As the one responsible for summoning you here, I would like to learn. I would like to hear just who you are, and what you plan to do from here on out. I want to have a frank conversation with you. If possible, I would like to completely clear the air between us."

Yes, that was the king's true intention without any pretense. Certainly, the previous matter would be settled as long as Felmenia and the king kept their mouths shut. They were the only two who knew about Suimei. And their silence would buy peace. If they stayed quiet, they could return to their everyday lives without any problems.

After calling a hero from another world, they would send him off to subjugate the Demon Lord. In a way, that was just abandoning the responsibility for having summoned them here. If something happened to the summoned children after they were brought to this world, if the king neglected them to save himself, even knowing that the children were strong enough to protect themselves, that would make him a horrible person. He wanted to get to know them in order to better understand their wishes. It felt like the least he could do.

"Naturally, you need not tell me. Forcing you to talk for my own gratification would defeat the point. But if you do not mind, then I encourage and welcome it. The choice is yours."

While sitting atop the throne, the king lowered his head. It was an unfitting gesture for the king of an entire nation, but it was his way of showing that he would not lose himself to his pride. When he raised his head again after a short time, Suimei looked shocked. "Why would you do such a thing?" and "Why would you go so far?" were the questions written all over his face. He stood there silent for a moment, and then let out a defeated sigh.

"Can I take that as your true intention beyond a shadow of a doubt?"

"Indeed, those are my feelings without any pretense or falsehood."

When the king clearly articulated that, Suimei straightened his posture.

"I apologize for my impolite manner of speaking up until now. Please, ask all that you will of me, Your Majesty. I, as one of the humble members of the Society, will answer all that I can within the permissible range."

The fact that he still did not kneel would have been called impolite by others, but the haughty atmosphere from just a while ago vanished like morning dew. Even Suimei's tone had changed completely. It was likely, finally, that this was his true self.

It wasn't his usual self when he was together with Reiji and Mizuki. It wasn't the haughty version of himself he became when he faced his enemies or unknown situations, either. It was just him as a lone mage, Suimei Yakagi. And to the king, this was the greatest respect he could show. He then began his inquiry in an attempt to unravel as much as he could about him.

"Who are you?"

"In my own world, I am what is called a magician. Something like a scholar who researches the mysteries to accomplish a thesis. In general, I do believe we are not all that different from what you call mages."

"A magician..."

The king repeated that strange word. Why was it that what he could only hear as "mage" before due to the effect of the hero summoning now sounded different? Was it because Suimei had used it in a way that revealed its true meaning? It was something different from a mage, and his ear could now properly appreciate the difference. His questions continued from there.

"Why do you hide this? Setting aside those of us from this world, why keep it even from Hero-dono and Mizuki-dono?"

"In our world, unlike this one, a technology known as science has developed. You may have heard this much from Reiji already, but magicka is something that has been driven into the underworld over there, and magicians have become a target for elimination by all powers. That is why, to the public, magicians do not exist. If we revealed our identities, we would be taken out mercilessly for going against the perceived normalcy of the world. That is why I do not openly identify as a magician. It is the reason I hide, even here. I'm just being careful."

"So Hero-dono and Mizuki-dono do not know, but Felmenia discovered your identity?"

"Yes. At that time, I couldn't know for sure if I'd been found out. So exactly what she knew and how she acted on it was a potential problem for me. And so, after investigating, I worked out a plan and sowed the seeds to lure her out, but some kind of dangerous automaton or something was put in place—well, since she didn't seem interested in talking, that's what it came to."

One word in particular there piqued the king's interest.

"Automaton?"

"Yes. It was a well-made one in the form of a heavy cavalryman. It attacked me, so I destroyed the spell that controlled it."

"Sage Slamas's golem, huh…?"

The king had an idea as to what had attacked Suimei. The only golem in the entire castle was the one Slamas had created. Naturally, if Suimei was talking about armor that attacked him, that was just about the only thing that came to mind. The golem Slamas created was well made, and powerful. If Felmenia had brought that out, it gave the king a glimpse of just how stubborn she'd gotten before being knocked down a peg by Suimei. However...

"I asked Felmenia the same question, but was it not a little too impatient to resort to force?"

In the end, the development of this conflict felt a little irrational. There would have been several opportunities for them to talk things out. Felmenia was the first to make a move, but the king couldn't help speaking his honest opinion. And in response to that, Suimei spoke with an extremely serious expression.

"Certainly I cannot deny that I was somewhat caught up in the moment. However, I am also one who walks the path of magicka. A magician has a magician's way of handling things, and when a simple braggart—no, someone conceited—enacts violence, we are ones who would seek revenge. Also, well, I was still resentful about being forcibly summoned here and was blowing off a little steam."

In the end, Suimei let out a laugh suitable for a boy his age, and seeing that, the king sighed.

"...What a brat."

"Magicians are often just like that. We are beings who only have interest in what we are selfishly trying to accomplish. It is normal not to think of those around us. Besides, I do not believe Your Majesty is in a position to complain after shutting your eyes to the matter in the first place."

"You certainly have a point."

Yes, the king was also responsible for turning a blind eye despite knowing what Felmenia would do. He wasn't in a position to strongly reprimand Suimei, and looking at the results, his way of dealing with her was arguably rational.

If he used his magic without restraint, there was a countless number of crimes Suimei could commit. If he wanted to satisfy his own greed, he could have freely done so all along. Yet he'd quietly stayed in his room in a way that didn't bother anybody. When investigating whether any harm had come of his sneaking around the castle, it was revealed that the treasury, the throne room, the depository, and any other place of material significance had gone untouched.

And when it came to Felmenia's violence, it could be said that Suimei had treated her sympathetically. He didn't know how things worked in this world, but after she'd used the golem against him, nobody would have been able to argue if Suimei had killed her in self-defense.

Suimei then looked to a pillar to his side. It couldn't be…

"That's how it is. That was just an extension of me venting my anger, so you can also relax. I have no intention of ordering you to do anything else."

He was speaking to someone other than the king—no, there was no need to be ambiguous. Suimei was talking to Felmenia. She was certainly there, hiding behind the pillar he was looking at.

"…"

Felmenia stepped out from the shadow of the pillar with a shocked expression. Suimei only gave her a cursory glance as if she didn't interest him, and then turned back to the king. Seeing this, he had a new question for the young magician.

"…Since when did you notice?"

"Counter-question: why would you think that I hadn't noticed?"

"..."

He certainly had a point there. Suimei had gotten the better of Felmenia at every turn. Rather than assuming he wouldn't have noticed her, it would have been safer to assume that he would.

"Suimei-dono, regarding this..."

"I can tell without you saying it. I was suspicious when you said you wanted to talk privately with just the two of us, but like you said, she's your precious retainer. If she's that important to you, then it's not like I don't understand your actions."

"I am sorry."

The king honestly apologized. The reason he'd had Felmenia hide there was not for his protection, but for her benefit. If Suimei knew Felmenia was there, there were likely things that he wouldn't talk about. And if she wasn't present, she would never get answers. Hiding her in the room was the king's compromise. In the end, Suimei saw right through it, but talked anyway.

Felmenia then called out Suimei's name with a pale face.

"S-Suimei-dono..."

"I said I wouldn't do anything, didn't I? Don't just fucking go pale. You really are good for nothing, aren't you? If you're also a magician, then stand up straight right until you're on the verge of death. Aren't you a court mage or whatever this kingdom prides itself on?"

"Auuugh..."

Felmenia didn't look away in the face of such sharp criticism, but tears formed in the corners of her eyes. It seemed she was unable to say anything back to that. As Suimei stood there waiting for the king's next question, he cut straight to it.

"So the reason that you're investigating the summoning circle after all…"

Indeed, it was because his will remained unchanged.

"I do believe I told you I wanted to return. I have things that I must accomplish back home. Besides…"

"Besides?"

"When Reiji and Mizuki happen to want to go back, I will have the path to return made ready for them. I am not accompanying my good friends as they run off into danger. As a magician, this is the least I can do for them."

"Aha…"

The king unintentionally let his admiration escape his lips. Naturally, Suimei's objective was motivated by his own desires. He wanted to return, he said so himself. However, he was also thinking of his friends. He wanted to give them the same chance. But even more surprising than that…

"Are you able to decipher that thing?"

"Given the time, to an extent. It's not impossible."

"T-Truly…?!"

The hero summoning magicka circle was said to be undecipherable by anyone, and Suimei had just rather offhandedly suggested he could do it. That summoning circle was passed down from a forgotten age. Using the precise amount of mana and reciting the proper chant was all that it took to activate. But the spell itself was too difficult to understand, and up until now nobody had been able to comprehend the principles behind the way it worked. Yet this young man had just declared that he could do so in a tone like he himself also found that to be unexpected.

"I have studied spiritualism and mediumship to an extent, but I never thought it would come up in a place like this. Seriously, it makes no sense."

However, if it was such good fortune, then…

"However, if you are thinking of Reiji-dono to this extent, why do you not speak of everything to him? If you open your heart to the hero, then…"

"Your Majesty, if my friends were to learn of my lineage, whenever we do return to our own world, it would only invite the possibility of harm befalling them."

Without holding back, Suimei admitted the real reason why he could not tell his friends the truth. It was a matter of danger and concern for their safety.

"Would not all be well if they simply kept your secret?"

"Your Majesty, I don't know how things are here, but the world I come from is a den of thieves."

"A… den of thieves?"

"Yes. Where I'm from, even if you keep your mouth shut, just having knowledge is dangerous. There are techniques to extract or steal one's memories, and spells that make one speak of their memories unconsciously. When it comes to magicka, the number of such methods cannot even be counted. If I carelessly let my identity slip in a world like that, there's no telling what the price would be. There are lunatics over there who would point their blades at those who don't even know of magicians."

"Is the path of magic in your world truly such a dreadful thing?"

"Yes."

Seeing Suimei nod clearly, a thought came to mind. If he was truly thinking of his friends, then it seemed he ought to be honest with them. But apparently that wasn't an option. The path of magic in Suimei's world went much deeper into darkness than it did here. Their enemies were many, and they spent their days with the danger of being exposed always hanging over them. Suimei's prudence then seemed perfectly reasonable.

"When the time comes that they say that they want to go back, I will probably have to tell them about it, but... After hiding it all this time, it makes it difficult to talk about."

"I can imagine."

As he said, when he revealed the return circle, he would probably have to explain himself then. And since they'd learned magic here in this world, they would have to be apprised of the dangers of returning home with it. There was certainly a long talk ahead of them, but it wouldn't be easy for Suimei and he was in no hurry to get to that. All of this carried another implication as well, and the king spoke of it with disappointment in his voice.

"This means you are indeed resolute to not go with them."

"I said something similar before, but I do not want to act recklessly."

"After defeating Felmenia, I do not think it would be all that reckless. Besides, Suimei-dono, would your presence not be a great boon to your friends?"

"That may be, but in the end, it is unnecessary."

"Why do you say such a thing?"

"We had a bit of an argument about it in the heat of the moment, but Reiji isn't a shallow person. He's the type to get caught up in crazy things, but he always thinks things through before making any judgments, he never forgets to be careful, and in addition to that, he has that terrifying power of a hero in his body now. Me worrying about him is as fruitless as being concerned he's going to trip over a pebble on the side of the road. I cannot say that he will definitely succeed in the Demon Lord's subjugation, but I do know that he will not just helplessly die."

"I see."

Suimei wasn't worried. He spoke with a smile on his face. Moreover, he trusted Reiji and Mizuki quite a bit. Despite the fact that he clarified that he thought Reiji should have to go through something horrible once in a while, he was still thinking of him. He didn't wish anything ill on either of his friends. And so the king questioned Suimei as if to confirm something.

"I will be repeating myself, but about Felmenia…"

"Just as I said before, nothing will happen as long as she doesn't talk, but—well, whatever."

With a knowing look, Suimei pulled out a pure white sheet paper. It looked completely normal other than the fact that it was a beautiful white like freshly fallen snow, but looking at it carefully, the front of it had words scribed on it and something that looked like a bloodstain. Suimei held the sheet with both his hands as if to tear it up.

"S-Suimei-dono?! W-Wait—"

Felmenia's face paled in an instant and she screamed for Suimei to show restraint, but her voice did not reach him. Without a moment's hesitation, the sound of ripping paper filled the audience chamber. Just how did Felmenia's ears interpret that sound?

As she was swallowed by emotion and fell to her knees, Suimei tore the paper many times over and scattered the shreds to the audience chamber floor. And with a snap of his fingers, they were all swallowed in a crimson light and vanished.

"Ah…"

"Court Mage. With this, the constraints that bound you are no more. Do show your gratitude to His Majesty until the day you die for putting his life on the line for you, understood?"

Setting aside Felmenia, who had fallen completely dumbfounded, the king moved on to question Suimei, who was scoffing at her.

"Is that alright?"

"Your Majesty, you said you wanted to clear the air completely between us, right? If anything would generate ill will, it would have been that. So I took care of it. After all, it was a guarantee no longer required between us."

Suimei smiled a bit, and then continued.

"However, I would still like you to promise not to speak of this to Reiji and Mizuki, and to not take any action that would lead to them to figuring it out. I hope I don't need to ask for your cooperation in that, but…"

"Understood. I will do as you ask."

The king accepted Suimei's terms. If he was willing to yield so much, then there was no reason for the king to refuse. The king then moved on to asking about one more thing he wanted to hear.

"What will you do after this? Until you have a rough idea of how to return, I do not mind if you wish to stay in the castle…"

They were guests that were called to this world against their will, including Suimei. The king accepted his responsibility in that. It only stood to reason that he should take care of him within the castle until he was able to complete a return circle and get home. That, however, was only if Suimei wanted to stay, which was why the king had to ask. And Suimei responded by shaking his head.

"No. After Reiji and Mizuki leave the castle, I was thinking of leaving as well."

"What do you plan on doing after leaving the castle?"

"I was thinking of going to the Nelferian Empire. It's a key point where three countries meet. I will be able to attain all sorts of information and goods that I'll need there, and I believe it's a suitable location for me to set up."

The king groaned upon hearing Suimei's plan. It was true that the Nelferian Empire was an important cross-section that bordered three countries including Astel. Trade was certainly more active there than it was here. As it was an allied nation of Astel, entry would be relatively easy, and it was possible to attain goods there that would be hard to find elsewhere in Astel. It perhaps was the optimal location for gathering information from every which direction.

Honestly speaking, the king didn't want a master of Suimei's level to leave the country, but be that as it may, it was impossible to stop him from going. Even if he had the power to do so, he wouldn't have wanted to restrict him in such a way.

"I see. Then if you have any needs, simply say so. As long as it is something that I can do, I will grant you all that I can, though it may be naught but a meager offering to you."

In order to make sure he was free to do as he wished, the king offered Suimei his support. However, Suimei shook his head in return.

"I thank you for your consideration, but please do not mind me."

"Why is that? You are about to venture forth into unknown lands. Do you not require some kind of aid?"

Suimei was a human from another world. He was unused to the culture and customs of this land. And he would be alone. It seemed he should require some sort of assistance, but…

"That's quite alright. From here, unable to endure living in the castle, I will selfishly run away. And there is no way you could show leniency after such a disgrace, much less reward that kind of behavior. Rather than myself, please think of your own reputation, Your Majesty."

"However…"

"After the uproar that came up last time and my shutting myself in my room, the rumors have only gotten worse. If you were to support me at your own discretion, there would undoubtedly be those who would praise your kindness, but the vast majority of people would decry such an act. That would be quite the inconvenience to Your Majesty."

It was just as Suimei said. If he left the castle, taking into consideration his public appearance up until now, things would go precisely as he surmised. Rumors of him running away would spread. There was no doubt about that. And if it was discovered that the king was supporting him after that, public dissatisfaction would be high. Why would the king go so far out of his way to be so generous with an ingrate?

"And… if I said that I would do so regardless?"

"I am grateful for your consideration, but you are being repetitious."

"Hmm…"

The king was at a loss for words at the sudden bit of upbraiding. Suimei was obstinate. He didn't mind. And he was telling the king not to mind. It could be taken as groundless confidence, but he was showing the right kind of spirit to back such a claim up.

Just what were those black eyes directed at the king really looking at? Something far beyond. His was the gaze of someone who was to challenge whatever difficulty lay on the path ahead of him. His personality was unexpected for a boy his age; it had far more gravity to it than his years would suggest. And then…

"To live in the world, one will always find themselves coming across walls that impede progress. No matter how broad or tall they may be, those who easily overstep such obstacles are known as magicians. I, Yakagi Suimei, am one of them. I leap over the walls known as the mysteries of the universe. And so, Your Majesty, I will say it once more. Just the consideration you've shown me is more than enough; I will graciously accept only that much."

Suimei's declaration was serious, confident, and left no room for argument. All he had was strength, but it was the strength of a boy who earnestly pushed to break through the deadlock known as impossibility.

In the end, he really was something else. This young man was definitely the kind of person who shouldn't have been dragged into the hero summoning. The king held his breath as he gazed at him, but Suimei then broke his stern expression and spoke in a self-deprecating tone.

"...Though I put on airs like that, it's really not something a man who refuses to face a fight out of fear for his own life should say, huh?"

"That wouldn't be limited to just you. Those who, frightened by the threat of the Demon Lord, have forced everything onto innocent children could also be accused of the same thing. And would include me."

Really, who had the right to say that Suimei's boasting was excessive? Only two people came to mind: those who were actually heading off to take part in the Demon Lord's subjugation themselves. Those who hid in safety and put their own lives before all else were in no position to criticize him. Suimei was throwing in his lot to strike out on his own and stand against all difficulties that would come his way.

Just how much had those who were all too ready to hurl insults obstructed this young man who was pushing forward towards his unfinished goal? How much had they held him back? The king had no way of knowing, but it must have been a serious blow. The cry he had unleashed in this very room that day had wounded the king's heart.

And what the king felt for him now was sympathy as much as anything else. Even though they were far enough apart in age to be parent and child, it wasn't like he didn't understand. And as he steeped in that strange impression, Suimei pushed the conversation forward.

"Is there anything else you would like to ask me?"

"If you don't mind, then…"

Taking him up on his offer, the king fired off several more questions, and about far more than just magicians. About him, about Reiji, about Mizuki, and even about the trivial foolishness between the three friends.

★

A spell had passed since the king and Suimei had begun talking. When the conversation came to a natural lull, Suimei suddenly changed the topic.

"Would it be alright for me to ask something small as well?"

"What's the matter?"

When the king asked that, Suimei turned his gaze to the side.

"No, not Your Majesty."

"You mean… me?"

"Yeah. I mean you. If I remember right, at the time, you told me that you had no intention of killing me, didn't you?"

Just when had they talked about that? The king wasn't aware, but Felmenia seemed to know.

"Y-Yes, and it's true. I swear to Goddess Alshuna."

Since Felmenia was willing to swear on her goddess, Suimei didn't bother asking again. He simply nodded to himself.

"I got a little curious when you said that, you see. After that, I did a bit of digging around, but I wound up stumbling across something even more interesting."

"Something... interesting?"

"Yeah. It isn't unrelated to you either—actually, you're more like a victim. How 'bout it? Wanna come with me and take a look?"

With the smile of a villain who had just concocted some sinister trick, Suimei began explaining the matter that he had thoroughly investigated.

Chapter 4 For That Which I Aspire to Be

On this particular day, in a large corridor of Royal Castle Camellia, somebody was in a hurry.

It was a man in a splendid robe—the court mage who had reported to Felmenia on Suimei's movements. After an emergency gathering in the audience chamber, he was now on his way back to his private quarters. His lean figure that looked like it might snap if he moved the wrong way was hustling down the hall with nimble steps. It was as if he was anticipating something, or perhaps like he was feeling high from an irrepressible joy, and that spurred him on.

"Hmm…?"

As he walked along in high spirits, something caught his attention out of the corner of his eye. He came to a stop in the middle of the corridor, and then as he focused…

"…Reiji-sama, Mizuki. Now is our chance. Quickly."

The man heard a familiar young woman's voice and shifted his attention to it. At the end of the training ground on the edge of the wall, he spotted the figure of Princess Titania beckoning the hero and his friend while keeping her eyes out on her surroundings in a furtive manner.

It was quite suspicious for them to be in such a place without actually doing any training. While the man was wondering what was going on, Reiji arrived and stood before the princess.

"I-Is this really alright, Tia? Isn't it bad to just sneak out of the castle on our own...?"

Reiji questioned Titania in an anxious tone. From the obvious way he was trying to stay low and out of sight, he hardly looked like the heroic figure who could challenge the captain of the guard and the court mages on an everyday basis.

"It is alright, Reiji-sama. This would not be the first time that I have slipped out of the castle without informing anyone, after all."

"No, that's not really what I mean. It's just..."

"It is alright. Please leave everything to me. I am certain you will be able to make some fun memories before departing. Though it is regrettable that Suimei-sama is not coming..."

As Titania said that, she cast her eyes down in disappointment. It seemed that they were planning to sneak out and go somewhere. Ever since the hero and his friends were summoned from another world, they had been confined to the castle. Knowing they must have felt stifled, this was most likely some considerate arrangement of the princess's. Just as the court mage was making that deduction, Mizuki noticed his presence and panicked a little.

"T-Tia, that..."

"What is the matter, Mizuki? You look flustered."

"Th-That... That..."

Titania didn't realize what she meant at first, but she saw the man when Mizuki pointed him out. Reiji looked up at the sky with an "oh crap" expression, and Titania's gaze started to swim around erratically.

"This is, um..."

Having been found by someone from the castle, she was shaken and unsure of what to do. Normally he would remonstrate her for her actions, but—to reiterate—right now, this man was truly in good humor. And so…

"Now then, I thought I heard something, but was I mistaken?"

Averting his gaze from the three teenagers, the man wondered loudly to himself if he'd imagined the whole scene. He'd let them go this time, and played the fool for their benefit. The three of them didn't seem to grasp what was going on for a moment, but Titania quickly figured it out and rose to that farce of a stage.

"Th-That's right. It's just your imagination. There is nobody here in the training ground."

"That must be it. There's no way I could be hearing the voices of Her Royal Highness and Hero-dono in the training grounds on a day with no scheduled training. It seems it's just my imagination after all."

With that, he snuck a quick glance and could see Titania sighing in relief. The other two seemed pleased as well. From what he could tell, they were all quite shaken at being caught, and had managed to calm down with this turn of events.

"Now then, let us go while we have the chance."

"Mm, you're right. Let's go, Reiji-kun."

"Thank you very much."

Reiji bowed his head to the man, and the three of them then made use of enhancement magic to leap off the wall surrounding the training grounds. The image of the princess and the hero's antics as they departed was most unusual and quite amusing.

"Heh heh… Oh dear, me of all people."

Recalling Titania in a complete fluster, the court mage leaked out a stifled laugh. Because something good had happened, he had lost focus and was unable to pin down his emotions.

"Heh heh…"

Still in high spirits, the man once more picked up his pace. A glorious court mage could not allow anybody to see them reveling in such a place. At the very least, he'd return to his private quarters before really celebrating.

Before long, the man arrived at his room and entered, shutting the door soundly behind him. He'd been using the same private quarters in Castle Camelia ever since taking up a position here, and his room was nice, tidy, and well organized.

"Now then…"

However, for some reason, he could smell an aroma wafting through his quarters that he'd never noticed before. It was likely that after one of the maids cleaned up, she'd burned some new incense to freshen up the place. It even seemed to be quite high-quality incense.

"She must have good taste…"

Thanks to the efforts of some unknown person, the man's good mood only improved further. When he had some time later, he was thinking of returning the favor with a gift. In any case, the pleasant aroma went a long way to stimulating his mood. Just from smelling it, his spirit soared to near euphoria. Yes, it was just as if his joy had multiplied several times over.

"Heh… heh heh…"

Urged on by the intoxicating scent, the man was no longer able to control the sensation welling up inside him. The moment he found himself by the window, that dam called self-control burst, and his joy came flooding out in a fit of laughter.

"Heh… HUAHAHAHAHAHAHAHAHA! Stingray, you stupid little girl, did you learn your lesson?! White Flame, my ass! Don't get carried away just because a stupid girl like you is a little good with magic! This is all your fault for making a fool of me in front of the hero and the princess! HAHAHAHAHA!"

Yes, the reason this man was in such high spirits was because the court mages had just gathered to discuss Felmenia's dismissal. Previously, when he was about to take on the role of being the hero's magic instructor, Felmenia had swooped in to steal the position and embarrass him. It was all petty and unjustified resentment on his part, but now that he'd gotten some good news in the way of revenge, he was unable to stop laughing. And as he ran out of oxygen from laughing too much, he paused to take in a deep breath and began talking to himself once more.

"Hmph. However, that stupid little girl... I never would have guessed she'd be deceived so easily. There's no way that cowardly friend of the hero's would even think of bringing harm to His Majesty. But to think with such simple magic and a little cajolery, she would end up doing exactly what I'd hoped and harming that youngster... It just goes to show it was far too hasty to appoint such a stupid little girl with zero insight as a court mage."

Indeed, on the surface, everything was just as he said. It was a hasty appointment and Felmenia was simply too immature for the job. That was what the court mages had discussed in the audience chamber earlier.

The king explained that after seeing Suimei take zero interest in joining the subjugation mission, Felmenia had gone to give him a little motivation, but took it too far and ended up injuring him. But from what the man knew of the real situation, Felmenia hadn't gone to motivate him. No, she'd gone to assassinate a young man with no power at all because of the glamor magic and lies he'd used to trick her.

However, this man was being quite talkative on the matter. It was as if he was being forced to speak all of his thoughts on the real situation out loud. He himself didn't know why he'd grown so passionate in his monologue, but it didn't faze him.

"Heh heh... And it wasn't just a reprimand, but a full dismissal from the court mages. I would have been fine with just teaching her a lesson, but the king was quite strict in his judgment. He's favored that stupid little Stingray girl up until now, so his indignation at her betrayal must have been that much greater."

The man continued to rant to himself. He had doubts as to why he was doing it, but in comparison to the joy he was feeling, it was a trivial concern. Nothing else mattered right now.

"At any rate, nothing could have been better than that face she made in the audience chamber! Such utter despair when His Majesty dismissed her in front of all the court mages was just—"

"Was just what?"

"Was just the greatest thrill!"

"Hahaha, the greatest, you say? She really was getting a little too carried away, wasn't she?"

"That's right! In fact, 'a little' is being generous! She was completely carried away! But now, even that... Wahaha... HAHAHAHAHA!"

"My, you seem to be enjoying yourself."

"Obviously! If this isn't enjoyable, then just what is it?! That impudent and stupid little girl of a Stingray who didn't know her place was knocked down from her seat as a court mage! Do you get it now? This feeling of joy that I... Ah?"

The man had been completely swept up in his joy. That was why, just like that, he was happy to continue the conversation like he was chatting with a friend. When he finally realized how strange it was that he was talking to someone, however, he stopped and turned around with a dumbfounded look on his face.

When he did, he spied an unfamiliar man wearing black clothes sitting on the couch in his office. This man crossed his legs, and with a sarcastic and derisive tone, asked him a question.

"Hmm? Aren't you gonna continue? You still have plenty you want to say, don't you? Right?"

He spoke in a quite casual fashion, first sounding like a small child looking forward to the sequel of a story, and then like a crafty villain who'd laid an inescapable trap. The latter proved itself to be more accurate. Before long, the sunlight pouring into the window dispelled the shadow that had obscured the man's face.

"Wh-Who the hell…?"

"Come on, no need to be so modest, mage. Or should I say Court Mage Sebastian Kran?"

Yes, the man who addressed him was none other than…

"S-Suimei Yakagi…?"

Sebastian Kran stammered his name as he pointed a shaky finger in his direction. Being so recognized, Suimei stood up and took a theatrical bow before him.

"The very one. It's a pleasure to meet you. This would be the first time that we've spoken face to face, no?"

"Wh-Why are you…? Since when were you there…? No, how did you get in?"

"It's not that exciting. I just opened the door and walked in normally. As for when, it was just a little before you came in yourself, I think? Yeah, that's about right."

As Suimei rattled off an awfully casual response, Sebastian recalled when he had entered the room himself.

Indeed, he'd entered the room with light footsteps and was so entranced in his mood that he was only looking ahead. He hadn't bothered to scan the room, but even so, that large couch definitely would have been in his line of sight. Yet no matter how many times he thought back on it, Sebastian didn't recall seeing anyone there.

"Ridiculous. When I entered the room, there wasn't…"

"Anyone there, you mean? I'm sure you thought that. I made it so that, in a sense, you couldn't see me. Really, I cast a spell on this room itself. There was no way you'd notice me like that."

"Wha… A-A spell? It couldn't be. A bastard like you can't…"

"Use magic? You bet I can. I am a magician, after all. By the way…"

What'd you think of my herbal magicka. Nice, huh?

Suimei followed up on his little comedy show by coldly curving his mouth into a grin and explaining what exactly had made Sebastian so talkative.

It was herbal magicka. In ancient times, it was used by shamans, and from the Middle Ages to the present, by witches. It was a form of magicka that made use of the mysteries hidden within plants, classified under witchcraft. It used magicka on the aroma from herbs, or mystified the herbs themselves by turning them into talismans. Suimei used the former method. It was a minor trap to bring Sebastian down.

And then, while still standing up from this theatrical greeting, Suimei began walking alongside the wall. Watching Suimei strut around someone else's room as if he owned it, Sebastian remembered something he had heard before.

"A-A mage, you said?! Th-That can't be! I heard the hero's world had no magic."

"I'm sure you did. The world as they know it certainly doesn't."

"The world... as they know it?"

"That's right. But you certainly don't fucking need to know any more than that."

As the darkness in the room seemed to be creeping towards him, a cold shiver ran down Sebastian's back. Just what was going on? The hero hadn't known anything of magic, and there was nothing to suggest he'd had magical ability and was just pretending to hide it. He was a man chosen by this world and by its goddess to be a hero. He was overflowing with talent and wisdom, yet he knew nothing of magic. So there was no way that this run-of-the-mill boy knew anything about it either.

Or was that why Felmenia had believed the story about Suimei's plans to harm the king so readily? Because she knew he was a mage?

"…"

Cold sweat traced its way down Sebastian's cheek. Was such a thing possible? This defied all expectation. After Suimei enjoyed the sight of Sebastian trembling for a while, with his back up against the wall, he began to coldly weave his words.

"Nevertheless, thank you. I already figured out most of it from looking into it, but thanks to you, I'm now able to grasp the entire truth. It just means that I was used as an excuse to accomplish your idiotic goal. Oh, and by the way, there's no point in trying to pretend you're innocent. His Majesty is already fully aware that you're really the one pulling the strings."

"Th-That's…"

When Sebastian tried to say something, Suimei mercilessly cut him off.

"That thing… The automaton that Stingray set up. You were the one who messed with it, weren't you?"

"Wh-What are you tal—"

"I thought I said that there was no point in trying to play innocent. The one who made the thing was your dear master. Golem manipulation is your forte, isn't it? Setting up a trick like that was a piece of cake for you, huh?"

"Ugh…"

Just how much more did he have in stock? As Suimei continued to fluently stab at all his weak points, Sebastian couldn't even protest. Suimei then unloaded another blow as he shrugged his shoulders.

"My my, having it suddenly go for the kill like that was a mighty nasty way of setting her up just because you were pissed. But I bet the one who's the most pissed off now is the victim who was set to be the punchline of your petty little revenge game, don't you think? So? Do you have anything to say?"

"...What do you intend to do with me?"

"I won't do a thing. The one to take action should be the one who suffered the most from all this, no?"

Sebastian kept himself on guard as he questioned Suimei, but Suimei turned around and fired off with questions of his own.

"Just who are you—"

Before Sebastian could even finish, the door to his office opened. On the other side was none other than...

"F-F-Felmenia Stingray?!"

Yes, standing just beyond that door was the young court mage that Sebastian had brought down over his grudge, Felmenia Stingray. Her beautiful and cold face that could hold any man captive, that even the women of the world would be fascinated by, was twisted with righteous indignation towards him, and a voice tense with rage poured out of her mouth.

"To think that this was a scheme by a bastard like you..."

Hearing her hiss those hateful words, Sebastian once more turned his attention to Suimei, who met his gaze with a searing sneer.

"Our special guest has arrived. Isn't that quite the clever development?"

"You bastard...!"

Sebastian shot daggers at Suimei like he was actually trying to kill him with his glare, but Felmenia was more than happy to interject.

"You had better come quietly! A bastard like you who would bring others down over your wretched envy doesn't deserve the title of court mage! I will expose all of your damn scheming before His Majesty the King!"

"Tch!"

Felmenia moved in to apprehend Sebastian with her valorous declaration, but he had no intention of letting her take him. He leaped over a desk and made a break for the exit.

"Out of the way!"

"Kyah!"

Felmenia was standing in front of the door and didn't seem to expect Sebastian's resistance. It took all her wits just to evade him as he hurled himself past her. By the time she collected herself, he was already fleeing down the corridor.

"H-Huh?"

Seeing Felmenia looking around trying to figure out what happened, Suimei put his hand on his head and brought her up to speed.

"Hey, HEY! What the hell are you doing? He ran off, you know?"

"M-My apologies. It was just so sudden…"

"Sudden? Aren't you a mage? Where's your magic?"

"Uh…"

"Come on…"

In reply to Felmenia's boneheaded response, Suimei let out an exasperated sigh. This would have been the perfect time for her *not* to go with the airhead routine, and Suimei was momentarily stunned this was how things had turned out. But then he quickly shifted gears and began moving.

"Well, whatever. We're giving chase."

"Alright."

With an acknowledgment, Felmenia followed Suimei and they went after Sebastian together. Since he had such a light body, he seemed to be good at running. He was already out of their sight, but he couldn't hide his presence. As Felmenia ran next to Suimei, she took an unusually meek attitude and called out to him.

"Um…"

"What's up?"

"My apologies, Suimei-dono. Although I was deceived, I have caused you a considerable amount of trouble… I want to apologize for all my impolite behavior up until now."

"Hmm? Ah, there's no need to really worry about that. It was all settled with our fight anyway, and it was sort of my bad for sneaking around in the shadows to begin with. You're not at fault for trying to challenge me for that, either… Well, let me put it this way. I'm the same in that I was deceived. I was splendidly duped by that man too, after all."

"Be that as it may…"

Despite Suimei telling her it was okay, she still looked troubled. Was that just her earnest disposition at work? Seeing Felmenia like that, Suimei made a very serious expression.

"Sorry. I really went too far with you in more ways than one."

"N-No! Th-There is nothing for you to apologize for, Suimei! You already pardoned my inexcusable rampage, and now you've even gone as far as orchestrating this opportunity for me to apprehend the mastermind. If you apologize on top of that, I really won't have a leg to stand on."

"…"

In response to Felmenia's excessively humble attitude, Suimei looked at her like he'd seen something quite surprising. Seeing his expression, Felmenia questioned him in a curious tone.

"…Is something the matter?"

"No, I just may have misunderstood you quite a bit."

"Misunderstood… me?"

"Yeah. Sorry about that."

"…?"

Suimei apologized as he looked at Felmenia's curious expression and thought to himself that he hadn't gotten the right read on her. He never thought she was a bad person, but if this was what she was really like, then the way he'd treated her seemed a bit evil, even if it had been to seal her mouth. Thinking back on it, he may have taken venting his anger too far. Suimei apologized once more and then focused his attention on Sebastian's presence.

"Actually, where's that guy going?"

"Judging from his current route, it would likely be the north wing, would it not?"

"...Isn't that basically a dead end?"

As Suimei recalled the layout of the north wing and asked for confirmation, Felmenia nodded.

"Yes, there are no exits there. If there's anything of note there, it's..."

"The room we were summoned to, huh? Ugh."

For some reason, Suimei had a bad feeling about this. He grumbled to himself as they ran along.

★

Before long, the two of them arrived in front of the ritual chamber that Sebastian had likely entered. Wary of the ambush that might await them, they burst into the room. Felmenia made a declaration to the man crouching down in the center of the summoning circle.

"There is no longer anywhere to run, you hear?! Surrender yourself!"

"..."

240

However, Sebastian remained silent. He didn't react to Felmenia at all. Seeing him quiet like that, Suimei pointed a chilling gaze in his direction as he questioned him.

"Hey, why'd you run somewhere like this?"

"Heh... Heh heh heh..."

"What is so funny?!"

Hearing Sebastian's scornful laughter, this time it was Felmenia who yelled back at him. But it hardly got under his skin. He simply countered as if seeing her enraged countenance was a delight to him.

"Naive... You're too naive, Stingray. It couldn't be that you thought that I would escape to this room without any sort of plan, did you?"

"What?"

"Hahaha, I am also a court mage! I have the means to break through exactly such a situation! Behold!"

With that, Sebastian activated the summoning circle. With only a mere mutter, a dark glow came out of the magic circle at his feet, and a boundless dark purple light flooded the rugged stone room. Seeing Sebastian's barbaric act, Felmenia broke into a panic.

"Wh-What are you doing?! That's the summoning circle for calling heroes from other worlds!"

"It surely is! However, if it is able to summon things from another world, then with some revisions, it can bring more than just heroes!"

"Wha... Then what are you..."

She was going to ask what he was trying to call instead, but she realized that wasn't necessary after seeing his behavior.

"Isn't it obvious?! It'll be a little something to rid me of you brats!"

"Is all you care about saving your own hide?! You've shown your true nature!"

"Enough of your prattling, you stupid little girl! Getting carried away just because you can use a flicker of magic! Just that would have been fine, but to steal the honor of summoning the hero from me, and then, of all things, to make a fool of me in front of so many people! Pay for the humiliation you brought upon me with your death!"

"Silence! You are nothing but vulgar trash possessed by fame and fortune…"

As Sebastian finally articulated the dark plan he'd been nursing, Felmenia spat back at him. Seeing her grimace with disdain, Suimei questioned her in a curious tone.

"…Hmm? You're not the only one who can use that thing?"

"Huh? N-No. In case something were to happen to the mage left in charge of summoning the hero, all of the court mages are taught the summoning spell, with the blessing of the Church of Salvation and the Mage's Guild. But more importantly, we must stop him from—"

As Felmenia stepped forward to begin to invoke her magic, Suimei grabbed her.

"Wait."

"What?! Why are you stopping me, Suimei-dono?!"

Felmenia couldn't understand why he'd do that, so she asked for clarification. Suimei made an expression like the answer should have gone without saying.

"Of course I'd stop you in a situation like this. That's obvious."

"What's obvious about that?! That's a summoning spell he tampered with! We don't know what will happen if it's used!"

It was true the summoning spell and circle that Sebastian was now using were things he'd altered. And since this didn't conform to the prescribed use for them, it could be completely unsafe. On top of that, the summoning circle was already taking action. The light emitted by the mana filled with power and grew stronger, and there was scarcely a second to waste.

Spurred by that sense of urgency, Felmenia was practically screaming. Her desire to act swiftly was perfectly understandable, but Suimei folded his arms as he grimaced with a slight amount of perplexity in his face.

"No, we can't stop it. It's been crackling and snapping for a while now, but that summoning circle seems to have a pretty good protection spell on it. Though it doesn't seem to have any defenses against what's coming from the other side, the defensive portion against obstructions from this side seems perfect."

The feedback was poor. Suimei had also attempted to obstruct the summoning while nobody was looking, but in the end, he couldn't stop it.

"Wha... Not even you can do it, Suimei-dono?!"

"I've got a bone to pick with you phrasing it like that, but even if we were able to stop him, forcing him out of the ritual right now... something outrageous is bound to happen, see?"

"Huh...?"

Hearing that warning from Suimei, Felmenia was struck by an uneasy premonition. The word "outrageous" wasn't a particularly strange one, but Felmenia felt ominously about Suimei using it in this situation. There was a terrifying disparity between what she would call outrageous and what he would. Suimei gazed at the pillar of light, which had started isolating its target, and tried to explain.

"That thing's using the same summoning circle created to call us to this world, but this is what we call a berserk summoning. It's like a summoning that jumps over the astral plane, or even dimensions. And when that happens, at the time the summoning wrenches a hole open, something called a repellent force is produced to maintain the hole. If we were to forcefully cut things off here without allowing the summoning to conclude, that repellent force wouldn't have anywhere to go, and it would come right back here."

"…If it returns, what will happen?"

"Let's see… Well, the worst-case scenario would be the entire region getting blown away."

"N-No way."

Suimei's conjecture left Felmenia at a loss for words. She must have been thinking of what would have happened if Suimei hadn't held her back moments ago. The potential disaster wasn't just limited to them or the castle. It could have been a national catastrophe.

"Well, that's what it means to wrench open the wall between dimensions. From my perspective, the out-of-date technology behind that hero summoning circle that makes such a thing possible for a single individual is far more outrageous, though…"

"H-Hahh…"

Naturally, Felmenia was lost. All Suimei got was a bewildered squeal from her.

"Well, don't worry about the summoning. The medium being used is only that old man's mana. Whatever is hailed over by it will likely conform to that scale. It'll be fine as long as nothing ridiculous comes through."

Suimei paused for a moment before continuing.

"That said, if the summoning succeeds, we're still probably looking at a portion of the castle getting smashed to bits."

"Th-That can't be! There are still so many people within the castle…"

Just as Felmenia was about to say something about the impending crisis, as if interrupting her, the purple pillar of light sealing in the summoning circle grew remarkably stronger.

"It's coming!"

"A-Ah!"

Felmenia shut her eyes before the surging torrent of light and yelped in startled surprise. Perhaps because she lost her senses for a moment due to the wave of power and light, the next thing she knew, she was being strongly embraced by Suimei's left arm.

"Ah…"

As she looked up, she could see Suimei gazing at something with a cold and indifferent look. The blue sky spread out behind him. It seemed it was just as he'd said. A portion of the castle, including the ritual chamber, had been obliterated. And below her…

"The power escaped upwards. With this, there shouldn't be any damage to the rest of the castle other than this room. Also…"

"Ah?! AAAH!"

Finding it strange that Felmenia suddenly started to raise a fuss in his arms, Suimei gave her a puzzled look.

"What's up?"

"F-Flying! We're flying!"

Smack in the middle of the blue sky staring down at the ground, Felmenia let out a surprised shriek. The two of them were indeed flying right now. Suimei had deployed flight magicka, and was carrying Felmenia with him. A glimmer of mana could be seen scattering from Suimei's feet. That was the shape of the power that suspended the two of them in midair. Suimei acted like this was nothing, but Felmenia nearly lost her mind at the shock of seeing it.

"Wh-What?! Just what is this?!"

Hearing her confusion, Suimei managed to guess what Felmenia was talking about.

"Ah, I get it. There's no flight magicka here, right? I thought that learning to fly after gaining the ability to use magicka was pretty much the first thing everyone did, though..."

"M-More importantly, Suimei-dono...!"

"I'm telling you it's fine. We won't fall, so calm down and hold on tightly."

"T-Tightly?! To a gentleman?! I cannot... N-No, I mean—"

And just as Felmenia was about to plead with Suimei to let her down because she was afraid of heights, a voice rang out from directly below them that was so utterly repulsive that it barely sounded like it could be of this world. It wasn't a sound that threatened to burst one's eardrums, but more one that outright assaulted them. Following it, the light around the summoning circle unraveled like a thin veil. And what was revealed was...

"Uh, ah..."

It was something like an eerie and gigantic four-legged beast colored by dusky shadows and a bloody red. The place where the ritual chamber was as well as its surroundings were now swallowed by its shadow. It stood easily half as tall as the castle spire, and its form resembled a starving dog or wolf. All around its body were belts of shadows whipping about.

"Wow, to think it'd be a B-class... Looks like we caught a big one, huh?"

"Wh-What? That monster...?"

Without even the composure to ask him about it properly, Felmenia simply stared at the monster wide-eyed. Suimei's only response was muttering a select word as if he were speaking a sneer.

"A beast."

"…Suimei-dono, do you know what that thing is?"

"Yeah. That's something from my world, after all."

Something from Suimei's world. Hearing that frightening fact, Felmenia recalled something that made her doubt it.

"From your world? But Hero-dono and Mizuki-dono said there were no monsters there…"

"That just shows how narrow their view of it is. They had no way of knowing because they were blinded by the developments of science. When it comes to things like monsters, our world has more than enough of them."

"…"

While Felmenia looked at Suimei and the beast in bewilderment, he continued elaborating.

"And that is one of them. Just like you have demons plaguing humanity here, in our world, there are systems which serve as humanity's enemy."

"Sis-stems?"

"That's right. The beasts of the apocalypse. In our world, they're nicknamed apparitions. To prove to the beings of our world that there is no such thing as eternity, they are the laws that accelerate the world towards its end."

"L-Laws? Are you saying that's not a living being?"

"Let's see… No, not really. That isn't a living being; it's a phenomenon. Just like lightning or a tornado. As long as the requirements are met for it to exist, it will come into being. That's one of the rules of the world. The reason it takes the shape of a living entity is because it's easier to plant fear in humans using a material form… That's what the leader said, but, well, just look for yourself. Doesn't that just inspire dread in you?"

Following Suimei's gaze, Felmenia took a hard look at the monster—no, the thing called an apparition. The information being passed to her brain from her eyes did have that effect. Its very appearance was triggering an indescribable fear up her spine. It was instinctual, and alarm bells were ringing out all over her body.

"Twilight syndrome. In our world, it doesn't assault people indiscriminately, but just like that, it ushers the world towards a determined endpoint. The moment the entire world is filled with them, humanity will begin its journey down the twilight path to being nothing more than myth."

Suimei's tone was flat, but his gaze conveyed a sense of discomfort that made Felmenia shudder. The world that they summoned the hero of salvation from was infested with things like that? It was a being that, just by looking at it, inspired pure terror that outclassed the fear felt at the sight of any monster. If that thing was the vanguard of the end of the world, then Suimei's world very well may be in more danger than hers.

Felmenia gulped.

Hearing Suimei's explanation, she could only stare at the beast with an odd fixation. And then…

"FUHAHAHAHAHA! Did you see that?! If you know how to use it, summoning is mere child's play! A brat like you isn't the only one capable of doing it, Stingray!"

Coarse, unpleasant laughter echoed through the air. Enraptured by the fact that his summoning had succeeded, Sebastian seemed far too caught up in his own excitement to make any sound judgment regarding the apparition. Even if he'd managed the summoning, he was worthless in this state. Hearing that man let out his pompous and intoxicated laughter, Suimei rolled his eyes despite the presence of the apparition.

"Wow, what an incredibly stereotypical line."

"Scoff while you can, brat! Next you'll be killed at the hands of the monster I summoned!"

Sebastian roared, but Suimei could only coldly deny that proud little speech of his.

"Yeah, that's not happening."

"What a sore loser! Go, monster from another world! Tear my enemy apart!"

Sebastian issued his command, but the apparition remained as it was and showed no signs of reacting to him at all.

"Wha…"

"See?"

"Wh-Why?! Why won't you listen to me?! Why won't you obey me?!"

With Sebastian fervently complaining at its side, the apparition pointed the crimson lights it had for eyes down at him as if scowling at something detestable.

"Eek, eh…"

And perhaps Sebastian finally realized the madness he himself had authored. Staring up at the apparition, he sank to the floor. And then…

"U-UWAAAAAAAAAAAAH!"

Sebastian's death cry was crushed into silence by the apparition.

"How foolish…"

From the skies, Felmenia curtly muttered her thoughts regarding Sebastian. Even if he was the worst kind of scum, she pitied him for meeting his end in such a way. But even so, she wouldn't forgive him for what he'd done. She then turned to Suimei again for answers.

"Suimei-dono, why would it not obey him?"

"Hmm? Ah, that's the summoning circle's—well, the foundation is entirely different, but portions of it closely resemble the ones in our world. In short, summoning spells and circles are fundamentally techniques that have the power to use a contract as a premise to put the being called over into servitude. Whether it's a phenomenon or a living being or whatever else, it normally does whatever it's asked without question—it's like that in this world too, right?"

"Yes. I do not know about the case of phenomena, but that does generally describe the way summoning spells work in this world."

Even though Felmenia couldn't say so with 100 percent certainty, it was just as Suimei said. The principles were largely the same. The summoning spells of this world, other than the hero summoning, primarily summoned beings bound by servitude.

"Summoning, evocation, petitioning, possession. Of the four categories of summoning spells, that one would fall under evocation. But there's a catch. That summoning circle's main purpose was summoning heroes. That's why it doesn't include the necessary part to bind the summoned creature into service."

"It doesn't?"

"A slave hero isn't really the kind of image most people are going for, right? Besides, try remembering it. The triangle within the circle was arranged upside down, wasn't it?"

"Now that you mention it, it certainly was."

"This applies to magicka just as it does with most anything else, but when a component is inverted, the aspect that component determines will also be inverted. Since the triangle in a summoning circle is what governs binding, its default orientation represents servitude, and the inverse of that would be liberation. In other words..."

"That thing was liberated into this world?"

"Yup. Well, I can't really imagine that thing obeying anything a human would have to say anyway."

"Th-Then a spell to bring it under control…"

"There isn't one."

Felmenia had no rebuttal to Suimei's declaration. Since he had walked much further down the path of magic than she had, she was willing to take his word on this. But if they couldn't bring it under control, then…

"Oh Fire. Thou art imbued with the essence of all flame, but burn unbound by the laws of nature. Now, turn everything in existence to ashes, the white calamity of truth! Truth Flare!"

Still being held by Suimei, Felmenia thrust out her arm, wove her spell, and let loose her magical white flame. She poured the maximum amount of mana she could into it. It was a strike in no way inferior to the one she'd once used to defeat that monster in the desert. The enormous and dazzling pillar of flame struck the apparition with a hearty roar, but…

"I-It didn't work…"

"Nope, 'fraid not."

The moment Felmenia thought that her magic was about to scorch the apparition, the white flame turned into particles and vanished. The apparition was perfectly unharmed. It was as if nothing had happened at all. Her full power was completely denied. She couldn't defeat it. Faced with that reality, Felmenia's heart was gripped by panic and fear.

"Wh-What can we do against that thing…?"

"Ain't it obvious? We beat the crap out of it."

All Felmenia could hear was manly bravado.

"M-Magic didn't work at all, you know?! Just how—"

"The magic from here didn't. But the magicka I know is something fucking else!"

And with that, just like last time, Suimei began reciting a chant in a language she had never heard before.

"The heavenly sky which dyes all in its perfectly clear blue light."

It began the instant Suimei started chanting. At his feet, despite there being nothing to draw on, an enormous blue magicka circle spread out in midair. Following that, the world began to tremble, and a shriek like that of metal being forcefully twisted consumed the area.

Brittle objects that were unable to withstand the power swelling up in the air crumbled, turned to dust, and were pulled skyward, swallowed by the countless bright blue lightning bolts created by the clamoring torrent of mana and reduced to nothing.

The world kept shaking indefinitely, and so did the shrieks of the earth and the crackling ovations of lightning that extolled it. The chant continued on from there.

"The invisible horizon where sea and sky are one. For only this moment in time, that boundary lies within my hand."

Before long, as if being drawn in by multiple magicka circles, the spectrum of blue which filled the sky converged in Suimei's hand, and he held it out like a blade. As if the blue gathering in his hand had been sucked right out of the sky, a portion of the sky fell into darkness as though it were night. And then...

"Sever the blue sky. Its name is the dazzling blue azure!"

Suimei swung down his right hand forcefully as he threw down the last of his chant.

"Azure Engraved Beheading!"

Those last words came out like a declaration of the slash created by the azure sword, Azure Engraved Beheading. Just like Starfall, its attribute was the void. It used all which existed in the void as power. If Starfall was star magicka, the Azure Engraved Beheading was sky magicka. The magicka circle was categorized as wide area deployment as well as multiplex convergence, a combination of Kabbalah numerology and weather magicka, another fusion of two systems.

And with his spell complete, Suimei wielded the azure in his right hand. The blue light was identical to that of a perfectly clear blue sky, but formed a massive blade that left a blue aurora trailing behind it. Just as the name of the spell implied, the enormous apparition was instantly decapitated.

The azure aurora which denied twilight.

When rent asunder, the apparition flailed in directionless pain. And before long, in the throes of death, it let out a chilling roar and began to convulse repeatedly.

"And that's that."

Finishing up with his magicka, Suimei slowly and safely descended from the sky, landing in front of the apparition and letting down Felmenia from his arms.

"There, it's alright now."

"Ah…"

Once he set her on her feet, Suimei began to put her clothes in order as if it were perfectly natural. Seeing this kind, caring side to Suimei again moved Felmenia. He'd done something similar for her once before, and it was an act of graciousness. He was largely selfish and brash otherwise, especially around her, but this was his true nature deep down. That seemed to be the inherent contradiction in his personality. He'd abandoned the hero and Mizuki, but was working hard to find a way to help them get back home. And just like now, he'd acted to save himself, but he'd also saved Felmenia.

She looked up. The apparition that Suimei had struck with magicka was now crumbling to pieces. The most impressive of her magic hadn't even scathed the beast, but it was cut down instantly by Suimei's magicka—an unthinkable feat with the knowledge of this world.

Their battle in the Garden of the White Wall, flying through the air, the phenomenon known as an apparition, techniques to combine various magicka into one. Everything that she had witnessed was like an experience right out of a dream.

"This is… This is what a mage can do…?"

Watching Suimei from behind as he drew closer to the apparition, she unwittingly muttered to herself again.

"So this is magic?"

Not by means of just chanting, not by means of the power of the Elements, but by using one's own power and the power of their surroundings to discover the laws of all creation and turn that into magic. That was the magic of Yakagi Suimei's world—no, its magicka.

If these were also the mysteries that humans could hold… The place that she was in, the people she competed against, the ones she gained victory over—this world was very small after all, wasn't it? Had everything up until this moment been a mere triviality?

Suddenly, Suimei turned around. There was neither exasperation nor fearlessness in his face. If one were to speak figuratively, it was the face of a man that did not need challenging.

"Didn't I tell you already? I'm a scholar of the mysteries. The objective of the mages of this world may just be to cast strong magic by simply chanting a spell, but we are different. The objective of the magicians of my world is to unravel all the laws of the universe and make ourselves omnipotent. Yes, so that we can surpass any and everything. The fundamental way we think is different from you mages."

"And this... all applies to you too, Suimei-dono?"

"That's right. I will definitely arrive at the truth of magicka, and accomplish the wish that my father was unable to. That's why—"

The apparition crumbled into nothing. It was so enormous and gave off such an overwhelming sense of despair, yet it was defeated so easily.

"I will definitely prove that I can return to my world. And then I'll prove that I can take hold of the Akashic Records."

And so the resolute voice of the victorious magician made a declaration as if swearing to something that could not be seen, and brought down the curtains on this battle.

★

After destroying the apparition summoned by Sebastian with a single magicka spell, Suimei began looking around at what was left of the room.

"Hahh... As I thought, it's totally gone."

Due to the impact from the apparition being summoned and its stamping around, there wasn't any trace left of the ritual chamber as it had been. That meant that the thing Suimei was looking for wasn't there either.

What he was hoping to find was the summoning circle that had brought him to this world. It was nowhere to be seen. The only reason he wasn't all that disappointed about it was because he'd already finished transcribing it. He had it copied down to all the finest details, so there wasn't any need to be aggrieved over the loss of his reference. Of course, what he had wasn't a match for the original, which was connected to the other side. Even without it, however, he was sure he'd work it out somehow.

But as he searched the area for signs of it, Suimei found a certain something else. Specifically, the man he had previously thought was crushed by the apparition.

"…He fucking survived. He's got the devil's luck. Seriously."

Indeed, it was Court Mage Sebastian Kran. Though the apparition should have stepped on him, he seemed to have managed to slip into the cracks in the rubble to save himself. He didn't appear to be seriously wounded, either. He was just unconscious.

Suimei left the court mage who had made all this racket lying face up on the floor unconscious, and simply shrugged his shoulders. Even if he was left alone, he wouldn't cause any more trouble. By the time he woke up, he'd likely be inside a prison cell already.

And then deciding that there was nothing left for him in the rubble, Suimei turned towards Felmenia. When he did…

"S-Suimei-dono…"

Felmenia was slightly blushing.

"…?"

She then suddenly stepped up to him, pulled his hand to her chest, and grasped it tightly with both hands. Just what was going on with her?

"U-Um, Miss Court Mage…?"

"There is no need to be so humble. Please call me Menia, Suimei-dono."

"Huh? Huh…?"

Shaking her head from side to side, Felmenia asked Suimei to call her by a nickname with a flushed face. Suimei was unable to hide his bewilderment at her sudden change in attitude. However, as if she was carried away by passion, Felmenia continued speaking.

"That magnificent spell you used to defeat the apparition just now… I am left in awe."

"Sure… Thanks."

"I cannot even express my gratitude to you for having gone out of your way to take care of the failures of my incompetence like this."

"Yeah, sure, but there's no need to be so courteous. Rather, um… is something the matter?"

Finding himself in the sudden and incomprehensible position of having praise lavished on him, Suimei's voice cracked as he spoke. What was with her? Seeing her suddenly take on such a formal attitude was somewhat unsettling. On the other hand, he couldn't tell whether or not Felmenia realized he was completely befuddled at her behavior.

"No, um… To speak of it aloud would make me somewhat self-conscious…"

"?"

Felmenia's cheeks turned even redder. She was clearly imagining something, and squirming on the spot as she did. In the middle of all this…

"Is somebody there?!"

From a distance, a loud voice called out towards them. Suimei didn't recognize it. As he turned to look to see who it was, he spied the figures of several of the castle's soldiers running over. Having seen the calamity… Or rather, having seen the calamity die down, they were likely coming over to investigate. Looking at them, Suimei called out to Felmenia in a troubled tone.

"Aah, sorry 'bout this, but…"

"Yes. I understand fully. It is preferred if I do not inform them that you handled this matter, correct?"

"Yeah."

257

After Felmenia properly surmised what Suimei meant with his brief words, Suimei nodded back to her as she immediately sprang into action.

"Acknowledged. As you wish, Suimei-dono."

With that, Felmenia's expression changed to a commanding one in an instant, and she dealt with the soldiers who came running over.

"Good work."

"White Flame-sama! Um, just what is this disastrous scene?"

"Well, just a moment ago, Sebastian-dono went mad and caused a disturbance. I have handled things here."

Felmenia gave a brief explanation without any unnecessary information. It seemed that she would be able to deal with this appropriately. One of the soldiers then suddenly looked over towards Suimei.

"That is, if I'm not mistaken, Hero-sama's…"

"Ah, yes. Suimei-dono happened to be in the area by chance. That is all he had to do with this."

"Is that so?"

"Sebastian-dono is lying on the floor over there. Since we do not know if he will attempt anything further when he wakes, seize him now while you have the chance."

"Acknowledged."

"Sorry about this."

It turned out that Felmenia was rather capable. She promptly put an end to the exact conversation Suimei was trying to avoid, and skillfully glossed over it as she changed the subject. There was hardly a shadow of the clumsy and incompetent girl he'd seen in her before. He honestly had trouble processing the disparity, but if this was how she normally carried herself in public, he could understand why the people all saw her as collected and talented.

Finishing her conversation with the soldiers, Felmenia once more turned towards Suimei. She'd returned to the normal personality he expected to see from her. The change was serious enough that he had to wonder where that gallant woman dealing with the soldiers just now had gone. Indeed, she was now blushing again full force.

"Was that to your liking?"

"Y-Yeah."

Felmenia tottered over towards him full of smiles and joy. She was acting like some kind of puppy who had gotten emotionally attached. Looking at her, Suimei could practically see a puppy wagging its tail and waiting for praise from its master as she stood in front of him expectantly. Suimei spoke to her with bewilderment mixed into his voice.

"Thank you, ummm... Menia?"

"Y-You are very welcome!"

Just what had her in such high spirits? The moment he thanked her, Felmenia hopped about as she spun in a circle. Her behavior only served to further Suimei's bewilderment.

After that, the arrest of Court Mage Sebastian Kran was completed without a hitch. Felmenia's mood, however, stayed girlish and giddy.

"What the hell's with her?"

It seemed this young man could no longer speak ill of Reiji in this regard.

★

The Kingdom of Astel, in front of the grand gates of Royal Castle Camellia.

There stood ranks of the kingdom's soldiers, a band, and groups of first-class knights to the front and rear. And in the midst of it all, a carriage carrying Reiji, Mizuki, and Titania appeared.

The moment they passed through the gates, they would be going out to meet the people of the royal capital of Metel for the first time. This would be the first leg of their journey. They were about to take their first steps towards the subjugation of the Demon Lord with their grand unveiling parade in town, and Suimei was none too happy about it.

"So it's finally come, huh?"

Just as Suimei said, the time had finally come. The day that they would depart on their quest. After the parade, Reiji would immediately leave on his journey with Mizuki and several of the knights. And as the hour approached, there was no helping the regret that showed on Suimei's face.

Reiji, however, looked cheerful. Was he that hopeful about his upcoming journey? Or was he just hiding his nerves behind a smile? It wasn't clear which it was, but he maintained his happy visage as he turned to Suimei.

"We're off."

"Don't treat it so lightly, damn it."

Suimei's regretful gaze changed to a suspicious one as he spoke, but Reiji's expression became extremely serious as he denied the accusation.

"I'm not treating it lightly. Even I've thought this through, you know? About how my answer that day was no mistake."

"No, it was definitely a mistake. No matter how you look at it, it was a mistake. How many times do I have to say it for you to get it? Seriously."

Even if Reiji said such a thing with a far-off look in his eyes, Suimei wouldn't allow himself to get swept up in the emotional atmosphere of it all. He spat some typical quip back at Reiji, but for some reason, Titania brought both her hands before her chest and clasped them together.

"Suimei-sama..."

She was the princess of the Kingdom of Astel. It was natural for her to have complex feelings towards such negative statements. She supported the subjugation, but even if it wasn't exactly the same as the king's, she must also have felt some guilt about her role in getting the hero involved. Her eyes turned sorrowful and her shoulders trembled. Reiji lightly patted them to try and disperse her anxiety, but turned to Suimei and made his intentions clear.

"Nah, you're wrong, Suimei. Whether I go or not, the fact remains that the demon armies are advancing into human territory. Those of us who can't return home have nowhere to run. I realized that whether I go to fight now or not, the day will come when we have to face the Demon Lord anyway. I can't say for sure when, but that's why I want to use this chance. If I fight against various enemies and grow stronger now, whether the time to take a stand comes sooner or later, I'll be all the more ready for it when it does arrive. Obviously, that's assuming we're keeping the goal of defeating the Demon Lord in sight though."

Reiji let his honest thoughts on the matter spill out. Despite his outrageous insistence on participating in the subjugation, in the end, he seemed to have thought out something of a plan for the future.

Suimei couldn't say that Reiji's outlook was bad. If they assumed that a standoff with the Demon Lord was inevitable, then his approach wasn't a bad one. Suimei did his best to stifle his usual snark and continue the conversation.

"You don't think that if you run away, someday someone else will come along and defeat them?"

"I can't count on things progressing so conveniently. Sure, it's a possibility. But if I bank on that assumption and it ends up being a bust, we're all gonna die."

It was good not to be optimistic, but...

"You *always* just pitch straight forward and slam into your problems, huh?"

"Is that bad?"

"I don't hate it, but just this time around, I don't think it would kill you to reel it in. This isn't anything like those delinquents and biker gangs in the neighborhood."

Suimei was talking about their past together. In their everyday lives, Suimei somehow or other always ended up playing sidekick to Reiji's superhero, and they'd tussled with all sorts of people because of it.

In the end, Reiji's physical strength and good heart always managed to find a way to resolve things, but this time around was completely different. Their opponents weren't even human; they were demons. The chances of them having the will of neighborhood bullies was predictably low. Yet Reiji spoke with confidence.

"Yeah, but you know, I'm not either now."

"...Seriously, you always have the last word, don't you?"

"Hahaha."

Seeing Suimei's tired expression, Reiji let out a good laugh. Did he find this kind of exchange between trusted friends to be that fun?

Suimei certainly didn't hate it either. And after having heard Reiji out, Suimei gave his reply.

"I get what you're thinking. If you're not going out there to die, but so that you can survive, I have nothing to say. It's just… Don't do anything stupid."

Suimei could understand his thought process. Even if it was reckless, it wasn't *just* recklessness. If he was doing what he thought he had to in order to survive, then he would by using his head more than normal. But even so, Suimei had to throw in a reminder. When he did, Reiji gave him a somewhat serious expression.

"It's alright. From here, we're going to head straight for the heart of the Demon Lord's territory and—"

"Hey."

"Hahaha, I'm kidding. First and foremost, I have to get stronger. Like I said, yeah?"

As Suimei interrupted him with a tired voice, Reiji laughed it off. With such a serious topic, how was it he could still throw a joke in the conversational gears like that? Reiji probably was anxious in his own way. If he was too tense all the time, it would be hard on him, so he was likely blowing off stress wherever he could. That's why he wanted to laugh away the tension in these lighthearted moments.

Suimei couldn't really find fault in him for that. How could he? Reiji was being pressured from every direction just by being the hero. This was his way of resisting the intense pressure those fetters created. That's why Suimei said what he needed to next in a whisper that only Reiji could hear.

"If you think it's getting bad, take Mizuki and run away to find somewhere to hide, okay? Just 'cause you became a hero isn't a guarantee you'll be able to conveniently defeat your enemy like in some manga or novel, you got it?"

"I got it. But I want to do everything that I can."

"How stubborn."

Seeing that he wouldn't yield, Suimei let out an exasperated sigh. This time, Reiji changed the subject entirely and turned the questioning on Suimei.

"But I'm surprised you got out safely, Suimei."

"Hmm?"

"You know, that thing that happened earlier... That."

Seeing that Suimei couldn't figure it out from Reiji's vague phrasing, Mizuki managed to guess what he was implying and spoke up.

"Ah, that thing where one of the court mages went on a rampage in the ritual chamber?"

"Mm. I heard you were a bystander, right?"

Reiji was talking about the time Suimei carried out his revenge on Court Mage Sebastian Kran. At the time, Reiji and Mizuki were out of the castle, so they had only heard about what happened after the fact.

"Well, yeah. Though I wasn't really all that close to the action."

"But you got dragged into it, right?"

"Well, more or less."

As Suimei gave Reiji nothing but vague responses, Mizuki spoke up like it was too much for her to take.

"When I came back with Reiji-kun and Tia, a whole section of the castle was obliterated. We heard a court mage went on a rampage, and there was a rumor of a giant monster appearing. It was all so surprising..."

After they returned from their little excursion, they'd heard all the gossip about what had gone down, but not the truth of it. In fact, Suimei had made arrangements to make sure that was the case long before they even went out. After being invited on their little field trip the other day, he consulted the king and Felmenia, and they decided to settle things while the three of them were away from the castle. Granted, no one had expected an apparition to appear.

"It's really good no one was hurt."

Seeing Reiji's relieved expression, Suimei replied with a quip.

"No one except the ritual chamber."

"As long as you're safe, Suimei, that's all that matters."

"I'm surprised you can spout such embarrassing crap with a straight face."

Reiji's concern for his safety and the delighted smile on his face were both genuine. And precisely because of that, they both made his embarrassing talk that much harder to listen to. While Suimei was thinking that, Titania called out to him apologetically.

"I'm sorry, Suimei-sama. The people of the castle have caused you so much trouble."

"No, in the end, Meni... I mean Stingray-san ended up saving me, so there's no need for you to lower your head, princess."

Titania let out a sigh of relief as he said that. It was perhaps to be expected, but both she and the king were feeling guilty about an awful lot. As she ruminated on that, Reiji spoke up in a delighted voice.

"That's our Sensei. Like I thought, she's amazing."

Nodding repeatedly, he sounded almost boastful. Did he have that much faith in his teacher? He seemed to have a deep admiration for her, if not an outright fancy for her, but...

"Don't you think so too, Suimei?"

"Hmm?"

"About Sensei. Don't you think she's amazing?"

"Ah, yeah, sure. You're right."

"Right?"

Reiji had gotten unusually adamant about getting Suimei to agree with him. What about Felmenia had struck him so?

Aaah...

Suimei then realized the heart of the matter. Thinking about it, he was quite sure his friend had a weakness for women with large breasts. When it came to the subtleties of women's hearts, he was devastatingly thick, but he certainly had a healthy appetite for their company.

The slight tinge of pink in his cheeks was more than enough to prove he was attracted to her. It was true that Felmenia was quite well endowed in contrast to her height. That wasn't all there was either, but in any case, it was fundamentally about the breasts for him. And Suimei wasn't the only one who'd arrived at that conclusion.

"Augh, is Felmenia-san also a rival...?"

"White Flame-dono is a formidable adversary, Mizuki. She has that beautiful silver hair as well as her cold and beautiful face. Felmenia is equipped with many weapons."

Mizuki turned her back to Reiji and was on the verge of tears, but Titania burned with a competitive spirit at the thought of adding a new rival.

"It's not fair... It's the jiggle..."

"Grr, if I had that, even Reiji-sama would immediately..."

The girls both aggrievedly put their hands to their own chests. Giving them a sidelong glance, Reiji seemed eager to move on to another topic.

"What are you going to do from here, Suimei?"

"Hmm? I'm thinking of leaving the castle."

"Oh...?"

This was the first Reiji had heard of it. Suimei had never mentioned his plans to him before. The same went for Mizuki and Titania, who were both also giving him puzzled expressions. The one to step forward as the representative of the group was Mizuki, and she questioned Suimei with a surprised and worried tone.

"Suimei-kun, what are you gonna do after leaving the castle?"

"No, I don't really have any goals. I'm just going to live outside the castle."

Suimei told a barefaced lie with a serious face. Reiji made a slightly tense expression as he asked him for details.

"What about living expenses?"

"I'll find a job or something and figure it out one way or another."

After Suimei replied to Reiji, this time it was Titania who had a suggestion for him.

"Suimei-sama. If you were to remain within the castle, my father would guarantee your livelihood. I do not believe that there is any need for you to leave in haste, is there?"

"That may be true, but even so, I want to go."

"Why is that? No matter how good public order is in the royal capital compared to other cities, you come from another world and have neither the knowledge of this land nor the divine protection of the hero summoning... It is difficult to say that life outside the castle will be safe for you. I cannot see any advantage to leaving..."

Certainly, nothing Titania said was wrong. She was operating under the assumption that Suimei had no talent and no power, and her suggestions were very reasonable, however mistaken.

"No, it's just... I will say this knowing full well that it is discourteous to you, but I feel ill at ease within the castle."

"Ah..."

An awkward expression. With just that, she seemed to have figured it out. Apparently the rumors about Suimei had reached even Titania's ears. Realizing the meaning behind his words, she fell silent and protested no more. It was Reiji who then got worked up, and made no attempt to hide his displeasure.

"Want me to go say something?"

Just what was he thinking? It couldn't be that he planned to find each and every one of the people who were spreading rumors and ask them to stop... could it? That was far too unreasonable, though it was proof of how great a guy Reiji was.

"No, it's fine. What are you gonna do by making a mess of everything right as you leave? It'll only complicate things, so give it a rest."

"Hmm, but you know..."

"It's fine. I have a good plan for how to handle things."

Mizuki questioned him in a doubtful tone on that note.

"A plan? What are you gonna do about money?"

"I'm gonna sell my textbooks and other stuff that I don't need."

"Can you even sell those? Aren't they all written in Japanese?"

"Someone curious will buy them. All I have to do is exaggerate a bit."

"Is that okay?"

"Well, yeah."

"Really?"

"Really. At the very least, I have a plan from here."

Hearing that, Mizuki made a complex expression. She was likely unconvinced. If he had studied magic, combat, and general knowledge together with them, she probably wouldn't have been so nervous—but little did she know that Suimei had in fact acquired all the necessary knowledge on his own. Of course she was worried.

So Suimei decided to try and sweep it all under the rug. He tried changing the subject with Mizuki, who still had a stiff expression on her face.

"But really, it's fine and all to worry 'bout me, but Mizuki, shouldn't you worry 'bout yourself?"

"I-I'm okay! 'Cause even I can use magic now!"

Just like Reiji, Mizuki had trained in the ways of magic. From what he heard from Titania, she had talent that was comparable to Reiji's. She may not have been all that worried about it, but that wasn't the point Suimei was focusing on.

"That's what I'm talking about. Magic. I'm saying that just 'cause you're able to use magic now, don't do things like you did in the past. Right, Reiji?"

As he turned to his buddy who knew the meaning behind such a statement, he got nothing but a dejected laugh in return.

"Ah, ahahah..."

"S-S-S-S-Suimei-kun! You promised not to talk about that!"

Meanwhile, Mizuki's face instantly turned bright red as she started to panic. It was a memory she'd long since tried to forget. It was her dark past from around the time Reiji and Suimei first met her.

"Your dad here is quite worried. No matter how much time passes, you're still wearing that mini belt and that red muffler and those fingerless gloves... What to do?"

"Just when did Suimei-kun become my dad?! I mean, the hero items have nothing to do with it, right?! Don't pretend to cry...!"

On one hand there was Mizuki, screaming and squawking as she made a racket, and on the other there was Titania, staring silently in confusion. She couldn't tell what they were talking about. She turned to Suimei with her head titled to the side.

"Something about the past?"

"Yeah."

"Suimei-kun! You absolutely can't say a thing about it, okay?! Absolutely not, you hear?! Absolutely not! I'm not kidding!"

This was easily the most desperate Mizuki had acted ever since arriving in this world. To her, the reveal of her dark past seemed to be a far more serious matter than being summoned to another world. As if to throw Mizuki a lifeline, Reiji turned to Titania, who was only growing more and more curious, and asked her not to pry.

"Mizuki also has a few things going on, Tia."

"I'm concerned."

"Don't be! It's a grave secret just between us! A secret garden! It's something no one else can know about!"

"If that is the case, then all the more, you should…"

And so Titania's expression stiffened in dissatisfaction and the slight sadness of being left out. Deciding that enough time had passed to completely divert the topic from what Mizuki was questioning him about earlier, Suimei turned to the girl who was self-conscious of being left out, and posed her a question.

"Incidentally, is it really alright for you to be participating in the Demon Lord's subjugation, princess?"

"Oh my, I would ask that you do not underestimate me, Suimei-sama. Even I have mastered magic here in the royal castle. I am certain that I will be of use to Reiji-sama."

Saying that, Titania proudly thrust out her chest, which was comparable to Mizuki's. Princess Titania… He didn't know what her skills with magic were like, but that was not what he was implying.

"I am certain that you excel in regards to magic, princess, but do you not have your position to consider?"

"There is no need to worry. Father will take care of the country. Because his advisors and my elder brother are also present, even in my absence, Astel will manage to get through."

"No, that is not what I mean—"

She was a beloved princess, something like a national treasure. So why was she accompanying them on the dangerous mission of subjugating the Demon Lord? And why was the king allowing it?

Parents naturally thought of their children as precious. So even if it was what the child wished for, could any parent really agree to thrusting them into the arms of danger? It was a poor way of putting it, but surely there were better things for a princess to be doing for her country. Suimei found it baffling. Why had the king really allowed it? However, before Suimei could ask why she would leap into danger despite her position as a princess, she cut him off and stole the initiative with a majestic declaration.

"Suimei-sama, this is the duty that has been charged to me."

"Duty, you say?"

"Yes. No matter how strong Reiji-sama is, this country cannot saddle him alone with the burden of saving us. It is only right that a representative of Astel do their part as well. And the one who was chosen to play that role was me. I have long since made up my mind."

"..."

Was that really all there was to it? It wasn't that Suimei doubted her determination. Her reassuring statement just now was certainly filled with unwavering sincerity. Because she had her own sense of responsibility, she was here in this position by choice. But what would drive her towards such a potentially grim fate? The excuse of defending the honor of the country seemed a little frail.

However, that didn't really have anything to do with Suimei. Titania was someone who was worth putting his faith in if she was offering to be of help to Reiji and Mizuki, so he felt no need to question her any further.

"Suimei-sama?"

"...No, excuse my discourtesy. Please take care of Reiji and Mizuki."

"Of course. Please leave it to me. I will make certain that all of us return safely."

Titania agreed happily to Suimei's request. The atmosphere coming from her in that moment was a strong, spirited, noble dignity that was perhaps best summarized as princessly. She then called out to him again.

"And one more thing, Suimei-sama."

"What is it?"

"I already consider Reiji-sama and Mizuki to be my irreplaceable friends. By proxy, since you're such a dear friend to them, I also consider you to be a good friend as well. I would like you to stop speaking to me so formally. Would that be alright with you?"

A modest request, but not something a woman of her station should ever really ask a guy like Suimei.

"Is that really okay?"

"Please, by all means."

He doublechecked to make sure, but she confirmed it all the same. And then, feeling just a tiny bit anxious, Suimei pulled himself together and tried to give her what she wanted.

"Got it. I'll do just that, prin..."

"It's Tia, Suimei."

Titania gave him a sweet and dainty smile. To someone who had no defense against girls, it was the kind of a smile that could fell a man in a single blow. In a sense, it bore a close resemblance to

Reiji's smile. But Suimei couldn't afford to fall victim, and returned hers with a smile of his own.

"Yeah. Best regards, Tia."

"With this, the four of us are all officially good friends."

In this world, the people she knew as friends were likely just those who paid needless attention to her. Yet as Titania declared the friendship between the four of them now, she looked genuinely happy—like it was her first time making true friends.

Suimei then turned and called out to Reiji.

"Hey."

"Hmm?"

"It's just…"

However, seeing Reiji's carefree expression as he looked back at him, Suimei changed his mind and stopped talking. On the spur of the moment, he'd almost said, "If there were a means to return, would you do it? If you wait, I'll make one."

But he stopped himself. Even if he'd asked such a thing, there was no way Reiji would stop. It would only needlessly cause him to waver. Since there was no real reason for asking, it would merely be a hindrance. And in that sense, Suimei thought it was better not to ask at all. Harboring the question in his heart, Suimei instead put on a smile and cheered Reiji on.

"Do your best. That's all."

"Mm, you got it. Thanks, Suimei."

"Yeah."

Suimei stuck out his fist, and Reiji bumped it with his own. That sealed their farewell, and anything else they were to discuss would have to wait for quite some time. What Suimei got in reply to his nod was a cheerful smile. It was the smile of a man about to take his first step into hardship, but a smile that would not quit or stand down. A smile filled with bravery. It was Reiji's way of telling Suimei not to worry.

Before long, the preparations for the parade were complete, and Titania called to Reiji.

"Now then, let us depart, Reiji-sama."

"Mm. Mizuki, stick close to me."

"..."

As Reiji held out his arm casually, Mizuki forgot to even speak, and shyly nodded with a smile. Reiji himself probably just thought that it was safer if she was closer to him, but there was no way that was what was going through Mizuki and Titania's minds. Despite being embarrassed, Mizuki happily clung to Reiji, and Titania stared jealously for a moment before shouting.

"R-Reiji-sama! Me too!"

"Huh? Tia?!"

She then scooped up Reiji's free arm. He raised a bewildered protest, but only for a moment. Though he was oblivious to her real feelings, he wrapped his arm around Titania as well and held her snugly.

"Mm, okay. You keep close to me too, Tia."

"O-Of course!"

Titania flashed a brilliant smile as she raised her voice in delight.

With a beautiful woman on each side, and not only that, but with his arms firmly wrapped around both of them, the hero grandly boarded the carriage. Looking around closely, the men in the area—the knights and the soldiers—were gazing at him with envy and even bloodthirst. Suimei felt similarly as he began to mutter to himself.

"Actually, I hope you guys stay here forever..."

It was jealousy. Pure jealousy. He couldn't stop it. It was a frustration most of the other men around understood. However, thinking carefully about what he said, Suimei realized his words could also be interpreted as a wish to let Reiji live a happy life surrounded by women. As Suimei was contemplating this, Reiji turned to him.

"Suimei, did you say something?"

"No, nothing at all."

"...Oh? No biggie."

Reiji sounded like he couldn't tell what was going on. Undoubtedly, for the rest of his life, he would remain oblivious to the nuances of the emotions of others in such situations, both women and men. And with that curious expression still on Reiji's face, he and the two girls happily stuck to him began to drive away from Suimei in the carriage.

Before long, the sound of the enormous gates opening rang though the air, and the sound of the band playing its music along with the tremendous roar of cheering and clapping could be heard in the direction the carriage had left in.

When the gate finally closed, the only one still standing around was Suimei, as if he'd been left behind. No. He was standing here because he wanted to be. He made that choice for himself. The melancholy and the loneliness he felt now were simply the result of having a hard time accepting that.

"I really did it, huh...?"

While staring off into the distance, Suimei muttered to himself. Because he wanted to go back, because he had to return, there was no mistaking the fact that he turned his back to danger. Watching the silhouettes of his friends disappear into the distance as they went to face the danger he shied away from, those feelings floated through his mind.

Right here. On his own. Was his decision to walk down a different path not unforgivable and gutless? Was it not an action unbecoming of a magician of the Society? But no matter how he thought of it, he could only see the choice of walking down the path to defeat the Demon Lord as the wrong decision.

As long as he had his thesis, there was no meaning to it if he didn't return. Once he accomplished it, he still had a promise he'd sworn to keep. He had someone he was already determined to save. That's why he felt like he was justified in not burdening himself with the problems of another world. He had his own. But he still couldn't fight the feeling that such thoughts may have been nothing but childish excuses in front of his two brave friends.

"..."

Ruminating on his situation, Suimei gazed into the sky. What he recalled as he stared up at the vast blue expanse were the figures of those he had gotten involved with up until now.

The one who raised him and taught him magicka, his father who collapsed partway down the path to his aspirations. The one who always forced unreasonable demands on him, the leader of the Society. Cursed by Ludwig, the girl with the blue shadow. The far too straight-laced radical of the Chivalric Order of the Rose Cross. The heiress to the neighborhood swordsmanship dojo, his childhood friend.

His choice was a selfish one. He was well aware of that fact. However, when he recalled their faces as he closed his eyes, he knew it was the only choice.

Epilogue I

Several days after Reiji and company left the castle, having made plans for what he would do next, Suimei left Royal Castle Camellia himself. Quite obviously, Suimei didn't have any sort of grand parade to send him off like Reiji did, and though the beginning of his journey was a lonely one, Suimei didn't care much about that. After informing Astel's King Almadious and a somewhat reluctant Felmenia, he descended towards the royal capital of Metel quietly at his own convenience.

His first destination was the so-called Adventurer's Guild in Metel. There, he had something that he had to attain no matter what. Well, before that, he had to do something about his clothes, but nevertheless…

Really, I didn't think he would hand over money…

Muttering in slight bewilderment to himself, Suimei gingerly lifted a heavy bag up to his face with the sound of jingling metal. When Suimei had actually left the castle, Prime Minister Gless had approached and handed him a bag containing some twenty odd coins. With a gaze showcasing disdain from the bottom of his heart, he'd told Suimei to thank His Majesty in a patronizing tone before yammering on full of hate, then finally pushing what amounted to charity money on to Suimei and shooing him out the front gate.

From what the prime minister had implied, it seemed to be an arrangement made by King Almadious. Suimei scratched his head weakly at the unexpected development.

Despite telling him not to, is that king trying to put me in his debt...?

Back in the audience chamber, Suimei had turned down his offer of support once before. So being handed money in spite of his polite refusal did lead him to suspect some sort of ulterior motive. But this was the king of Astel. He wasn't the type to act so craftily in such a transparent way. It was likely just a simple act of goodwill. But speaking frankly, Suimei didn't want to be bound by any such fetters, so he couldn't quite bring himself to be happy over the generous little gift.

For example, if the king made it publicly known that he'd helped Suimei and that Suimei had a connection to Astel, Suimei would feel obligated to repay the kindness somehow. That was the kind of thing he was worried about. He didn't want to have his hands tied in any way. He doubted the king had anything like that planned, but it still put him in a precarious position.

Making use of Suimei's conscience and naiveté, there was no mistaking that he was set up in such a way that it would be simple to entice him into action. Favors sowed could be reaped later threefold, and the king was an expert tender of his fields in that regard. He'd planted all the right seeds for himself and his kingdom.

"Hahh... What are you gonna do? Well, if he couldn't do this much, I guess he wouldn't be a king..."

Perhaps he knew that if he handed the money over to Suimei himself, it would have simply been handed right back to him. That's why he'd used the prime minister to send it. Suimei wouldn't be able to refuse him. Certainly, if he rejected the king's goodwill when that barcode baldy was in such a poor mood, he knew he wouldn't be able to escape the castle without incident. Though Suimei could deal with whatever may come, he didn't want to get involved in anything serious. So in the interest of leaving quickly and quietly, he took the money.

It would be a different story if there had been more harm in accepting it, but since he had no articulate reason to refuse, that would make it even more difficult to do so. And what he had received was money. It was something he would require a significant amount of in the very near future.

There were traveling expenses, the acquisition of a base, the production of magickal items, everyday necessities. There would be no end to it if he listed it all out. Right now, that was one of Suimei's weak points. So when he weighed the overall pros and cons of taking the money, he knew he was right to quietly accept it.

Besides, even if someone tried to extract a favor down the line from him for it, it wasn't like Suimei was obligated to do anything just because he'd accepted the money. That would be something for Suimei and his conscience to fight out when the time came.

Suimei lowered his gaze to the money pouch and the letter he was handed together with it. Written on a fine piece of paper was a note from the king stating that he hoped Suimei would accept both the money and his apology. Reading it, Suimei's heart swayed, and he unintentionally let out a sigh.

Suimei knew he should be grateful to the king. Turning around and glancing back at the gate that was already in the far distance behind him, Suimei respectfully bowed his head.

"You damn sly old fox."

But that old man would never forget his abusive thanks.

Epilogue II

Today, Court Mage Felmenia Stingray—rather, former Court Mage Felmenia Stingray—was in the library finishing up work on a towering pile of documents. Several days had passed since Suimei had departed. Felmenia was in the process of putting together all the necessary materials needed to hand over her work, and putting the fruits of her magic research on temporary hold.

This was naturally so that she could chase after Suimei, who had departed on a journey to find the spell to return to his own world. Between her personal feelings and wanting to be even just a bit useful to him...

"Suimei-dono, please wait for me. Once these documents for the transfer are put in order, I'll hurry to your side with all haste."

As she imagined Suimei wandering through Metel, Felmenia put the feelings in her heart into words. It was true that she wanted to be helpful to Suimei, but she also just wanted to see him again.

It began with what happened in the corridor that fateful day, and led all the way up until his help in the arrest of Sebastian. At first she had been hostile to him, and though she was defeated utterly and completely by him that night, she was now at the point where she fully understood that it was an essential process that she had to go through with him.

What was completely unexpected to her were the feelings she found herself harboring for him. Indeed, feelings often known as love. That pure emotion born at the limits of fellowship between man and woman was something that always felt far away for her as a court mage. Felmenia had abandoned the idea of it, assuming that it just wasn't meant for her.

"Aaah, Suimei-dono…"

While working, she was reminded of Suimei and let out a languishing sigh.

What she was reminded of were the few days before he departed. Ever since they had cleared the air between them, their relationship had improved, and she had started to get somewhat(?) clingy with him. He'd kindly talked with her on all sorts of subjects, and even though it was only for a short period of time, he even taught her the foundations of his world's magicka. She had questions as to why a lethargic and perplexed expression would float up on his face here and there, but that was a mere triviality.

While Felmenia was stretching out in her chair, her eyes idly passed over the spine of a certain book.

"Hmm?"

It was the title of the book that had caught her attention. She stood up, walked to the bookshelf, and took it into her hands.

"*A Study of the Hero Summoning Ritual and the History of the Summoned Heroes*…?"

She then opened it and scanned its contents.

"This is…"

Felmenia was surprised at this most serendipitous discovery. What was written inside was all about the hero summoning. It was likely that this information would be useful to Suimei. When she chased after him, she would be sure to take it with her.

"But if this brings Suimei-dono closer to his goal…"

What crossed Felmenia's mind in that moment was a sense of anxiety that she had never felt before. If she delivered this book to him, he would certainly draw one step closer to his goal, and that meant returning to his world that much faster. When he did eventually find the spell he needed, it was almost certain that she would never be able to see him again.

And if that happened, what would she do with these strange feelings welling up inside her?

"Tch, no! Don't think about that, Felmenia! Our first priority is helping Suimei-dono! The rest can wait until after that!"

Felmenia knew that she was really just choosing to abandon all thought on it. But no matter what she felt, she knew she couldn't abandon her morals.

Afterword

To everyone who picked up *The Magic in this Other World is Too Far Behind!* on this occasion, as well as those of you who are checking out the afterword, thank you very much. Thanks to all who bought this book, and everyone who checked it out while browsing. I'm happy just to have people picking it up to read.

This would be my first meeting with those of you who only learned of me after lining up at the book store, but for all of you who have read the web version, I am the one who was active on Syosetsu with the stupid and noncommittal pen name of "Beef from the Nose" Hana kara Gyuniku. Hitsuji Gamei is also a strange pen name, so not that much has really changed. And yes, I am also one of the ones pulled from Syosetsu into the field of light novels... Eh? Rank and file? I can't hear you, I can't heeear youuu!

God, not in my wildest dreams did I think that I would be publishing a book like this. I just thought I'd write something down and make the best of a setting I casually thought of, and wrote on a different platform than usual... I think.

From getting an award at Syosetsu to the beginning of the convention rush... At that time, I could only think, "wow, is this really happening?" and just went with the flow.

I started writing this story at the end of July in 2013, and it was first made public at the end of August that same year. After finishing the first stage, as I was pumping myself up for continuing the story on the same site at the end of September that year, the invitation for a publication came.

I was shocked. Very much so. At all sorts of things. I guess I still am, honestly.

Ummm, about the story! It's something like a transported to another world fantasy crossed with a modern fantasy? It's sort of about a probable concept that hasn't come up much. I wanted to write a story where the friend caught up in the protagonist's summoning was actually the stronger one, so then I thought, "Well, how do I make him strong, I wonder?" This is how it turned out. When a magician from Earth touches upon the magic of a fantasy world, just what kind of mystical reaction will occur?

I'm a chuunibyou. I love chuuni settings, so I wrote about someone who was unable to escape from one—that kind of story. And so I hope everyone who reads it contracts chuunibyou as well. Multiply, my chuunibyou patients! Viva chuunibyou!

Finally, to the person who put in so much work to get this book published, the chief editor S-san, thank you very much for jabbing at my poor writing all the time. To the one in charge of the illustrations, himesuz-san, thank you very much for the cool and cute cover picture and illustrations. To all the dear readers who read my work on Syosetsu, and all the dear readers who sent me words of support, thank you very much. There are many others that I need to extend my thanks to, but this time around, I think I will put an end to the acknowledgments here. To everyone who's reading this and thinking "Where's my thanks?!"—please contact me.

If I'm still alive by the time volume 2 comes out, let us meet again in the afterword there.

-Gamei Hitsuji

Gamei Hitsuji
illustration=**himesuz**

2

The Magic in this Other World is Too Far Behind!

Available in Stores Now!

novel club

HEY///////
▶ **HAVE YOU HEARD OF**
J-Novel Club?

It's the digital publishing company that brings you the latest novels from Japan!

Subscribe today at

▶ ▶ ▶j-novel.club◀ ◀ ◀

and read the latest volumes as they're translated, or become a premium member to get a *FREE* ebook every month!

═══ Check Out The Latest Volume Of ═══
The Magic in this Other World is Too Far Behind!

Plus Our Other Hit Series Like:

▶ The Master of Ragnarok & Blesser of Eihenjar
▶ Invaders of the Rokujouma!?
▶ Grimgar of Fantasy and Ash
▶ Outbreak Company
▶ Amagi Brilliant Park
▶ Kokoro Connect
▶ Seirei Gensouki: Spirit Chronicles

...and many more!

▶ The Faraway Paladin
▶ Arifureta: From Commonplace to World's Strongest
▶ In Another World With My Smartphone
▶ How a Realist Hero Rebuilt the Kingdom
▶ Infinite Stratos
▶ Lazy Dungeon Master
▶ Sorcerous Stabber Orphen
▶ An Archdemon's Dilemma: How to Love Your Elf Bride

In Another World With My Smartphone, Illustration © Eiji Usatsuka   *Arifureta: From Commonplace to World's Strongest*, Illustration © Takayaki

J-Novel Club Lineup

Ebook Releases Series List

Amagi Brilliant Park
An Archdemon's Dilemma: How to Love Your Elf Bride
Ao Oni
Arifureta Zero
Arifureta: From Commonplace to World's Strongest
Bluesteel Blasphemer
Brave Chronicle: The Ruinmaker
Clockwork Planet
Demon King Daimaou
Der Werwolf: The Annals of Veight
ECHO
From Truant to Anime Screenwriter: My Path to "Anohana" and "The Anthem of the Heart"
Gear Drive
Grimgar of Fantasy and Ash
How a Realist Hero Rebuilt the Kingdom
How NOT to Summon a Demon Lord
I Saved Too Many Girls and Caused the Apocalypse
If It's for My Daughter, I'd Even Defeat a Demon Lord
In Another World With My Smartphone
Infinite Dendrogram
Infinite Stratos
Invaders of the Rokujouma!?
JK Haru is a Sex Worker in Another World
Kokoro Connect
Last and First Idol
Lazy Dungeon Master
Me, a Genius? I Was Reborn into Another World and I Think They've Got the Wrong Idea!
Mixed Bathing in Another Dimension
My Big Sister Lives in a Fantasy World
My Little Sister Can Read Kanji
My Next Life as a Villainess: All Routes Lead to Doom!
Occultic;Nine
Outbreak Company
Paying to Win in a VRMMO
Seirei Gensouki: Spirit Chronicles
Sorcerous Stabber Orphen: The Wayward Journey
The Faraway Paladin
The Magic in this Other World is Too Far Behind!
The Master of Ragnarok & Blesser of Einherjar
The Unwanted Undead Adventurer
Walking My Second Path in Life
Yume Nikki: I Am Not in Your Dream